Bad Unicorn

Bad Unicorn

by **Ellis Michaels**

Infinite Summer Publishing, LLC

FIRST INFINITE SUMMER PUBLISHING EDITION
AUGUST 2019

ISBN: 1-7333240-1-1
ISBN-13: 978-1-7333240-1-4

Dedicated to Ellice for teaching me that maybe –
just maybe – unicorns really do exist.

1.

Deep within the forest, miles from the nearest village, lived a blessing of unicorns. It's of little wonder why a group of unicorns were called a blessing: They were mystical, magical creatures, pure of heart, overflowing with kindness and love. The unicorns kept to their part of the forest – Unicaria, as it was called – safely hidden from the outside world. It had everything that a unicorn could ever need or even want. From a young age, every unicorn was taught to stay within the boundaries of Unicaria. And they all did – all except one.

"I can't believe my eyes," a man whispered to his hunting partner, crouching down behind a tree deep within the forest. "Are you seeing what I'm seeing? Is that..."

"Yup," his elven partner replied. "It sure is. It's a unicorn. It's a living, breathing unicorn."

"Do you realize how many gold pieces we could fetch if we brought its alicorn back to the village with us?"

"It's what?"

"You know, it's alicorn. That's what a unicorn's horn is called. And it's supposedly where their magical powers come from – some of them, anyway. A long, thick alicorn like that should bring in tons of gold."

"Forget about the gold," the elf whispered, slowly pulling an arrow out of his quill. "Do you know how famous we'll be?"

"I still can't believe my eyes," the human replied, tightening his grip around his freshly sharpened spear. "I've heard the stories like everyone else, but I didn't think that unicorns were actually real."

"Well, now we *know* they are," the elf said, lining up the arrow and taking aim at the unicorn's head. "And so will everyone back in Edgewood when we return with the horn – or alicorn, as you say it's called."

"Okay. On three, take your shot and I'll run in for the kill."

The elf nodded.

"One," he whispered, slowly rising to his feet.

"Two."

"Three!"

The human hunter charged at the unicorn. His partner's arrow screamed through the air, missing its target by a fraction of an inch. The arrow came so close to the unicorn's head that it was both heard and felt.

"Oh shit," the unicorn muttered, looking up from the wild grass it had been munching on.

"Get him!" the elf yelled.

The human ran straight for the unicorn, ready to attack with his spear. The magical creature snapped into action, darting away from the open field of wild grass back toward the thick woods. A second arrow flew through the air, again narrowly missing a head shot – but this time it wasn't the unicorn's head that the elf almost hit.

"Watch it!" the human hunter yelled, chasing the unicorn through the woods. "You almost hit me!"

"Don't let it get away!" the elf yelled, pulling another arrow from his quill as he followed after his partner.

The human chased the unicorn through the woods as it weaved its way between the trees. With every passing second, the distance between them grew. Realizing he wouldn't be able to catch up with the unicorn, the hunter launched his spear in a desperate attempt to stop it.

"Ugh!" he grunted, throwing it as hard as he could.

The two hunters watched the spear fly through the air. For a moment, both of their faces lit up. It was a perfect throw, right on target. Their eyes followed the spear as it came down at the unicorn. If only it had been thrown just a little bit harder, the spear would've hit the the creature right in its backside.

"No!" the human yelled, falling to his knees as he watched his spear stick into the ground and the unicorn disappear into the forest.

"I can't believe you let it get away," the elf said, catching up to his partner.

"Me? I can't believe *you* missed it – twice!"

"You're blaming *me*?"

"You're always going on and on about what a great archer you are," the human replied, getting back up to his feet. "Yet you can't even hit a massive animal that's standing perfectly still."

"You know exactly how skilled I am," the elf said, throwing his bow to the ground and crossing his arms. "We've been hunting together for years. You're just mad because *you* missed."

Neither of them said anything for a moment. The human took a deep breath, then finally replied.

"You're right. You *are* a skilled hunter. We both are. And we *both* just botched the opportunity of a lifetime. But it could've happened to anyone."

"You're right, too," the elf replied, uncrossing his arms. "I did miss what should've been an easy shot. That thing was just standing there. It looked like it was completely oblivious to its surroundings."

"I know," the human said, picking up the bow and handing it to his partner. "He was just chewing on some grass with no idea we were here. And I think he was talking to himself."

"He?" the elf asked.

"Oh yeah. It was a he alright. No question about it."

"So what now? Are we going to try to track it – track *him* I mean?"

"Yeah," the human answered. "He's a big creature. It shouldn't be too hard to track him. Although... I don't know if you noticed, but he didn't make a sound even when he was running through the woods. Strange. But surely he left a trail we can follow. Maybe we can still get that horn after all."

The hunters were right: It wasn't hard to track the unicorn. The massive creature left an easy-to-follow trail of hoof prints and broken branches through the forest. They followed the trail for the better part of an hour. Eventually it led to a wide, fast-moving river.

"I don't get it," the elven hunter said. "This river is impassible. There's no way that thing could've crossed it."

"Then how do you explain it? His hoof prints clearly lead right to the water. It looks like he just walked right into it." The human got down on his hands and knees next to the river. Being careful to maintain his balance, he stuck his hand in the water. The current was so powerful that it was impossible to hold it steady. "You're right. There's no way that thing – or *any* thing, for that matter – could cross this river."

"So how do *you* explain it?" the elf asked.

"I can't," the human replied and stood up, defeated. "We've lost him. Come on. Let's get back to our camp. It'll be dark soon."

2.

"Where have you been, Xavier?" Astra asked as she saw her friend – if you could call him that – come walking by, breathing heavily. "I hope you haven't wandered away from Unicaria again."

"And *I* hope *you* haven't been eating too much wild grass," Xavier replied, poking Astra in the side with his horn. "Your hips have been looking a little wider than usual lately."

The mostly blue unicorn didn't react. She casually swallowed the grass she was chewing and replied, "I'm serious, Xavier. You're going to get yourself in a lot of trouble. The elders said that..."

"The elders said this. The elders said that," Xavier interrupted. "The elders say lots of stuff. I'm not worried about the elders."

"Well, I'm worried about *you*. I just don't want anything to happen to you."

"Awwwwww. You care about me. How touching."

"I *do* care about you, Xavier. Believe me, sometimes I wish I didn't. But I'm a unicorn and I care about all of us – just like *you're* supposed to. The only thing you seem to care about is yourself."

"That's not true at all," Xavier replied and looked Astra in the eyes, their heads just a few inches apart. "In fact, I'm hurt. I care a lot."

"Really?" Astra asked, tilting her head slightly. "You care about me a lot?"

"About *you*?" Xavier replied with a smirk. "Not so much. But I do care about having fun and taking naps. Speaking of which, I just did one and now I'm ready for the other."

Astra shook her head. She was used to dealing with Xavier. They'd known each other since they were little. Both Astra and Xavier were in their late teens – in unicorn years, of course.

"Whether you admit it or not, I know you care deep down," Astra said. "And I also know that you're going to get in some serious trouble if you keep wandering off."

"You're not my mother," Xavier replied.

"Thank goodness for that!" Astra replied with a smirk of her own. "But speaking of moms, we should both be getting back to our families. It's getting late."

"Don't tell me what to do."

"Fine," Astra replied and started walking off. "Suit yourself. I'm going back to *my* family. You do whatever you want to do. That's all you ever do anyway."

"Yeah, yeah," Xavier said, watching Astra's hips sway from side to side as she walked away.

He munched on some wild grass for a few minutes before heading back to his parents, siblings, and grandmother. Unicorns lived with their families until they were ready to start a family of their own. Xavier stayed with his parents, grandmother, younger sister, and older brother, Auris.

"Where have you been?" Auris asked as Xavier casually strolled into his family's part of the forest.

"It's kind of a secret," Xavier whispered. "I really shouldn't tell you. But since you're my brother, I guess I will. Come here."

Auris walked over to Xavier suspiciously – and rightly so. Even though Auris was older than Xavier, he was often the target of his younger brother's pranks. Like all unicorns, Auris was pure of heart, always looking for the good in others. This made him an easy target for Xavier.

Buuuuuuuuuuuurrrrrrrrrrrp!

Xavier unleashed a deafening, grass-scented burp right in his brother's face, then burst out in laughter. Auris turned around and walked away without saying a word.

"Never gets old," Xavier said, smiling.

"Xavier!" his mother and father yelled at the same time.

"Yeah?" he replied, as if he didn't know exactly what they were talking about.

"What did we tell you about being mean to your brother?" his mother asked.

"That it isn't funny and that I shouldn't do it," Xavier answered.

"That's right," his mother said.

"Maybe I should, maybe I shouldn't," he replied. "But it *is* funny."

Xavier's mother shook her head. That was something a lot of unicorns seemed to do around Xavier – shake their heads.

"Your behavior is absolutely unacceptable, Xavier," his grandmother, Civia, said. "I heard that you wandered away from Unicaria again today, in spite of being warned by me and the other council members."

Civia was on the Council of Elders. They were a group of nine unicorns chosen to govern over all the others. Each elder served for a term of one-hundred years. It wasn't uncommon for unicorns to live to be thousands of years old. She was about halfway through her term and was well-liked by all her peers – in spite of her grandson.

"Oh?" Xavier replied. "And where'd you hear that? Did Astra tell you?"

"It doesn't matter who told me," Civia said.

"So it *was* Astra."

"No," Civia stated. "It wasn't. I'm not telling you who it was, but it wasn't Astra."

"Whatever," Xavier said, rolling his eyes. "Who cares. You're right. It doesn't matter."

Civia was getting frustrated with her grandson. You'd never know it from the elderly unicorn's voice, but her face was a dead giveaway. Even though her hair was a beautiful shade of light pink, Civia's face turned red when she was angry.

"I probably shouldn't be telling you this," she said, "but the elders are having a meeting about you first thing tomorrow morning."

"I feel like the elders have lots of meetings about me," Xavier replied. "I'm not worried about it."

"Well, you should be. This isn't a regular look-what-Xavier-did-this-time meeting. It's much more serious. Every time you wander away from Unicaria, you're putting us all at risk. And not only that: The elders are sick of the way you treat other unicorns."

"It's not just the elders," Xavier's little sister said.

"Mind your own business, Ebelle," Xavier replied to his sister, then turned to his grandmother. "The elders can be as sick of it as they'd like. We all know they're not going to do anything about it. I *am* a unicorn after all."

"You're a *bad* unicorn, Xavier," Civia said. "In all my years, I've never seen anything like it."

"Wow," Xavier replied. "Never? Thank you. That's a huge compliment. Because you're really, *really* old. Aren't you like a thousand?"

"I'm eleven-hundred-and-sixty-two-years old, to be exact," Civia stated proudly, though her face was now beet red. "And I've never met such a selfish, foul-mouthed, trouble-making unicorn in my entire life. I just don't understand how it could've happened. You have loving parents who somehow have managed to put up with you for as long as they have."

Both of Xavier's parents nodded.

"You have two wonderful siblings," Civia continued, "who have done nothing but try to be friendly with you, yet you treat them like dirt."

Auris and Ebelle both nodded.

"And most importantly: You're a unicorn!" Civia concluded. "You're supposed to be full of joy and kindness and friendliness and happiness – not full of..."

"Shit?" Xavier interrupted.

"I was going to say... Well, I wasn't going to say *that*! I don't even think I'm capable of saying that. And you're not supposed to be, either! I don't know how you turned out to be the way you are, Xavier. Actually, you didn't turn out like anything – you came out that way. You've been nothing but trouble since the day you were born and everybody's sick of it."

Xavier's parents and both of his siblings nodded.

"Well, you might as well get used to it," Xavier said. "Because I'm never going to change."

"That's what I'm afraid of," Civia replied. "And so are the other elders."

Xavier didn't reply. He just picked his head up high and blew a massive gust of air from his nostrils before walking off. As soon as he was out of earshot, his family started talking.

"What are the elders going to do about Xavier, grandma?" Ebelle asked.

"I'm not sure, dear," Civia replied. "But even if I knew, I wouldn't be able to talk about it. I shouldn't have even told him that we're having a meeting about him tomorrow morning. But he makes me so angry sometimes that I just couldn't help myself."

"I don't want anything to happen to him," Ebelle said. "I know a lot of unicorns don't like to be around him. I feel really bad about it, but sometimes even I don't like being around him. He *is* my brother though and, even if I don't always *like* being around him, I do *love* him."

"We all love Xavier," Civia replied. "We're family. And not just that: We're unicorns! We're supposed to be loving. But your brother has been nothing but trouble for our whole community and something needs to be done about it."

"I hope the elders find a way to put an end to Xavier's nonsense once and for all," Auris said.

"Don't say that!" Ebelle replied to her brother.

"I don't mean hurt him or anything," Auris clarified. "I just hope they find a way to turn him into a decent unicorn. Maybe cast some sort of spell on him so he has to be nice from now on."

"Could you do that, grandma?" Ebelle asked. "Could the elders make Xavier act nicer?"

"Unfortunately," Civia replied, "I don't think we can. That would go against what us unicorns are all about."

"What do you mean, grandma?"

"Us unicorns are supposed to accept others exactly as they are – no matter how unlikable they may be. We can't use our magic to change someone's personality. That's just not something us unicorns can do. And we're not allowed to intentionally cause harm to others in any way."

"So what *can* you do?" Auris asked.

"That's what me and the other elders are meeting to discuss in the morning. Speaking of which, I'm going to turn in early so I'm well rested for the meeting. You all have a wonderful night." Civia walked over to Ebelle and gently pressed the side of her face against her granddaughter's. In a soft, warm tone, she whispered in Ebelle's ear, "Don't worry, sweetheart. We'll figure out something that's good for both Xavier and the community at large. I know how much you love your brother. We all do. But things can't continue like the way they've been going. He's not just putting himself in danger every time he wanders away from Unicaria. He's putting us all at risk. I'm sure you can understand that."

"I do," Ebelle replied and smiled. "Thanks, grandma."

Civia smiled back, then walked off. She curled up in her favorite resting spot and soon fell asleep thinking about her grandson. The rest of the family soon did the same. Ebelle laid down in her spot but was having trouble falling asleep.

"Psst," Xavier hissed, sneaking up to his sister a little while later.

"Xavier!" Ebelle replied, whispering. "What are you doing here? Why aren't you asleep?"

Xavier dropped a massive mouthful of fresh grass next to his sister. Ebelle loved the grass that grew wildly in a part of Unicaria she wasn't yet allowed to travel to by herself.

"I brought you some of the grass you like," Xavier replied.

"Thank you, Xavier. It's my favorite!" Ebelle replied, whisper-yelling. Then, her tone got more serious. "I don't want the elders to do anything to you, Xavier. I know you're not a bad unicorn."

"Don't worry about the elders. They're not going to do anything. They're all talk," Xavier said. "Now, get your little ass to sleep!"

He rubbed the side of his face against the side of his little sister's, putting a huge smile on it, then walked off. Ebelle nibbled on some of the grass and soon fell asleep. Xavier found his way to a comfortable spot not too far away and, within seconds of closing his eyes, nodded off.

The whole family had Xavier on their minds that night. They were all anxious to see what the elders were going to do about him. Xavier had been right: The elders *had* met to discuss him several times before. But this time was going to be different and his grandmother knew it. The elders were fed up with Xavier's behavior – Civia included – and planned to finally do something about it.

3.

"There you are!" Savius said to Xavier. "I've been looking all over for you."

"What do *you* want?" Xavier replied. "Shouldn't you be off licking some elders' alicorn or something?"

Savius was the secretary and messenger of the Council of Elders. While it was true that he had a reputation for being somewhat of a brown-noser, Savius was well liked throughout the unicorn community. It was the next morning and the elders had met for several hours to decide what to do about Xavier.

"The elders sent me to come get you," Savius answered. "They want to talk to you."

"I'm busy," Xavier replied. "I'll go see the elders when I'm done doing what I'm doing."

Xavier was doing a whole lot of nothing. He was just standing by a slow-moving river, taking swigs of water and practicing how far he could spit it. To his credit, Xavier was getting quite good. He could spit water up to ten feet.

"They want to see you right now," Savius said in a stern tone.

"And *I* want to see *you* all wet!" Xavier replied.

He slurped up a huge mouthful of water and spit it at Savius, who was standing only a few feet away. It hit him right in the face, splashing all over Savius' golden-yellow coat. With water dripping from his face, he shot Xavier a dirty look.

"Not funny!" Savius yelled.

"I couldn't possibly disagree more," Xavier replied, laughing.

"Go see the elders before you get yourself into even more trouble," Savius said.

"Yeah yeah," Xavier replied, still laughing a little bit. "I'm going."

Xavier leaned down and took one more massive sip of water. He picked his head up and turned toward Savius, as if to spit at him again. Savius turned quickly and closed his eyes. When he heard the unmistakable sound of water being swallowed, he cautiously reopened them.

"Made you flinch," Xavier said.

Savius didn't reply. He just shook his head as Xavier started walking away from the river. It was the first head shake of the day that Xavier would be responsible for, but it wouldn't be the last. Savius followed behind Xavier, making sure he was walking to the elders and not wandering off to somewhere else. To his pleasant surprise, Xavier went right to the elders' meeting spot.

"What happened to you?" one of the elders asked Savius. "You're all wet."

Savius didn't answer. He just looked at Xavier with accusatory eyes.

"Thank you, Savius," the elder said. "You may go."

Savius clip-clopped off, leaving Xavier alone with the nine elders. He stood before them in silence as they eyed him up and down. Xavier leaned to one side, calm as could be, already bored. It wasn't the first time that he'd been called to stand before the Council of Elders. Little did Xavier know that it would, however, be the last.

"Good morning, Xavier," Brina, the eldest of the elders said.

Xavier didn't reply. He just nodded his head, slightly.

"You've been called before the Council of Elders this morning because we've made a decision regarding your standing in our community."

Xavier let out a long, dramatic yawn. A couple of the elders shook their heads.

"Despite being given several chances to change your behavior, you've continuously been a problem for your family, your friends – if you still have any – and the unicorn community as a whole. We've tried to help you, to nurture you, to bring out your good side – but our efforts have been in vain. When Savius told us that you left Unicaria again yesterday, despite our warnings, you made us realize that..."

"So it was *Savius* who told you?" Xavier interrupted, looking right at his grandmother. "That ass-kissing, good-for-nothing piece of..."

"Don't blame Savius for *your* actions," Brina said, interrupting Xavier. "He did the right thing by telling us. But Savius didn't just tell us that you left Unicaria. He told us that you led two hunters right to the edge of our part of the forest. If it wasn't for the elemental magic that protects our land, we'd be in real trouble right now. You've put us in a very difficult position, Xavier, one that is without precedent in the unicorn community. After discussing a number of options, we've made our decision about what to do with you. Before we tell you, is there anything you'd like to say?"

Xavier didn't speak. He just stood there, still casually leaning to one side.

"Anything?" Xavier's grandmother asked, her voice a little shaky. "Anything at all you'd like to say?"

"There's no need to draw this out," Xavier said. "We both know you're just going to give me a slap on the hoof and send me on my merry way. Now, would you like to give me a slap on one of my right hooves," Xavier asked, holding out his front-right hoof, then the other, "or one of my lefts?"

"Not this time. We've given you plenty of chances. You've left us no choice but to take serious action," Brina said and paused for a moment. Then, she continued slower with sadness in her voice. "From this moment onward, Xavier, you are hereby banished from Unicaria."

Xavier let out a short laugh and replied, "Oh, really? You realize that, even if you force me to leave our hidden part of the forest, I can find my way back here whenever I want, right?"

"We *do* realize that," Brina answered. "Which is why we have no choice but to do what we're about to do."

"I'm sorry, Xavier," Civia said to her grandson, tears dripping from the corners of her eyes. "But it's for the good of the whole unicorn community."

Xavier stood up straight for the first time since he'd gotten to the elders' meeting spot. Though you never would've known it by his poker face, Xavier was starting to get worried. Maybe this *wasn't* just another slap-on-the-hoof meeting with the elders. Xavier had only seen his grandmother cry one other time in his entire life, when his grandfather died. Between the tears and her shaky voice, Xavier could tell that something very serious was about to happen.

The nine elders gathered in a circle around Xavier. He slowly turned all the way around, eyeing each of them. His worry quickly turned into panic. Xavier didn't know what was about to happen and the uncertainty was eating away at him.

Starting with Brina, she turned and tapped her alicorn against the alicorn of the elder to her right. That elder then turned and tapped *his* alicorn to the alicorn of the unicorn to *his* right. This continued all the way around the circle until it came back to Brina. After the ninth elder tapped his alicorn against hers, Brina started walking toward Xavier. He took a step back but had nowhere to go – he was completely surrounded. Brina took one final step and touched her alicorn to Xavier's.

"What the..." he yelled. "What did you do to me?"

In an instant, Xavier's alicorn was gone. The elders used their magic to remove it so he'd never be able to return to Unicaria ever again. The unicorns' part of the forest was protected on all sides by powerful elemental magic. Hundreds of years earlier, the Council of Elders created a magical barrier to keep the unicorns safe. Though they were taught to never leave Unicaria, their alicorns allowed them to find their way home and easily pass through the barrier should they ever accidentally wander off.

"We did what we had to do," Civia said, tears still in her eyes.

"You can't do this to me!" Xavier protested.

"We're sorry," Brina replied. "We really are. We all wish there was another way. But you've given us no choice. We gave you more chances than you deserved. We didn't do this to you. You did it to yourself."

"What am I supposed to do?" Xavier asked, his eyes still looking up at where his alicorn used to be.

"You'll be fine, Xavier," Brina answered. "You're still a unicorn. You still have most of your magical abilities. You'll find a nice spot in the forest to call home where you can behave however you'd like."

"Still a unicorn? Who's ever heard of a unicorn without a horn? That's what unicorn means! It means one horn. Now I have no horn. No horn!"

Xavier was incredibly angry. Not at himself, as he probably should've been, but at the elders. He huffed and puffed, stomped his hooves, and screamed at the top of his lungs.

"Arrrggghhh!" Xavier yelled. "You know what? Forget you. Forget all of you. I'm out of here. I don't need you. I don't need any of you. In fact, I'm better off without you. You just did me a huge favor. Now get out of my way so I can leave."

Of course, Xavier didn't actually believe what he was saying. He was trying to convince himself more than anyone else. The elders moved out of his way and he started walking off.

"Should we have Savius follow him to make sure he actually leaves Unicaria?" Brina asked.

"That won't be necessary," Civia answered, confidently. "I know my grandson. He's leaving."

Civia was right. Once Xavier started walking, he didn't stop until he was gone from the community he'd been a part of his entire life. Truly alone, Xavier wandered through the forest with nowhere to go and no place to call home.

4.

Though Xavier had wandered away from Unicaria several times before, he'd never traveled more than an hour-or-so away from his now-former home. For the first hour after being exiled from Unicaria, Xavier huffed and puffed as he walked away from everyone he'd ever known, stomping his hooves along the way. But once he got to a part of the forest he'd never seen before, farther from Unicaria than he'd ever traveled, Xavier's anger gave way to a new set of emotions as the reality of his situation set in.

"What I am going to do? I've got no one to talk to and nowhere to go," the hornless unicorn said to himself. He stopped for a moment, turning around and looking back toward Unicaria. Xavier's eyes started becoming a little glassy. As he turned back around, the unicorn continued, "I don't even have any fresh..."

Before Xavier could finish his sentence, he noticed a small field of wild grass up ahead.

"Hmmm. Ask and ye shall receive, huh?" the unicorn said, giving him an idea. "I also don't even have a cute female unicorn with a long alicorn and a big, bushy tail to play with."

Xavier eagerly looked around, hoping an attractive companion would appear as soon as he mentioned *her*, just as the field of grass had appeared when he mentioned *it*. Much to his disappointment, she didn't.

The unicorn walked over to the small grassy area. He began nibbling in an attempt to forget about his situation for a moment. The grass didn't quite do the trick, but something else did.

"Now that's weird," he said, noticing a strange knot high up on a tree.

Xavier put his grass munching on hold for a moment and looked up at the knot. Though he knew it wasn't an actual eyeball, it certainly looked like one to him. Without taking his own eyes off it, Xavier took a few steps to his left.

"And that's even weirder."

Xavier took a few more steps to his left, still staring at the knot high up in the tree. He then took several steps backward. Finally, his eyes still glued to the knot, Xavier walked all the way to the right side of the grassy area. A chill ran down the unicorn's spine. No matter where he moved to, the strange knot appeared to be looking at him.

"It's just my imagination," Xavier muttered, his legs a little shaky. "It's just a tree. That's all it is. It's not a real eye, just a knot in a tree. It's not looking at me. It *can't* look at me."

Xavier stood motionless on the right side of the grassy field, trying to shake the feeling that the tree was watching him. The air was mostly still that morning and the forest was silent, which made it seem even creepier. Xavier's eyes had been so focused on the knot in the tree that he hadn't noticed the massive hawk circling the field from above. It had spotted a couple of mice in the grass and was waiting for its moment to strike.

Swwwooossshhh!

Suddenly, the hawk swooped down to catch its prey. The massive bird flew within inches of Xavier, startling him so much that all four of his hooves left the ground. The terrified unicorn bolted out of the small grassy field and into the woods.

Xavier ran through the dense forest, zigzagging between trees. He got what he'd wished for – to forget about being kicked out of Unicaria – for a few minutes, at least. Now all the scared creature could think about was getting as far away from the eerie knot in the tree as possible. Xavier ran as fast as he could for several minutes, ducking under fallen trees and leaping over prickly vines along the way. He came to a narrow path and galloped down it, eventually slowing and finally coming to a stop.

The unicorn stood in the middle of the path to catch his breath, looking over his shoulder every few seconds. Even as Xavier's breathing slowed, his body continued to shake. He'd never been so scared or felt so alone in his entire life. Though Xavier had always been somewhat of a loner – especially by unicorn standards – he never actually *felt* alone. Even when he'd been chased by hunters a day earlier, Xavier knew that the safety of Unicaria was nearby. Now he was truly alone.

For several hours, Xavier traveled down the narrow path. It was obvious to him that the path was rarely used, as it was somewhat overgrown. Still, Xavier used one of his magical abilities, something that all unicorns were able to do: move silently. Unlike most humanoid magic, no incantations or ingredients were necessary in unicorn magic. All Xavier had to do was think it and it happened. The large creature continued traveling down the path without making so much as a clip *or* a clop.

An added benefit of being able to move silently was that Xavier could keep his ears peeled for trouble without the sound of his own hoofsteps getting in the way. A while later, a little before sundown, he heard voices and movement coming from up ahead.

Xavier briefly considered his options: hide or basically do nothing. He went with the former. Not knowing who or what was coming up the path, he thought it'd be best to get off the path and hide in the dense forest. Xavier silently worked his way through the woods up a small hill until he found a good hiding spot. He laid down behind a fallen tree, poking his head out just enough to look down at the path.

A minute later, Xavier saw who was coming up the path and was glad that he'd hid. Though he'd never actually seen one before, Xavier had been warned about hobgoblins and instantly recognized their greenish-orange skin and skinny bodies. All young unicorns were taught about the humanoid races and especially about hobgoblins since they're known to live in the forest not far from Unicaria. Though Xavier barely paid attention to his lessons, he did recall learning that hobgoblins were to be avoided at all costs.

"Garg m'nar!" the hobgoblin in front yelled as they marched single-file up the path.

Xavier couldn't understand the hobgoblin's words but could tell they meant something along the lines of "Move faster," since the hobgoblins' speed nearly doubled after the leader shouted them. The unicorn didn't speak hobgoblin, but he did speak two languages: unicorn and common. Most intelligent species had their own language. But there was also a language simply known as "common" that was spoken by dozens of different species. Among them were humans, elves, dwarves, centaurs, gnomes, and even unicorns – but not hobgoblins.

Before long, the hobgoblins had come and gone. Xavier counted six of them including the leader. Just to be safe, he waited a few more minutes before returning to the path. The unicorn continued walking down it with no idea where it led. Even with no destination in mind, Xavier found that walking took his mind off things better than sitting around and doing nothing. However, it soon got dark and he had no choice but to find somewhere to settle in for the night.

5.

The next morning, after tossing and turning all night, Xavier got up and continued wandering aimlessly down the narrow path. He walked for days stopping here and there for a drink of water or to munch on some wild grass before continuing onward. Eventually, the narrow path led to a much-wider one and Xavier started walking down it.

"What in the world is that thing?" Xavier mumbled, seeing movement in the woods.

He spotted a wild pig – or so he'd thought it was wild – eating acorns. It was actually a domesticated pig that had wandered off from a nearby village. Little did Xavier know that he was approaching the end of the forest and getting close to the village of Edgewood.

Oink! Oink, oink!

"What?" Xavier asked, mistaking the pig's grunts for words.

Oink!

"I don't know what that means," Xavier said. "Speak more clearly."

The pig looked up at Xavier, then went back to nibbling away at some grass and acorns. Xavier stood there for a moment, not quite sure what to make of the pig. He'd never seen one before and mistook its normal pig behavior for rudeness.

"Hey!" Xavier yelled. "I'm talking to you. What's your name? Are there more like you around here?"

Xavier was so caught up in his interaction with the pig that he didn't hear the approaching footsteps coming from a nearby path.

Oink, oink, oink!

        Hiding behind a large oak tree not too far
away, a young man and woman watched Xavier
trying to talk to the pig. Both of them looked on with
wide eyes, shocked by what they were seeing and
especially what they were hearing. Even though the
world was filled with magic and wonder, neither of
them had ever heard what they thought was a horse
talk like that before.

        "What should we do, Murin?" the young
woman whispered.

        "I don't know," the man whispered back. "I
need to get my pig back. But I've never seen a talking
horse before. I don't know what it'll do if we go near
it."

        The young man was a farmer from the nearby
village. One of his pigs wandered off and he was in
the forest tracking it with his best friend, Luna. Both
of them were shocked by what they were seeing and
hearing.

        "You know," Xavier continued, still talking
loudly but not quite yelling, "you're no better than the
elders. Actually, you're worse. At least they talked to
me. All you do is keep making that stupid 'oink'
sound. Maybe that's it: Maybe you're so stupid that
'oink' is the only word you know. Or maybe you're
just a rude little... whatever you are."

        Murin and Luna stayed behind the tree for
several minutes, listening to Xavier talking to the pig.
It was mostly a rant about how the elders had
wronged him. The pig, even if it wasn't talking back
to him, was the first animal larger than a rabbit that
Xavier had run into since leaving the unicorns. On
some level, he was just happy to have another living
thing to talk to.

        "Do you think it's true?" Luna whispered to
Murin from behind the tree.

"What?" he asked, whispering.

"Do you think it's really a unicorn? I've heard that they live somewhere in this forest."

"I don't know. It doesn't look like a unicorn – it just looks like a horse."

"Or a unicorn with no horn. It keeps going on and on about how the other unicorns removed its alicorn. What if it's true? What if it really *is* a unicorn?"

"I don't know," Murin replied. "I find that very hard to believe."

"Then how do you explain it being able to talk?" Luna asked.

"Magic, obviously," Murin stated, matter-of-factly.

"Cast by who? Talking animal spells usually only last for a few minutes. There's no one around to have cast it."

"I have no idea."

"I'm going to go try to talk to it," Luna said, still speaking quietly but no longer whispering.

"No, don't!" Murin protested. "We don't know what it's going to..."

Before he finished his sentence, Luna walked out from around the tree and approached Xavier and the pig. Murin, knowing that their cover was blown, followed his friend.

The pig heard them coming before Xavier, who was too busy ranting about the elders and the other unicorns to notice. The runaway farm animal looked over at Luna and Murin which caused Xavier to look. As soon as he saw them, he immediately stopped talking.

"Hi there," Luna said in a friendly tone, cautiously approaching Xavier.

He didn't respond. Xavier didn't do much of anything. He just stood there, staring at the approaching woman.

"It's okay," Luna said. "I'm not going to hurt you."

While she was trying to talk to Xavier, Murin ran up to his pig and put a harness on it, attached to a leash. The pig was enjoying the grass and acorns so much that it barely seemed to notice. As Luna got closer to Xavier, he started stepping backward.

"Don't be afraid," she said, smiling. "You're a handsome one, aren't you? What's your name?"

Xavier still didn't reply. He kept backpedaling, keeping his eyes locked on Luna. Murin tied the leash around a tree branch so the pig couldn't go anywhere, then walked over to join his friend.

"Easy, big fella," Luna said. "I just want to pet your beautiful white hair."

Xavier kept moving backward, his legs shaking so badly that he could barely hold himself up.

"Here. Let me," Murin said, brushing past his friend with a smug look on his face. "I've had a lot more experience with horses than you have."

Xavier kept moving backward, his eyes fixed on the approaching humans. He didn't realize that he was about to back right into a tree – and that's exactly what he did. Xavier's butt hit a massive oak tree, preventing him from backing up any farther. Murin caught up with him a moment later and ran his hand down the long, white hair on Xavier's head – or, at least, that's what Murin *tried* to do.

The unicorn stood up on his hind legs and unleashed a deafening roar before Murin had even touched him. The young farmer jumped back several feet, unsure of what he'd done wrong.

"Good thing I let you try to touch him first," Luna said, a smug look now on *her* face. "All that horse-handling experience of yours really came in handy."

Again, Murin tried to pet Xavier. And again, the unicorn got up on his hind legs and growled at the top of its lungs. Luna laughed.

"You think it's so funny, huh?" Murin shouted. "I bet he would've freaked out even more if it was *you* who tried to touch him."

"It would've been me if you didn't rudely step in front of me. You obviously spooked the poor thing somehow. Now, let's see if he lets *me* pet him."

"Maybe we should just get my pig and head back to Edgewood," Murin suggested. "He clearly doesn't want either of us touching..."

Before Murin finished his sentence, Luna reached up and stroked the unicorn's long, white mane. Xavier was still quite scared but made no attempt to avoid being touched this time.

"That's a good boy," Luna said, running her hand down Xavier's neck over and over again. "You're a handsome one, aren't you? Yes you are. You sure are. Don't be scared. We're not going to hurt you."

With crossed arms, Murin stood there and watched his friend pet what he still thought was a runaway horse. Xavier was still shaking a little bit but found Luna's touch to be very soothing. It was the first contact he'd had with another living thing since being kicked out of Unicaria.

"Maybe he was afraid of me because I'm male," Murin said. "He was probably intimidated by me. He seems to be calmer now."

Murin approached Xavier again. The unicorn turned his head and gave the young man what any other unicorn would've known was a stay-away-from-me look. Murin, of course, didn't recognize it as such. He mistook it for a friendly face. The farmer reached up and tried to touch Xavier's flowing white mane once again. Much to his surprise, Xavier stood up on his hind legs and growled at him for a third time. Like before, Murin jumped back several feet.

"I guess he just doesn't like you," Luna said, trying to hold in a laugh. When Xavier's front legs returned to the ground, she resumed petting him. Luna ran her hand gently over the unicorn's head and noticed a bump just above his eyes. "This is strange. Look."

Murin looked at Xavier's head, being careful not to get too close to him. Sure enough, there was a small bump in the middle of Xavier's forehead where his alicorn used to be. It was barely visible and neither of them had noticed it at first.

"That *is* strange," Murin agreed.

"And it's consistent with what he was saying to your pig. If he really is a unicorn who had his horn removed, he might have a little bump or something where it used to be."

Murin was still having a hard time believing that Xavier was a unicorn. He was a lot more skeptical than his friend in general. Xavier just stood there silently while they talked. Luna kept petting his head, which Xavier really liked. He was still a bit on edge but found Luna's touch to be calming. It reminded him of when his mother used to lick his head when he was a baby.

The son of two experienced farmers, Murin spent his whole life working with animals. His parents owned the largest farm in Edgewood and he spent his days working there. They were teaching him and his siblings everything they knew so that they could one day take over the farm. Murin was in his late teens, as was Luna. He didn't love working on the farm, but he did take pride in it. The one part of working on a farm that Murin did enjoy was taking care of the animals. He considered himself to be an expert animal handler. But Xavier's refusal to let Murin touch him had the young farmer questioning how much of an expert he really was.

6.

"You're a good boy, aren't you?" Luna asked Xavier, running her hand down the unicorn's side. "Aren't you? Yes you are. You *are* a good boy. But a minute ago you were a talking boy. How were you doing that? Did somebody cast a spell on you? Why'd you stop talking when you saw us come out from behind the tree?"

Xavier almost answered Luna, but resisted the urge. He was still a bit scared and didn't know what to do. However, Luna's insistent questions and especially her tone of voice were starting to annoy Xavier. Luna was talking to him the same way the older unicorns often talk to the babies. He thought Luna was being condescending when she was really just trying to be caring and comforting.

"Such a big, healthy, handsome boy!" Luna continued, walking around Xavier, running her hands over the unicorn's soft hair. "Yes you are! How'd you get all the way out here in the forest all by yourself? Did you get away from your master?"

With every passing second, Xavier was getting more and more annoyed with the way Luna was speaking to him. He did his best to contain his annoyance but was finding it to be very difficult.

"And such beautiful hair!" Luna continued. "And eyes. Look at those eyes! Who's got the bluest eyes in the whole entire forest? That's right: You do! Who's a handsome boy with beautiful hair and..."

"Enough!" Xavier shouted.

Murin and Luna both jumped back. Xavier couldn't take it any longer. He had to say something. Luna's constant baby-voiced questions were driving him crazy. The young man and woman stood there staring at Xavier. Neither of them said anything. They were both in shock.

"Who's a good boy? Who's a big boy?" the unicorn yelled. "So many freakin' questions. Who's an annoying pain in my ass? You want to know the answer to that one?"

"You can talk!" Murin exclaimed.

"I told you he wasn't just a regular horse lost in the woods!" Luna replied equally excited, then turned to Xavier. "You really *are* a unicorn, aren't you?"

"An extremely annoyed one, yeah," Xavier answered.

"But how..." Murin asked, a bit in shock. "Where did you come from? Where's your horn?"

Xavier wanted to tell them the truth. He'd never felt more alone in his entire life and wanted to make friends with the young man and woman. But after hearing all the cautionary tales about human alicorn poachers from his parents, he was hesitant – at first. Then Xavier looked between his eyes and reminded himself that he had nothing to worry about. As angry as it made him, he no longer had an alicorn to be poached.

"It's a long story," Xavier answered. "Maybe I'll tell it to you at some point. Let's just say I'm a long way from home and I won't be going back any time soon. What about you two? You guys don't live here in the forest, do you?"

"No," Luna replied and resumed petting Xavier, cautiously. "We live in Edgewood."

"Edge what?" Xavier asked.

"It's a village only a twenty-minute walk from here," Luna said.

"A village, huh?" Xavier replied. "I've never been to a village before. It's got to be more exciting there than it is out here."

"I don't know if 'exciting' is the right word," Luna said. "It's just an average, everyday village. But being in the village is certainly more exciting than hanging out in the forest all day. You want to come back with us?"

"You sure that's a good idea?" Murin asked Luna, then tried to pet Xavier.

Like before, Xavier jumped back onto his hind legs and growled at Murin. Luna took a step backward and Murin took several. He couldn't understand the unicorn's reaction every time he tried to touch him. It was starting to make him feel really self-conscious.

"I don't..." Murin muttered. "Why won't... Is it me? Did I do something?"

Making others feel better wasn't exactly Xavier's strong suit. If anything, he excelled at doing the exact opposite. But he could tell that Murin was upset and didn't want them to leave him in the forest. So, he decided to try to make Murin feel better by telling him the truth.

"No, it's not you," Xavier replied. "You didn't do anything. It's me. I can't be touched by anyone who isn't pure."

"What do you mean, 'pure?'" Murin asked.

"You know," Xavier replied. "Pure."

Murin gave Xavier a look that Luna easily recognized: confusion. But the unicorn, having never been around humans before, did not.

"Look, it's nothing against you personally," Xavier continued when Murin didn't say anything. "That's just how us unicorns are. We can't be touched by anyone who isn't pure of heart. If it makes you feel any better, I'm pretty sure most humans aren't pure. Your girlfriend here is special."

Murin and Luna both replied at the same exact time.

"I'm not his girlfriend."

"She's not my girlfriend."

Xavier looked curiously at Luna and said, "So... You're not a girl?"

"Yes. I am," she replied, trying not to be offended.

For a moment, Xavier looked just as curiously at Murin as Murin had looked at him. Then, the unicorn looked back to Luna and said, "So... You two aren't friends?"

"We are," they both replied.

"Okay, let me get this straight," Xavier said. "You're a girl. You're a friend. But you're *not* a girlfriend."

"Right."

"Exactly."

"No wonder you're having a hard time understanding what purity means," Xavier said. "You clearly don't understand how words work."

Murin opened his mouth to speak but Luna blurted out a question before he had the chance.

"We can talk more about what exactly purity means later," she said. "But I'm curious to know, how did you know that I'm pure and Murin isn't?"

"I'm a unicorn – we just know. It's not like I thought to myself, 'What a super-pure girl this one is. Not this dude, though. Better not let *him* touch me!' It ain't like that. It's more of a feeling than a thought. It's instinct, really."

"If we're going to go, we should get going," Murin said, untying his pig's leash. "It'll be dark soon.

You going to come back to the village with us, um... Do unicorns have names?"

"We sure do," Xavier replied.

"Well?"

"Well, what?" Xavier asked.

"What's your name?"

"Xavier."

"Why didn't you just say that when I first asked?"

"I did. You just asked and I just answered."

"No," Murin said. "I mean when I asked if uni..."

"It's nice to meet you, Xavier," Luna interrupted. "I'm Luna and this is my good friend Murin."

"Cool," Xavier said. "So, are we going to your village or are we just going to stand around here introducing ourselves all night?"

Luna and Murin exchanged looks. They both nodded.

"Let's go," Murin said.

They all started walking to Edgewood, getting on the well-worn path nearby and following it until they got to the edge of the forest. The sun was on the horizon and it was getting dark, but it was still bright enough for Xavier to get a good look at the village. He'd never seen anything like it. The brick and wood houses with smoke billowing out of some of the chimneys. Roads going every which way. People and animals out walking around, heading home after a long day of work or to the tavern for a stiff drink. Xavier was blown away by all the sights and sounds... but that wasn't all.

"Yuck!" he said. "What is that smell?"

"What smell?" Luna asked.

"You don't smell that? It stinks!"

"I don't smell anything," Murin said.

"It smells like... Well, it smells like you two times a billion!" Xavier said.

He was used to the pleasant smell of the forest and of his fellow unicorns. They were magical creatures, after all. Sayings like, "Don't act like your shit don't stink" didn't exist in the unicorn community because, well, their shit *didn't* stink.

"That's just how our village smells," Luna said. "That's how *all* villages smell. It's normal."

"It's disgusting," Xavier replied.

As they walked down the main road, Xavier's head went back and forth from one side to the other, his eyes wide.

"What's that?" he asked.

"That's a house," Murin answered.

"Cool," Xavier said, then a few seconds later asked, "What's that?"

"That's a signpost," Luna replied.

"I see. What's that?"

This went on and on as they walked up the main road, which went right through the middle of the village. There weren't many people outside, even though it was a mild night. They did, however, occasionally pass someone on the road, usually going to or coming from the tavern.

"Good evening Murin, Luna," a middle-aged man said as he approached them. "Well, look at him! I don't recall ever seeing you with that horse before, Murin. Did you just get him?"

"Who are you calling a horse, huh?" Xavier questioned. "Talk about rude. That'd be like me asking Murin, 'Hey, who's this two-legged beaver talking to us.'"

The man put a hand over his mouth, self-conscious about his big, buck teeth. Luna looked away, trying to hold back a laugh. Murin, on the other hand, was incredibly embarrassed.

"We're so sorry," Murin said. "He didn't mean it."

"How did he just talk?" the man asked. "I know you're getting good with your healing spells, Luna, but I didn't think healers could cast *that* kind of spell – only wizards."

"It *was* a wizard," Murin blurted out. "A real trickster. In fact, we need to go find him right now so he can reverse the spell. Got to go!"

They continued down the road, hurriedly. The man shook his head and continued walking, nervously touching his teeth every few seconds.

"You probably shouldn't talk around anyone other than me and Luna," Murin said to Xavier. "For now, at least."

"Yeah, that's probably a good idea," Luna agreed.

"And why is that?" Xavier asked.

"Because not all humans are as kind and caring as we are," Murin answered. "Most people are good – but not all. There are certain people who might try to hurt you if they found out you're a unicorn."

"Even thought I don't have a horn?" Xavier asked.

"Sadly," Luna replied, "I think the answer is still yes. There are some evil people in this world. If you want to keep yourself safe, you should do what Murin suggested – don't talk to anyone but us for now."

"Alright," Xavier said. "I guess I won't talk to anyone else. Hey, where are we going?"

"Where *are* we going?" Murin asked.

"I just assumed that Xavier would stay with you on the farm," Luna answered. "You should have plenty of room for him in the stable."

"Stable?" Xavier asked.

"It'll be perfect for you," Luna told him. "You'll love it."

7.

"I hate it," Xavier said. "No way am I staying out here with these stupid creatures. Even the slowest of unicorns can at least put together a few sentences. These horses can't even talk. Not to mention they smell absolutely disgusting. They're basically stupid, smelly, useless unicorns."

"Oh, come one," Murin replied. "It's not that bad. You've got all the hay you can eat and all the fresh water you can drink. You only have to stay here in the stable overnight. I'll come get you first thing in the morning. Luna has the day off from her studies and I only have a few small responsibilities around the farm. Then, we can show you around some more."

With nowhere else to go, Xavier reluctantly agreed to stay in the stable. Murin got him settled in his own stall with some fresh water and hay.

"What are you doing?" Xavier asked.

"I'm closing the door," Murin replied. "I do it for all the animals at night."

"Did I not mention that I'm a unicorn? Because I'm pretty sure I mentioned that I'm a unicorn."

"Yes, Xavier, you mentioned that you're a unicorn. And?"

"Well, first of all, I don't like being confined. Us unicorns are free-spirited in general and I've been told that I'm more free-spirited than most."

"I'm sorry, but my parents would kill me if they saw that I left a stall door open. It's just for the night. I'll come open it as soon as I'm awake. Were you going to say something else? You said 'first of all,' which implies there's at least a second of all."

"Yeah, I'm a unicorn and..." Xavier said, then stopped himself. "Actually, that was it. Just a first of all. No second of all. You have to shut the door. It's cool. Wouldn't want your parents getting angry at you."

What Xavier was going to say was that, as a unicorn, he had certain magical abilities. Those abilities included being able to get out of most confined spaces, especially ones not created with magic. Xavier knew that he could easily unhook the latch and get out. It occurred to him that if he told Murin, he might try to make things a little more secure.

"Okay," Murin replied, a little surprised that Xavier didn't put up more of a fight. "Good. Well, I'm off to bed. I'll come get you first thing in the morning. Get some rest."

Xavier nodded his head and half-smiled. Murin wasn't sure if Xavier was smiling or not, as he was still learning the unicorn's different expressions. Regardless, Murin smiled back before heading into the house.

Feeling alone once again, Xavier's mind began to wander. He thought about the Council of Elders and how he'd been exiled from his home. Xavier went back and forth between feeling incredibly angry and incredibly sad. He thought about Astra and the other unicorns he liked to spend his time with. He thought about Auris and Ebelle, his siblings. Though he didn't want to admit it to himself, Xavier missed them all – a lot.

"Forget about them," he muttered. "Forget them all. They turned their backs on me. They don't need me and I don't need them."

Xavier laid down and shut his eyes but was unable to fall asleep. He hadn't had a good night's sleep since he left Unicaria. Whenever he closed his eyes, all he could think about was being exiled from his home. After a little while, Xavier gave up on sleep and stood up. He wanted to find something to do to take his mind off things.

Xavier looked in the stalls to his sides. His eyes widened when he saw a young female horse with a roan coat in the stall to his left. Her head and legs were solid black, her body a mixture of black, white, and brown hair. She was lying down but not sleeping.

"Well, look at you," Xavier said. "How are *you* doin'?"

The young horse glanced over at the unicorn. Her eyes widened when she saw *him*, just as his had done when he first saw *her*. She'd never seen a horse with such a flawless white coat of hair before. Little did she know that Xavier wasn't a horse at all.

"You want to get out of here and have some fun?" he asked.

Obviously, the horse didn't reply, not that Xavier expected her to. She just kept looking up at him. Knowing that she couldn't speak, Xavier answered for her.

"Yeah you do. Let's get out of here."

Xavier walked over to the door of his stall. He nodded his head, trying to touch his alicorn to the door. After it being there his entire life, Xavier still wasn't used to not having his horn.

"Oh, right," he said and sighed. "The damn elders took my alicorn."

Again Xavier nodded his head, this time touching his nose to the door. The latch magically moved up and Xavier pushed the door open with his head. He walked out of the stall and over to the stall to his left. Touching his nose to its door, he magically unlatched that one, too.

"Come on," he said to the female horse. "We're free. Let's go do stuff."

The female horse was intrigued by Xavier and stood up. She hadn't taken her eyes off him since he started talking to her. Like he'd done, she used her head to push the unlatched door to her stall wide open.

"Follow me," Xavier said.

He started walking out of the stable. The female horse followed right behind him – at first. As soon as they got out into the yard, she began wandering off.

"Hey," Xavier whisper-yelled, not wanting to wake up anyone in the house. "Where are you going? Get back here!"

The horse kept walking away. Xavier silently ran over and got in front of her. She turned and started walking in a different direction. Again he got in front of her and again she changed course. This happened a few more times before Xavier started getting frustrated.

"Stop being difficult. I let you out of your stall and this is how you repay me? By being a pain in the ass? Fine. You're going right back in the stall. Let's go."

Xavier gently nudged the horse back toward the stable by tapping his butt against hers. He thought he was being gentle, anyway. Unicorns are stronger than horses and his butt-tap was just hard enough to spook the young horse.

Like a bolt of lightening, the roan mare started galloping away. Within seconds, she was out of the yard, running down the main road.

"Uh oh," Xavier whispered. "This isn't good."

For a moment, he considered going after the horse. But Xavier knew that even if he caught up to her, he'd struggle to get her back to the stable. His unicorn magic would be useless, as they're not allowed to use it to influence the behavior of living things – even animals. Xavier thought about galloping out of the yard himself and returning to the forest, leaving the village behind. But then he reminded himself of how lonely he was with no one to talk to. Ultimately, Xavier decided to return to his stall.

He silently trotted back to the stable. Xavier backed into his stall and tried to close the door. Closing the door proved to be much more of a challenge than opening it, but he eventually pulled it shut with his chin. Then, Xavier tapped the door with his nose and the latch dropped back into place as if he'd never left.

The unicorn laid down again and shut his eyes after having a drink of water. As frustrating as it may have been, the experience with the female horse wasn't a complete waste of time for Xavier. It did serve its intended purpose – to take his mind off things. Now all he could think about was what had just happened. But Xavier wasn't particularly worried about the consequences of his actions. He was just frustrated by the whole thing.

Xavier finally managed to fall asleep. He had several dreams that night, all of them about unicorns. In one dream, the female horse made an appearance and *was* a unicorn. She still smelled like a horse, though, and Xavier did his best to stay as far away from her as possible. He slept soundly through the night and, although not a perfect night's rest, it was the best night's sleep he'd had since leaving home.

8.

"Oh no!"

Xavier was woken up the next morning by the sound of Murin's voice. He picked his head up and opened his eyes. Murin was standing outside the female horse's stall freaking out, both of his hands on top of his head.

"Xavier, what happened?" Murin asked. "Where'd Lily go? Did you have anything to do with this?"

"To do with what?" Xavier asked, pretending not to know what Murin was talking about. "Where'd who go?"

"Lily, the roan horse that was in this stall. Where'd she go?"

"How would I know? I was asleep all night long. You locked me in this stall, remember?"

Murin looked at Xavier suspiciously for a moment, then looked back to Lily's empty stall.

"You didn't see or hear anything? Nothing?"

"See or hear?" Xavier replied. "Nope. Smell, on the other hand..."

"My parents are going to kill me," Murin said, pacing back and forth. "I can't believe I left the latch up. I must've been so preoccupied with you that I forgot to put it down. We have to go look for Lily."

"Sure," Xavier replied. "Let's get right on that. Let me just eat a little bit of this stale grass and maybe go back to sleep for another hour or two and we'll go find your horse."

"No!" Murin shouted as he unlatched Xavier's door. "Now! Come on!"

"Fine," Xavier agreed.

The unicorn stood up and stretched his legs, then slowly walked out of the stall. He and Murin looked at each other when they heard someone approaching the stable. Murin started freaking out even more, but pulled himself together quickly. If he was going to hide what had happened, he needed to remain calm.

"Come with me," Murin whispered to Xavier. "And don't say a word."

"Yeah, yeah," Xavier replied. "We went over this last night."

"I'm just reminding you," Murin whispered, a little annoyed.

They walked out of the stable just as Murin's father was about to walk in. Murin and Xavier stood in front of the entrance, blocking it.

"Good morning, dad," Murin said. "How are you today?"

"I'm fine," his dad replied. "I thought I heard yelling. Is everything alright in there?"

"Oh yeah. Everything's fine. I just stubbed my toe. It really hurt, so I yelled a little bit. I'm better now."

"Mmm hmm," Murin's father replied, then looked at Xavier. "And who's this? I know he's not one of ours."

"This is Xavier," Murin answered. "Luna and I found him wandering around in the forest yesterday."

"Who does he belong to?"

"We haven't figured that out yet. But we're going to look into it today since we both have the day off from our responsibilities – well, after I take care of the animals, of course."

Murin's father, Mr. Fieldstone, looked over his son's shoulder into the stable. His eyes went back and forth between Murin's face and the horse stalls behind him.

"You sure nothing's going on in there?" his dad asked.

"Like what?" Murin questioned. "What would be going on in there?"

"Anything out of the ordinary?"

"Nope."

"You sure about that?"

"Yup."

"Okay then," Mr. Fieldstone said. "I'll let you get back to what you were doing."

Murin smiled at his father and he half-smiled back before turning around to walk away. A huge wave of relief crashed through Murin, but that relief didn't last for very long. After taking a few steps, Mr. Fieldstone turned back around.

"Oh, I almost forgot to ask..." he said.

"Yes, dad?" Murin replied.

"If everything's fine," his dad said, each word louder than the one before it, "then maybe you can explain to me why Mary, the fortune teller who lives all the way on the other side of the village, just showed up at our front door with Lily?"

"I... I was going to tell... I didn't want to..." Murin tried to answer but couldn't complete a sentence.

"I'm not mad that Lily got out," Mr. Fieldstone replied, walking over and putting a hand on his son's shoulder. "But I *am* mad that you weren't honest with me. One person can't run a farm by him or herself. It's a group effort. In this case, a family effort. When something goes wrong – and things *will* go wrong – you need to let the rest of us know so we can help to fix things. This is your life, Murin. This is your livelihood. And it always will be."

"You're right," Murin said, his head down. "I should've told you as soon as I noticed that Lily was missing."

"Yes, you should've. Your mother and I are very understanding, son. You should know that by now. We want you to feel comfortable being honest with us."

"Actually, I wanted to..." Murin started saying before his dad cut him off.

"Good talk. Now go get Lily and the other animals ready for the day. Then, you and Luna can take your new friend here to go look for his owner."

Murin exhaled and replied, "Yes, father."

Again, Mr. Fieldstone turned and walked away. This time, he kept going until he was back in the house. Seeing Murin interacting with his father reminded Xavier of his own dad.

Xavier wandered around and munched on some hay while he waited for Murin. The young farmer took care of his animals and brought Lily back out to the stable. When she saw Xavier, the horse stopped dead in her tracks.

"What is it, Lily?" Murin asked.

"Don't bother," Xavier said. "She doesn't talk. Believe me, I tried."

"I know she doesn't talk," Murin replied. "I was just..."

"You want to say hi to the wall while you're at it?" Xavier said. "Or maybe have a lengthy conversation with one of those weird, long-necked things over there. How about this pile of hay? You want to ask it why it tastes like shit compared to fresh grass? Better yet, you could ask..."

"I talk to all my animals," Murin replied, already getting annoyed with Xavier and he hadn't even been awake for an hour yet. "I know they can't respond to me. But I like to think they find it comforting. And those long-necked animals are called ostriches."

After eyeing Xavier for several seconds, Lily cautiously continued walking past him. Murin got her settled in the stable and finished taking care of the other animals.

"Okay," he said to Xavier once he was done. "All set. Now, let's go get Luna."

"Jeez," Xavier replied. "Finally."

Murin shook his head. That seemed to be a common response to Xavier from both humans *and* unicorns. They left the farm and walked to Luna's home. She lived with her mother. Luna's father had been a respected healer and adventurer but passed away when she was just a little girl. He was the one who inspired her to take up the healing arts.

"Good morning, Murin," Luna's mother said, opening the front door. "Luna just walked to the bakery to get some fresh bread. She should be back any minute. This must be the horse you and Luna found in the forest yesterday. She told me all about it."

Out of the corner of his eye, Murin saw Xavier open his mouth as if he was about to talk. He quickly and loudly replied to Luna's mother before Xavier had the chance to speak.

"Yes! That's right. It is. This is Xavier," Murin replied to Luna's mother, then turned and looked the unicorn in the eyes. "The *horse* we found in the forest."

"How do you know his name?" she asked. "Luna didn't tell me his name was Xavier. Was he wearing a name tag?"

"Um, yes," Murin answered. "He was. How else would we know his name? It's not like he told us himself!"

"No, I suppose not," Luna's mother replied, laughing, then pointed down the road. "Here comes my daughter now."

Luna was walking with two large loaves of fresh bread in her hands. Though Murin didn't pick up on it – he never did – Luna's face lit up a little bit when she saw him.

"Who wants fresh bread?" Luna asked.

"I do!" both Murin and Luna's mother said at the same time.

"I'm going to save a loaf for later," the mother said. "But I'll slice one up for us now. Are you two hanging around here or are you going somewhere else?"

Murin and Luna looked at each other. They'd been friends for a very long time and were quite good at reading each other's facial expressions – most of the time.

"We're going out," she replied to her mother. "Probably for the day. Do you want me home at any particular time?"

"Nah, just come home whenever."

"Okay," Luna replied. "Can we take the bread to go?"

"Of course!" her mom answered.

Luna's mother sliced up a loaf of bread and after taking a couple of small pieces for herself, gave the rest to her daughter. Murin and Luna said goodbye to her mom and started walking down the road with Xavier. She broke the bread in half, giving Murin the bigger of the two pieces.

"What's that smell?" Xavier asked.

"We told you last night," Murin replied. "That's just the way our village smells. It's normal."

"No, not that. What you're eating. It smells amazing. I've never smelled anything like it."

"You want to try a piece?" Murin asked.

"Yeah," Xavier replied.

Murin broke off a piece of bread and held it up for Xavier. He looked at the bread, then at Murin. Back to the bread, then back to Murin. Bread, Murin. Bread, Murin.

"Can *you* hand it to me?" Xavier said to Luna.

"What, my bread's not good enough for you?" Murin asked, visibly upset.

"No, it's not that," Xavier replied.

"Oh, I get it. *I'm* not good enough for you."

"Don't take it personally," he replied.

"Here," Luna said and handed Xavier a piece of bread.

Without hesitation, he took the bread out of Luna's hand. As Xavier began chewing on it, his eyes widened and his nostrils flared. Aside from wild grass and hay, Xavier had never really eaten anything else. That bread was the most delicious thing he'd ever had in his entire life.

"You like it?" Luna asked.

Xavier swallowed the last of the bread in his mouth and replied with a single word: "More."

"I guess that's a yes," Luna said.

She gave Xavier another piece of bread and then another a minute later. Before long, the three of them finished it all. Murin didn't say anything for several minutes, still upset by Xavier's refusal to eat bread out of his hand.

They walked around the village all morning. Luna showed Xavier where the healer lived that she was apprenticing for and some of her favorite spots around town. Murin showed him some of *his* favorite spots, including the blacksmith's and the weapons shop. Although he was destined to be a farmer like his parents, Murin often dreamed of being a powerful warrior or a traveling adventurer. One of his friends who *was* training to be a warrior had been giving Murin some basic swordsmanship lessons when they got together.

Xavier found the village to be extremely interesting. But by the time the sun was at its high point, he was also feeling a bit overwhelmed. Being around so many humans, elves, dwarves, and other bipeds was something that Xavier needed time getting used to. Just a day earlier, he'd never even met a humanoid before.

"I want to go back out into the forest," Xavier said.

"Are you sure?" Murin asked. "Weren't you lonely out there all by yourself?"

"I don't mean forever. Just for a little while."

Murin and Luna looked at each other, both shrugging their shoulders.

"Okay," Murin said. "Sure. We can go into the forest for a bit."

The three of them followed the main road until it brought them to the edge of the woods. The main road turned into a well-worn path that led all the way through the massive forest. Both Murin and Luna had traveled down it quite far, but never all the way to the end. There were several smaller paths that branched off from it along the way but they had never been down most of them. The main path was well-traveled and considered to be very safe. But both Murin and Luna had been warned from a young age to never stray from the main path, as the forest was full of dangerous monsters.

For the better part of an hour, they followed the path through the woods, enjoying the mild weather. All of a sudden Luna, who was walking a few steps ahead of Xavier and Murin, stopped. She turned her head so the others could see her and put a finger over her lips. Murin knew that it meant to be quiet, but Xavier had never seen anyone do that before. It would've been quite difficult for a unicorn to hold a hoof over its mouth.

When Murin saw Luna stop and put her finger over her mouth, he stopped. Xavier didn't. The unicorn almost walked right into her.

"What are you doing?" Xavier asked. "Why'd you stop? And what's with the finger to the face?"

"Shhhhhhhhh," Luna hissed.

Xavier didn't know what that mean, either. He had never been shushed before but found it to be rude.

"What's *that* supposed to mean?" Xavier asked.

"It means be quiet!" Luna whisper-yelled. "I hear something. It sounds like it's coming from over there."

Luna pointed ahead to the left. Xavier finally stopped talking and the three of them listened closely. What they heard blew all three of their minds – especially Xavier's.

9.

"I can't really hear what they're saying," Murin whispered. "We're too far away."

"We can't get any closer without making a lot of noise," Luna replied. "They're out in the middle of the woods, far from the path. They'll hear us coming."

"They won't hear *me* coming," Xavier said. "I can walk silently when I want to."

Luna smacked herself in the forehead.

"I can't believe I didn't think of that!" she said, again whisper-yelling. "I can cast a silence spell. It's really easy. It was one of the first spells I learned."

"I thought you were studying to be a healer?" Murin asked.

"I am," Luna replied. "But healers can use other white magic besides just healing spells. You should know this. We've talked about it plenty of times."

"Right. Of course," Murin said, looking away. "Then do it. Make it happen."

Luna walked over to Murin and began reciting the silence spell. As she whispered the words, she took Murin's hand. The spell made it so the caster and whoever she was touching wouldn't make any sounds when they moved. Xavier, being a unicorn and all, didn't have to recite anything. While Luna was finishing the spell, Xavier began silently walking through the woods in the direction the voices were coming from.

A few seconds later, the spell was cast. Murin tested it out, lightly stepping off the path. He didn't hear anything, so he cautiously took another step... and another... and another. Now confident that the spell worked, Murin followed behind Xavier, walking normally. Luna followed right behind him.

As they walked farther into the woods, the voices got louder and louder until they could clearly make out what was being said. Xavier saw three humans – a young man, a young woman, and a much older man – standing around, talking. They were still far enough away that he couldn't see their faces or make out any details. Xavier took a few steps over to a large tree and hid behind it, lying down. Murin and Luna both laid down next to him so they wouldn't be seen. The three of them listened carefully.

"And what were you able to find out?" the old man asked. "You better have good news for me."

"We do, Involore," the young man answered.

"We do indeed," the young woman said.

Murin and Luna looked at each other when they heard Involore's name. He was a well-known wizard that had been living in Edgewood for years. He was also rumored to be one of the most powerful wizards in the entire world.

"Well?" Involore asked, impatience in his voice.

"We've narrowed it down to just two parts of the forest," the young man said. "They have to be in one or the other. There's nowhere else they could possibly be."

"You're sure?"

"Oh yes, we're sure," the young woman answered. "There's nowhere else in the forest that they could possibly be. Before long, we'll know which one of those two areas the unicorns live in and then you can proceed with your plan."

Luna and Murin both looked at Xavier. As soon as he heard the word "unicorns," he picked his head up and his eyes widened. Now extremely interested in the conversation, the three of them listened even more closely.

"Excellent!" Involore said. "As soon as you find out exactly where the unicorns are, I can proceed with my ingenious plan."

"Isn't the unicorns' part of the forest protected by some sort of super-powerful magical barrier?" the young man asked.

"Yeah," the young woman added, "I've heard that it's impenetrable. Unicorn magic is said to be incredibly powerful."

"Incredibly powerful? Yes," Involore said. "But impenetrable? No. Not anymore. I've devised a way to break through the unicorns' magical barrier – once we find out precisely where they are. Then, I can slaughter them all and take their alicorns. Do you realize what I'll be able to do with those things? Once I grind them down, I'll be able to make the ultimate potion – an immortality elixir. I'll be the most powerful wizard in the world and I'll have all of eternity to enjoy it!"

Murin and Luna couldn't believe what they were hearing. Though they didn't know him personally, both Murin and Luna had heard quite a bit about Involore. He had a reputation for being a powerful but malevolent wizard who had adventured all over the world. They'd each heard a number of stories about him and the legendary quests he'd been on. They'd even heard that their village wouldn't exist if it wasn't for the old wizard. It was rumored that Involore once single-handedly saved Edgewood from a violent dragon who threatened to burn the village to the ground. The good people of Edgewood, including Dessa, the leader of the village, were thankful and let him live there regardless of his evil reputation.

Even though Murin and Luna were well-aware of Involore's reputation, they couldn't believe he was planning something so evil. Murin clenched his fists and started grinding his teeth as he listened to Involore speak. The thought of dead unicorns brought tears to Luna's eyes and she wiped them with the back of her hand.

Xavier, on the other hand, had a very different reaction. The unicorn did everything he could to stop himself from breaking out in maniacal laughter. He found the wizard's plan to be poetic justice. By kicking Xavier out of Unicaria, the Council of Elders might have unknowingly saved his life.

"Good work, you two," Involore continued. "I need to go back up to Briarville to take care of some business. You two know what you need to do now. I'll be back in a few days after I'm done in Briarville. And don't mention a word of any of this to the other apprentices – especially Anora."

"Anora?" Murin whispered to Luna. "Isn't that your friend?"

"Sure is," she whispered back. "She's one of Involore's apprentices."

Murin, Luna, and Xavier stayed hidden behind the large tree as the wizard walked off in one direction and the other two started walking in the other. They walked over to the path that Murin, Luna, and Xavier had come from. The robed figures walked within just a few feet of them but didn't seem to notice they were there. They were too busy gloating about how happy they'd made Involore. Murin, Luna, and Xavier listened as the robed figures began walking down the path.

"I told you our master would be pleased with what we found out, Drixius," the young woman said.

"I'm surprised," the young man replied. "I thought for sure he'd be angry that we only narrowed it down to two areas."

"It sounded like he still needs some time to put together his plan, whatever it is. Do you know how he's going to get through the unicorns' magical barrier?"

"I have no idea," Drixius replied. "I don't know anything that you don't know. What I *do* know is that after being out in this forest for the past few days, I could use a big piece of mutton and a nice hot bath."

"That does sound good," Evia said. "I wonder what Involore keeps doing up in Briarville."

"Me, too. I'd bet a gold piece that it has something to do with..."

Drixius and Evia got far enough down the path that Murin, Luna, and Xavier couldn't hear them anymore. They got up and brushed themselves off.

"I can't believe what we just heard," Luna said.

"I know," Murin replied. "I can't believe Involore is planning on killing all the unicorns. You must be furious, Xavier."

"Furious?" he said and laughed. "Are you kidding me? I'm as happy as a unicorn on Tuesday... or Wednesday... or any day, really. Unicorns are generally a pretty happy bunch. But they won't be happy when Invalid..."

"Involore," Luna corrected.

"When Involore breaks through their magic and destroys them all. Serves them right. All of them. Especially the elders. That's what they get for kicking me out of the forest."

"You're happy about this?" Murin asked.

"Yeah, I thought you'd be beyond angry," Luna added. "Or sad or worried or something."

"Why would I feel bad about them? They turned their butts on me. They kicked me out. And they took my long, thick alicorn – one of the best-looking alicorns in all of Unicaria. Well, we'll see how they like it when *their* alicorns get removed."

Murin and Luna glanced at each other. They were both still in shock about what they'd heard the wizard and his two apprentices talking about. Even being aware of Involore's reputation, neither of them thought he was capable of doing something *that* evil. They didn't think *anyone* was capable of doing something so terrible, especially for such a selfish reason. And they were surprised by Xavier's reaction as well – but not *too* surprised. They both sympathized with the unicorn. Neither of them could imagine how much it must've hurt to get kicked out of a community you've been a part of your whole life.

After giving the apprentices a few minutes to get a ways down the path, they started walking back to Edgewood.

"Should we do something?" Luna asked Murin. "Should we tell someone?"

"I think we have to," he replied. "We have to do something."

"We should tell Dessa," Luna suggested. "If anyone can do anything to stop Involore from killing all the unicorns, it's Dessa."

"Who?" Xavier asked.

"She's the oldest citizen in Edgewood," Luna explained. "Dessa's been living in Edgewood since before it was called Edgewood."

"I've heard that she's over five-hundred years old," Murin said.

"I thought you humans croak long before you even reach one-hundred," Xavier said.

"That's true," Murin replied. "Humans do usually *pass away* long before they reach a hundred. But Dessa isn't a human. She's an elf."

"A what?" Xavier asked.

"An elf," Murin replied. "They're a lot like humans. But one thing that's different is that they can live a lot longer. I've heard that some elves live to be over a thousand years old."

"Huh," Xavier said, disinterested.

"So, do you agree?" Luna asked Murin. "Do you think we should tell Dessa what we heard?"

"Yeah, I think that's the best course of action."

Just as they got to the end of the path where it turned into the road leading through Edgewood, Xavier stopped.

"What are you doing?" Murin asked him.

"I think I'm going to stay out here tonight," Xavier said.

"Are you sure?" Murin asked. "You don't want to sleep in a nice, cozy stall with all the hay you can eat and all the fresh water you can drink?"

"Hay? You mean stale grass? And those stalls might be fine for your horses and other livestock – although, for *live*stock, they certainly don't seem to be very full of life. What a boring, morose group of creatures. And don't even get me started on how they smell."

"You're not going to come see Dessa with us?" Luna asked.

"Why would I? I really don't care what happens to the unicorns. That's their problem. Not mine. If I was still part of their community, it would be my problem. But they kicked me out. So it's not."

"Will we see you again?" Murin asked.

"Couldn't tell you," Xavier answered. "Maybe you will, maybe you won't."

"What are you going to do?" Luna asked.

"I'm going to find some nice *fresh* grass to munch on, maybe have a drink from that stream we passed a little while ago, and then curl up somewhere comfortable and go to sleep."

"I mean, like, tomorrow," Luna said. "And from now on. What are you going to do?"

"What's with all the questions? Jeez," Xavier replied. "What are you going to do? Where are you going to go? When am I going to see you? The answer to all the questions you've asked and all the questions you're probably going to ask is: I have no freakin' idea."

"Okay," Luna said, looking down. "Sorry."

"Well, take care," Murin said. He raised his hand to pet Xavier, then dropped it remembering what would happen if he tried. "I hope I get to see you again. You know where to find me. You're welcome to come to my family's farm whenever you'd like."

"Yeah, cool," Xavier replied, casually. "Later!"

The unicorn turned and started walking back into the forest. Both Luna and Murin hoped that they'd see Xavier again. They watched him walk away until he disappeared into the woods. Luna and Murin turned around and walked back to the village.

"It's late," Murin said. "Why don't we go see Dessa first thing in the morning."

"Okay," Luna replied. "Do you think we'll see Xavier again?"

"I hope so," Murin said, solemnly. "He's kind of a jerk – but I like him."

10.

The next morning, Murin woke up earlier than usual. He wanted to make sure he had time to go see Dessa and to tend to all his responsibilities. Luna did the same. She woke up a little early so she could go see Dessa with Murin before her healing lessons began for the day. The two of them met in front of Luna's house right at sunrise, something they'd planned the night before. Dessa lived not too far from there and it was a sensible place to meet.

"I can't remember the last time I saw you up this early," Murin said to his friend.

"Um, how about never," Luna replied, half awake. "I hate getting up early unlike you, you weirdo. It's so unnatural."

"You'd make a terrible farmer," Murin said with a smirk.

"I didn't get up early to be insulted by my so-called best friend," Luna replied with a small smirk of her own. "You ready to go see Dessa?"

"Yeah, I'm ready. I've been waiting for you," Murin said.

They took the short walk to Dessa's house. The sun was just coming up over the horizon and most of Edgewood was still asleep. Dessa had a reputation for staying up late at night and getting up early in the morning. Some Edgewood residents questioned whether she slept at all. Both Murin and Luna were aware of her reputation and assumed she'd be awake by the time they got there. They were right.

"Good morning," Dessa said in a warm tone, opening the door. "Come in."

The elderly elven woman was tall and thin with long silver hair. Dessa looked good for her age

– great, even – but it was still obvious that she was quite old. Her movement was slow and her hands a bit shaky. She'd been in charge of Edgewood for over a century and was well-liked by its citizens.

Dessa's home was extravagantly decorated. Beautiful paintings hung on the walls and her furniture was made from rare, expensive wood. Several bookshelves were visible in the living room, all of them overflowing with books and scrolls. Dessa also had a number of trinkets displayed that she'd collected while traveling during her younger years. Both Murin and Luna were extremely impressed. They'd never seen so many valuables in one place before.

"Something urgent must be on your minds," Dessa continued, shutting the door behind Murin and Luna. "Otherwise, you wouldn't have come to see me so early. Please, have a seat."

She pointed to a couple of wooden chairs in the living room. Murin and Luna sat down in them and thanked her. Dessa disappeared into another room for a few seconds, then returned to the living room wearing a pair of thick glasses. She walked over to a rocking chair that was next to the fireplace and slowly turned it to face Murin and Luna. Just as slowly, Dessa sat down in the rocking chair and leaned forward, slightly.

"Now, what's troubling you at such an early hour?" she asked.

Both Murin and Luna started answering at the same time.

"You're not going to believe..."

"This is going to sound crazy but..."

They turned and looked at each other.

"You tell her," Luna said.

"You sure?" Murin asked.

"Yeah, go ahead," Luna answered.

"Well," Dessa said, "*somebody* tell me!"

"I know this might sound crazy," Murin started, "but we were out in the forest yesterday and we overhead voices. Me, Luna, and... I mean just me and Luna. We were out there going for a walk, something we do often. We snuck closer to see if we could see who it was and hear what they were saying. It was Involore and two of his apprentices. They were talking about how they found out where the unicorns have been living in the forest. And then Involore started talking about how he is planning to kill all the unicorns so he can steal their horns."

"He said that he knows where the unicorns are?" Dessa asked.

"Not exactly," Murin replied. "He said something about narrowing it down to two places they could be. But I think he said he'd know which of the two soon."

"Yeah," Luna agreed. "He did."

Dessa sat silently on the edge of her rocking chair, suspiciously eyeing Murin and Luna up and down. Both of them noticed that Dessa was aggressively tapping one of her feet against the bottom part of her chair.

"I don't find this even the least bit funny," Dessa said, her tone no longer warm.

"What?" Luna asked, a bit confused. "Funny? Neither do we."

"I don't know what would possess you two to come over here first thing in the morning and say something like that," Dessa said, crossing her arms. "I don't know what you're trying to accomplish, but it's not going to work. If you're trying to be funny, you've failed miserably."

"We're not trying to be funny," Murin replied, his voice raised. "Neither of us think it's funny at all. Luna and I both agree that what we overheard was incredibly serious, which is why we came here to see you first thing in the morning."

Again, Dessa didn't respond right away. She just sat on the edge of her rocking chair, arms crossed, tapping her foot. After a long, uncomfortable moment of silence, Dessa finally uncrossed her arms and spoke. Her tone warmed a bit, but still wasn't nearly as friendly as it had been when they'd first arrived.

"There's just no way," Dessa said. "It's not possible. I know that Involore has a reputation around here for being an evil wizard. But he's really not as bad as everyone makes him out to be. In fact, Edgewood wouldn't even exist if it wasn't for Involore. Years before either of you were born, he used his magic to drive away a powerful dragon that was threatening to destroy our village. Believe me: If I thought Involore was capable of something as horrible as you're describing, I would've kicked him out of Edgewood a long time ago. But I don't believe he'd ever do something like that. I've known Involore for a very long time and he's no more evil than your average wizard. If anything, he's less. Involore spends a lot of his time teaching young, aspiring wizards the craft free of charge. Would an evil person do that?"

"No," Murin replied.

"I know it's hard to believe," Luna said, ignoring Dessa's question. "But it's true. Everything Murin said is true. We really did hear Involore talking to his apprentices about how he's planning to use his magic to kill all the unicorns. He said he figured out some way to disrupt the magic that protects them and that with all their horns, he could live forever."

"Look," Dessa said, slowly getting up from her rocking chair, "I thought you were messing with me at first. But the two of you seem sincere and I believe you now."

"You do?" both Murin and Luna said at the same time.

"Yes," Dessa replied, walking over and opening the front door. "I do. I believe that you heard someone say something and your imaginative young minds crafted it into the story you just told me. But I don't believe that Involore is conspiring to kill all the unicorns and take their horns – not for a second. That's just silly. My guess is that you really were out in the woods and something spooked you, causing your imaginations to run wild. Now if you'll excuse me, I have a lot to do today as I know both of you do, too."

"But if you'd just..." Luna protested before being cut off by Dessa.

"If *you'd* just be on your way, I have a lot to do today. Now to make myself perfectly clear, I don't want to be bothered with this again. Consider this topic closed for discussion. And *I* don't want to hear that you've been going around telling people what you *think* you heard. Involore has a bad enough reputation in this village as it is without you two running around spreading rumors. Have I made myself clear?"

"Yes, Dessa," Murin replied.

Dessa looked at Luna.

"Please, at least..."

Dessa's eyes remained focused on Luna, her head tilting back slightly, nostrils flaring.

"Fine," Luna conceded. "You've made yourself clear."

"Good!" Dessa replied, her friendly tone returning instantly. "Luna, tell your mother I said hello. And Murin, please tell your folks and siblings that I said hello to them as well."

"Thanks for your time, Dessa," Murin said.

Dessa smiled as Murin and Luna walked out of her house. She closed the door behind them and watched them disappear down the road through a window.

"I'll have to have a word with Involore about this," she muttered to herself. "He's getting sloppy in his old age."

"So, what are we going to do now?" Luna asked as they walked down the road.

"The only thing we *can* do: nothing," Murin replied. "All we can do is hope that Dessa was right. Maybe Involore and his apprentices weren't talking about what we thought they were. Maybe we misheard them like she said."

Luna stopped walking.

"What?" Murin asked.

"Are you kidding me right now?" Luna asked.

Again, Murin asked, "About what?"

"This is so typical of you," Luna answered, shaking her head.

"What's *that* supposed to mean?" Murin asked, crossing his arms.

"It means you roll over and submit to the nearest authority figure you can find the second he or she opens his or her mouth."

"Oh, please. I do not."

"Yes, you do. And you always have. You're not a little boy anymore, Murin. You're a grown man. Act like it. You need to start advocating for what you believe and for what you want for yourself."

"I do," Murin replied, a slight quiver in his voice.

"Do you believe that Dessa was right? Do you honestly believe that we misheard Involore and his apprentices out in the forest?"

"No," Murin reluctantly answered.

"Of course not!" Luna yelled, throwing her arms up in the air. "Because we *did* hear him say all that awful stuff. But the second Dessa suggested otherwise, you agreed with her even though you knew she was wrong. It's the same thing with your father."

"Oh, here we go. This again!" Murin said, now throwing *his* arms up in the air.

"Face it. You're afraid to confront anyone with any authority over you. I don't know if it's because you don't want to disappoint them or you're afraid that they'll do something to you or what. But you need to learn to stand up for yourself, what you want, and what you believe. Otherwise, you're in for one miserable life. You know, you could actually learn a thing or two from Xavier."

"Oh, this ought to be good," Murin replied, again crossing his arms. "What does the all-knowing, all-wise Luna think I have to learn from a rude, selfish unicorn?"

"You're right: Xavier *is* rude. And he *is* selfish. But at least he's not afraid to speak his mind. He says what he's feeling and doesn't care what anyone thinks about it."

"You want to know what *I'm* thinking right now?" Murin asked, shooting Luna a dirty look.

"I need to get ready for today's lesson. And you need to go take care of the farm for the next fifty years so you don't have to explain to your parents that you hate it and would rather follow your own path in life," Luna said, then stormed off down the road.

Murin opened his mouth to yell at Luna as she walked off but nothing came out. Her words really stung and Murin knew that there was at least some truth to them. He stood in the middle of the road for a moment and watched her walk off before returning to the farm.

All day long, both Murin and Luna struggled to stay focused on their duties. They did the best they could, but their minds kept returning to the events of the morning. Murin couldn't help but replay Luna's words over and over again in his head. To take his mind off things, Murin planned to go for an evening walk in the woods after he was done on the farm for the day. Long walks usually made him feel better when he was upset and he wanted to see if he could find Xavier. Little did Murin know that he wouldn't have to.

11.

"I'm so freakin' bored," Xavier mumbled.

After parting ways with Murin and Luna, Xavier wandered around the forest aimlessly. While his assessment was partially right – he *was* bored – he was also starting to get lonely. But more than anything, Xavier was feeling troubled by what he'd overhead Involore and his apprentices saying the day before. At first, he was almost happy to hear that the unicorns were going to be destroyed. Xavier felt betrayed by them and saw it as karmic retribution. But after letting it really sink in overnight, Xavier's feelings were starting to change.

Over the course of the day, as he wandered around the forest, Xavier did a lot of thinking. It might not have been by choice, but he couldn't take his mind off what Involore had said. In fact, Xavier did everything he could to distract himself from thinking about it. But no matter what he did, his thoughts kept returning to what he'd overheard the day before. It ate away at him over the course of the day, no matter what the unicorn did to try to distract himself.

"Astra used to love nibbling on fresh green grass like that," Xavier said out loud as he came to a small area filled with wild grass. "Ebelle, too."

He started eating some grass with thoughts of his family and friends back in Unicaria bouncing around in his head nonstop. Xavier picked his head up high and stood there motionless, looking up at the sky. He couldn't take it any longer. His emotions had been heating up all day and were finally about to boil over. Unable to contain himself, he yelled at the top of his lungs. Unicorns had long vocal chords and it was loud enough that it could've been heard for a mile in all directions. Fortunately, there was no one around to hear it.

"Arrrgggggghhh!" Xavier screamed and stomped his hoof at the same time. "Why can't I stop thinking about what that stupid wizard said?"

Deep down inside, Xavier already knew the answer. He might not have wanted to admit it to himself, but Xavier cared about his fellow unicorns. Even after having been exiled, he still loved them. Xavier was a unicorn himself, after all, even if he was a bit different than the others. All unicorns had love in their hearts, even if that love was buried deep underneath a rough exterior – several layers deep, as it seemed to be with Xavier.

"Uggghhh," Xavier yelled at the top of his lungs, then calmed himself. "I can't just sit back and let this happen. I can't let that wizard destroy my kind, no matter what they did to me."

Xavier knew that there probably wasn't much he could do on his own. He needed to recruit the help of some friends. And the closest thing to friends that Xavier had were the only two humans he knew: Murin and Luna.

Xavier found his way back to Edgewood, doing his best to steer clear of anyone out on the road. When Xavier got to Murin's farm, he wasn't sure what to do. Unicorns didn't have front doors to knock on, so he didn't know that was how you'd usually announce your presence at someone's house. Xavier walked around back to the stable, which was locked shut for the night. He could've magically opened the latch but knew that, if the gate was shut and locked, Murin probably wasn't out there.

Xavier walked up to the house, confident that Murin must be inside. The house had two doors – a front door and a back door. Xavier had only seen people going into and coming out of the back door, so he walked up to it. He thought about simply yelling Murin's name, but knew that wouldn't have been wise. Xavier tried to recall what Murin had done when they went to Luna's house the morning before. He remembered Murin tapping on the door and then Luna's mother opening it just a few seconds after.

With no fist to use to knock on the back door, Xavier first tried using his horn. He still wasn't entirely used to it not being there. When he bobbed his head forward, Xavier was expecting the horn to hit the door. Since it was no longer there, it didn't. He was thrown slightly off balance and whacked his head against the door.

"Stupid elders," Xavier mumbled, looking up to where his alicorn used to be.

Accidentally hitting his head against the door gave Xavier an idea. He headbutted the door several times, hoping it would be loud enough to get someone's attention. It wasn't.

Xavier was starting to get frustrated. Again, he considered calling out Murin's name but knew it was probably a bad idea. He thought of one more thing to try before he would resort to that. Xavier turned around and backed up to the door. With one of his back hooves, he lightly tapped on it – or, at least, he *tried* to lightly tap on it.

Crash!

Xavier's hoof went right through the back door. Once again he underestimated his own strength. Getting the attention of someone inside the house was no longer a problem. Xavier had managed to get the attention of *everyone* in the house.

"What the..." Murin's father said as he opened the door. "Murin! Get over here right now!"

"What is it dad?" Murin asked.

As soon as he came around the corner, Murin knew the answer to his question before his dad had a chance to reply. He saw the hole in the door first, then saw Xavier standing outside right after.

"That horse you found the other day just put a hole in our back door!" Mr. Fieldstone yelled. "A hole that you're going to fix right now!"

"Yes, dad," Murin agreed. "I'll take care of it right away."

Murin went outside, closing the door behind him. He wasn't thrilled about having to fix it after working all day long, but he was happy to see Xavier.

"You came back!" Murin exclaimed. "I wasn't sure if you would. I was just getting ready to go out in the woods to look for you."

"Yeah," Xavier replied, "I didn't think I'd ever want to return to this smelly village."

"So, what changed?"

"I haven't been able to stop thinking about what we heard that wizard say out in the forest yesterday. Did you and Luna go talk to the elders like you said you were going to?"

"Elder," Murin replied. "Just one. Our village has one elder, an elf named Dessa. Remember? And yes, we talked to her. Well, we tried to."

"What do you mean, 'tried to?' What did she say? She's going to stop the wizard, right?"

"I'm sorry," Murin said, looking down.

"What does that mean?" Xavier asked. "She isn't going to stop him? Doesn't she care?"

"She didn't believe us. Dessa thought we were making it up or exaggerating or something. She insisted that it couldn't possibly be true."

"What if you brought me to go talk to her?" Xavier asked. "Do you think she'd believe us then?"

"Dessa made it very clear that she doesn't want to be bothered by this again. *Very* clear. Even if I brought you to her, I doubt she'd believe that you're actually a unicorn. She'd think we were playing some sort of trick on her. Dessa told us that she doesn't want us to bother her with this again and she definitely meant it. The last thing we want to do is make her angry."

"So, what? That's it? There's nothing that can be done?"

"I don't know what to tell you, Xavier. Luna and I did the only thing we could think to do. We tried to get help. I don't know what else to do."

"Maybe you, me, and Luna can come up with a plan together," Xavier suggested.

"She's not very happy with me right now."

"Trouble with the non-girlfriend girl friend, huh? What'd you do?"

"Nothing, really," Murin replied, scratching the back of his head. "She just thinks I should be more vocal about what I want and what I believe. She actually said I should be more like *you*."

"She's a smart girl," Xavier said with a smirk. "I think everyone could benefit from being a little more like me."

"Uh huh," Murin replied, cracking a half-smile. "I guess we can try to talk to Luna to see if the three of us can come up with some sort of a plan. Hopefully she's calmed down a bit since I saw her this morning."

"All right!" Xavier said. "Now you're talking. What kind of plan?"

"I have no idea," Murin replied. "But between the three of us, maybe we can figure something out. There has to be something we can do."

"All right," Xavier said again, this time with a little less enthusiasm. "That evil wizard isn't going to destroy the unicorns if I have anything to say about it. If anyone's going to do that, it's going to be me!"

"And here I was thinking that you actually wanted to help the other unicorns," Murin said with a slight smirk.

"What? I can't want to save them and destroy them at the same time? I'm a complicated unicorn." Xavier replied.

"Yes, you certainly are," Murin said with a full smirk.

"It's not like I could destroy them even if I really wanted to. Unicorns can't kill other living things. If we could, I wouldn't be talking to you. I'd just go find that wizard and kick his stupid face in."

"Kind of like you did to our door?" Murin asked, still smirking.

"Yeah. That was my bad."

"Uh huh," Murin said. "Come on. Let's go get some wood and nails so we can fix it."

Murin patched up the door while Xavier stood outside and watched. It didn't take very long and was easy enough for him to do.

After he finished fixing the door, Murin apologized to his father for a second time and told him that he was going for a walk with Xavier for a while. They headed down the main road to Luna's house and a few minutes later were at her front door.

"You want me to knock on it?" Xavier asked.

"No," Murin replied. "I've already patched up one door today. I don't want to have to fix another one."

Murin knocked on the door and Luna answered it a few seconds later. She was wearing her evening gown. Murin couldn't help himself from looking her up and down. He'd always thought that Luna was pretty and her gown left little to the imagination.

"Hey," she said to Murin, then looked at Xavier. "You're back."

"Yup yup," the unicorn replied.

Murin and Luna looked at each other. After the way they'd left things that morning, Murin wasn't sure how to go about asking Luna if she'd come out with them for a while. Xavier didn't have that problem.

"We need your help," the unicorn said.

"Oh?" Luna asked, her eyes never leaving Murin's.

"We're trying to come up with a way to help the unicorns and could really use your help," Murin said.

Luna looked at Xavier for a second, then back to Murin and replied, "Let me get changed."

Murin and Xavier waited for Luna in her front yard. She came out a few minutes later wearing a long, white dress and her favorite pair of sandals. Without saying a word, the three of them took a walk down the road to a spot that Murin and Luna liked to sit and talk. There were two large rocks, just big enough for each of them to sit on one. The rocks were about twenty feet away from the main road next to a small, fast-moving stream. Xavier walked over to it and started drinking while Murin and Luna sat down on the rocks.

"So, what's up?" Luna asked, finally breaking the silence.

"Well," Murin replied, "Xavier had a change of heart. He wants to stop Involore from destroying the other unicorns."

"That makes me happy to hear," Luna said. "Maybe he's not as cold-hearted as I'd thought. But how? Did you tell him that Dessa isn't going to do anything?"

"Yeah, I told him. He doesn't know what to do and frankly, neither do I. I was hoping that the three of us can brainstorm and come up with some kind of plan."

"Brainstorm," Xavier parroted, looking up from the stream. "What a great word. I've never heard it before." Immediately, he went right back to drinking from the stream.

"Well," Luna said, "what do we know?"

"We know that Involore is planning to use his magic to destroy all the unicorns and take their horns," Murin replied. "We know that his apprentices are helping him to find out where in the forest the unicorns live."

"We know that *two* of his apprentices are helping him," Luna said. "Involore has four apprentices, each one studying a different type of elemental magic: earth, wind, fire, and water."

"How do we... How do *you* know that?" Murin asked.

"Because I'm friends with Anora, Involore's water apprentice. Remember? Her and I have been friends for years. She's a real sweetheart."

"That's great!" Murin exclaimed. "I forgot you two were friends. Do you think she knows anything about what Involore's up to? Do you think she's involved?"

"No way," Luna replied. "There's no way that Anora would have anything to do with Involore's evil plan, even if he is her master."

"Would you talk to her?" Murin asked. "Maybe tomorrow you could go see her. Find out if she knows anything. Anything at all."

"Yeah," Luna replied. "I can do that. I've been meaning to go visit her, anyway."

"You hear that, Xavier?" Murin asked.

"Yup," he replied in between sips of water. "Sounds good."

"You don't sound too thrilled," Murin said to Xavier. "I thought you'd be happier. It might not be a detailed plan to stop Involore, but it's a starting point. Anora might be able to give us something we can work with."

"I'm happy, I'm happy," Xavier said, briefly looking up at Murin. "Good brainstorming. It's just... This water is so freakin' good! I can't stop drinking it."

The water from the stream was the freshest water Xavier had drank since leaving Unicaria. He went right back to drinking it as soon as he finished talking. Both Murin and Luna looked at him and smiled.

"While I'm visiting Anora, maybe you could go snoop around the magic shop," Luna suggested. "Usually, one of Involore's apprentices is working there in the morning. Maybe go ask a few questions, but don't make it obvious that we know about Involore's plan."

"That's not a bad idea," Murin replied. "Magic shops kind of creep me out, but I'll suck it up and do it. I doubt I'll be able to find out much, but I'll try. And don't worry: I'll be smooth about it."

The three of them stayed there for a little while. Luna and Murin talked while Xavier drank from the stream. At times, they had to raise their voices because he was slurping so loudly. Eventually, they decided to call it a night. Murin and Xavier walked Luna back to her house, then returned to the farm. After a brief protest, Xavier agreed to stay in the stable for the night. He really didn't like being confined and, even less, being around a bunch of smelly animals. But Xavier preferred the stable to being alone in the forest for another night. He slept soundly, as did Murin and Luna. All three of them fell asleep wondering what they'd be able to find out the next day.

12.

"Luna!" Anora yelled, running over to the door.

"Anora!" Luna yelled back, holding her arms out wide.

Anora ran right into Luna's arms and the girls shared a long, tight hug. They were both in their late teens and had known each other for a long time. Anora lived right down the road from Luna. When they were children, they used to spend just about every day together. Now that they were young adults and both studying different types of magic, they didn't get to see each other nearly as much as they used to. Their bond remained nonetheless and after catching up for a few minutes, the girls felt as close as ever.

"So, how are your studies coming along?" Luna asked.

"Good!" Anora answered. "I'm starting to get a lot better. Want to see something cool?"

"Sure," Luna replied.

Anora started speaking in a language Luna didn't recognize, her words getting louder and louder. She shouted the final sentence and pointed at a nearby puddle in her yard. As Anora slowly raised her hand up, the water raised with it several feet into the air. It was wide at the bottom, narrowing until it formed a point at the top. Anora shouted one more word, snapped her fingers, and the water froze.

"Wow!" Luna said. "That was really cool!"

She walked over to the puddle, now a large spike of ice. Luna touched the tip of it, though not for any particular reason. The ice was already starting to melt. It was still early in the day but the sun was shining brightly. Before long, it all melted and the puddle was back to normal.

"Thanks!" Anora replied. "I thought you'd like that."

"How do you like studying under Involore?" Luna asked.

"He can be really strict at times. But he's a great teacher. Involore is incredibly smart. I've never met someone who knows as much as he does. But sometimes he..." Anora started, then paused.

"What is it?"

"Sometimes I feel like I'm the least favorite of all his apprentices."

"Why do you say that?" Luna asked, putting her hand on Anora's shoulder.

"Because he spends more time with the others. Like, a *lot* more time. He's always out on some secret adventure with this one or that one. But never me. I always get stuck having to stay in town, working at the magic shop. I'm off today, though."

"Who's working there today?"

"Galan, Involore's fire apprentice. He's a little, um, slow. But he means well. I actually kind of like Galan."

"You don't like the other two apprentices?" Luna asked. "Is that what you're saying?"

"It's not that I don't like them," Anora replied, looking away. "I just don't trust them. I feel like they're always up to something."

"Like what?"

"Who knows. They've been going out into the forest a lot. I can tell you that. I'm pretty sure Involore's got them working on something out there, but I have no idea what. They just weird me out a little bit."

Luna thought about telling Anora what she'd heard out in the forest. She knew that Anora was trustworthy. In fact, Anora knew more about Luna than anyone else, even Murin. As close as they were, Luna always felt more comfortable talking to Anora about certain things. Girl talk. But after giving it some thought, Luna decided to hold off on saying anything to Anora until she found out if Murin was able to learn anything from Galan.

"A couple of weirdos, huh?" Luna said and smiled. "Well, unlike you, I don't have the day off, so I should be going. It was so nice to catch up a little bit."

"Agreed!" Anora replied. "Let's get together again soon. I want you to tell me a little about Murin."

"What about Murin?" Luna asked, her eyebrows raised slightly.

"I don't want to keep you from your studies," Anora replied. "We'll get together and talk some other time."

"Okay," Luna replied.

The girls wrapped each other up in their arms, exchanging another long, tight hug. They said goodbye and Luna left Anora's yard, heading to the healer's for her daily lesson.

Meanwhile, Murin was finishing up his morning routine. He let out the animals, fed them, and took care of his other responsibilities. Xavier stayed in his stall the entire time, which made Murin happy. He was able to take care of everything quickly without being distracted by his unicorn friend. While Murin worked, Xavier napped, floating in and out of consciousness. By the time he actually got up, Murin was done with everything he needed to do.

"You want to come with me to the magic shop?" Murin asked Xavier.

"Noooooo," Xavier replied, the sarcasm in his voice incredibly obvious. "I want to sit around here all day with these stinky, smelly, dirty, nasty..."

"I get it," Murin said. "Come on. Let's go."

13.

Murin and Xavier walked to the magic shop. They passed a few people along the way that were going about their morning business. Several of them said hi to Murin but paid little attention to Xavier. They were used to seeing him with horses and other animals. The magic shop was an old, eerie building, one of the oldest in all of Edgewood.

"Wait out here while I go inside," Murin said to Xavier as they got to the shop.

"What if I want to go in with you?" Xavier asked.

"You want to go inside?"

"Nope," Xavier answered. "I don't. But what if I did?"

"Then you'd need me to hold the door open for you," Murin said as he opened the door for himself. "Otherwise, you'd have to kick your way through it like you did to my back door."

"Still mad about the hole I put in the door, huh?" Xavier replied, but Murin was already inside the magic shop. "Jeez, get over it. That was forever ago."

Murin had never been in the magic shop before. Even walking past it gave him the creeps. As soon as he was inside, the hair on the back of his neck stood up and a chill ran down his spine. The few windows that the old building had on the first floor were covered and it was very dark inside. The only source of light were two small candles burning on the counter. Behind it was a door that led into the back room where Galan was putting away some fresh herbs that had been delivered that morning.

"Hello?" Murin yelled.

"One minute," he heard someone say from the back room.

Murin leaned against the counter and looked around. Dozens of different herbs, gems, and other items were neatly organized on shelves around the room. There was a scent in the air that Murin didn't recognize, but he kind of liked it.

A minute later, Galan came out from the back room. He was Involore's fire apprentice and looked the part. His hair was long, wavy, and bright red. Galan was wearing a black cloak with a hood, his hair poking out from all sides. He looked like he hadn't bathed in quite some time. Murin had never met Galan before, but he'd seen him around the village.

"Can I help you?" Galan asked.

"Hi," Murin said. "I've never been in a magic shop before. I see you've got a lot of different plants and gems."

"Aren't you a farmer?" Galan asked, recognizing Murin from around town. "That's probably why you've never been in a magic shop before. There's nothing special about that. If you told me you've never been on a farm, now that'd be something. Imagine that? A farmer who's never been on a farm?"

Galan started laughing at the thought of a farmless farmer. It didn't take much to make him laugh. He was a simple young man, especially for an aspiring wizard. Involore often got frustrated with Galan, but kept him around because he was trustworthy and willing to do the jobs that others refused.

"Yes," Murin replied. "That's right: I'm a farmer. My name is Murin. It's nice to meet you. You're one of Involore's apprentices, right?"

"That's right," Galan answered, followed by an inappropriately-long smile. "I'm Involore's fire apprentice. You want to see?"

"That's not really necessary," Murin replied.

Galan paid no attention to Murin's response. The fire apprentice reached under the counter and took out a brand-new candle. He placed at the end of the counter and took several steps backward.

"Watch this," Galan said with pride.

He rubbed his hands together and started speaking softly in a language that Murin didn't understand. As he cast the spell, Galan's voice got louder and louder. Finally, he clapped his hands together and pointed at the candle. It didn't catch on fire, but a jar of dried herbs on the shelf behind it did.

"No!" Galan yelled. "Not again!"

He grabbed a book from under the counter and ran over to the burning jar of herbs. Galan held the book over the top of the jar, depriving the fire of oxygen. Gradually it went out and Galan eventually removed the book from the jar. Smoke poured out of it and the pleasant scent in the room was replaced with a foul odor.

"That wasn't supposed to happen," Galan said, visibly embarrassed. "I thought I'd figured out how to stop that from happening."

"No worries," Murin replied, trying to make him feel better. "We all make mistakes. You might not have lit the candle on fire like you intended, but you did light *something* on fire. That's more than I could do. And it certainly proves that you're a fire wizard."

"I'm just an apprentice," Galan said and smiled. "But thank you for the kind words. It's nice to meet someone who's so understanding."

Murin could tell that his words made Galan feel a lot better. It was also obvious that Galan wasn't used to being treated so kindly. Murin knew that he could use this to his advantage.

"I take it Involore isn't very understanding?" Murin asked.

"He treats me like..." Galan started, then paused. "Involore's a good teacher. But I mess up a lot. It takes me a long time to learn things and the other apprentices make fun of me."

"That's not nice. I try not to ever make fun of people. Involore has four apprentices, right? They all make fun of you?"

"Four: That's right. They don't *all* make fun of me. Anora is really nice. But Evia and Drixius can be really mean."

Murin knew that those were the two apprentices they'd seen out in the forest with Involore. He was happy to hear that they frequently made fun of Galan, but not because he wanted Galan to be treated poorly. Murin knew that it meant he'd be more likely to give up information about the other apprentices.

"Evia and Drixius," Murin said. "Does Involore favor them over you? Does he spend more time with them than he does with you?"

"He does. And he spends *a lot* more time with them. He barely spends any time with me, aside from our lessons."

"That's not right. He should spend *extra* time with you if you're having a hard time with your magic. What does Involore do with them when they spend time together? Where do they go?"

"Usually, they don't tell me," Galan answered. "Involore just tells me that they'll be gone for days and that I need to take care of the shop. I feel like me and Anora work here twice as often as they do, but we're all supposed to work the same amount of time."

"You said they *usually* don't tell you," Murin said. "Do you ever know where they go?"

"Sometimes. Like right now, I know where Involore is. He told me. But I'm not sure where Drixius, Evia, and Anora are. Actually, I *do* know where Anora is. She's probably at home. She has the day off. Involore doesn't send her on quests like he does with the other two."

"Where is Involore now?" Murin asked.

"I don't know if I'm supposed to say," Galan replied.

"I'm sure he wouldn't mind," Murin said and smiled. "I'm just curious to know how wizards spend their time. You're the only wizard I know in Edgewood and you've already told me how you spend your time."

"Again, I'm not a full-fledged wizard," Galan replied with a smile of his own.

"Yet," Murin added. "But you will be someday and I bet you'll be a great wizard. Involore might not make you feel that way, but I think you will be. Where is he?"

Murin's words had the effect he'd wanted. Galan was smiling on the inside and out. He'd never met anyone who was as kind and encouraging as Murin. And he loved being called a wizard, even though he was technically only an apprentice. That word was music to Galan's ears and it made him smile every time Murin said it, even though he did his best to hide it.

"Involore went to Briarville," Galan replied. "He said he had urgent business up there and that he'd be gone for a few days."

"Wizard business, huh? What kind of business?"

"He's going to see Thall the Explorer. But I don't know why."

Now Murin was smiling on the inside. He knew who Thall was – everyone did. Thall was a legendary explorer who lived in Briarville, a town about a day's walk north of Edgewood. Murin had been hearing stories about Thall since he was a child. He couldn't imagine why Involore would need to see him urgently. It could be for any of a number of reasons. Thall had his hand in just about everything: map making, buying and selling rare gems, identifying cursed items, getting his hands on hard-to-find items, and a bunch of other pursuits. Murin was eager to find out why Involore would need to see the seasoned explorer.

"That's cool," Murin replied, trying not to seem too interested. "Well, I should go. My horse is waiting for me outside."

"You don't want to buy something?" Galan asked, coming out from behind the counter. "How about if I try to light that candle one more time. I know I can do it."

"I really need to go," Murin replied.

"Please," Galan said, lightly grabbing Murin's arm. "Let me try one more time."

Murin really wanted to get out of there. He'd accomplished what he'd set out to do and was eager to tell Xavier. But Murin saw the look on Galan's face and it made him feel bad.

"Okay," Murin said. "One more time. I know you can do it."

Galan ran back behind the counter. He put the new candle at the end of it again and took several steps backward. Murin was silently rooting for Galan but took a couple of steps back himself – just in case. With a determined look on his face, Galan began chanting. He rubbed his hands together and his voice got louder. Finally, he clapped his hands and pointed at the candle.

Nothing happened – at first.

"Oh man," Galan mumbled. "This is strange."

Just as Murin was about to ask what the apprentice meant by "strange," the candle that Galan was trying to light started melting. There was no flame or smoke – it just melted. The entire candle turned into a puddle of wax on the counter. It quickly began cooling and hardening up.

"Damn it!" Galan yelled, slamming his fist on the counter.

"Don't be so hard on yourself," Murin said as he walked to the door, not wanting to get stuck there for a third demonstration. "Your magic *did* work. It just didn't work the way you wanted it to. Keep practicing and eventually you'll get it. See you!"

"Bye, Murin!" Galan yelled as he walked out the front door. "Maybe sometime we can..."

The door to the magic shop closed and Murin was happy to be out of there. He genuinely felt bad for Galan but was happy to have gotten some useful information out of him. When he got outside, Murin didn't see Xavier anywhere.

"Xavier!" he yelled.

Nothing. Murin cupped his hands around his mouth and tried again, this time much louder.

"Xavier!!!"

"What?" the unicorn asked calmly, walking out from behind the magic shop.

"Where were you? What were you doing?"

"You were in there for so freakin' long that I went in the shade and took a nap. I thought maybe the apprentice put some kind of spell on you or something."

"You thought he put a spell on me so instead of trying to help me, you went around back and took a nap?"

"I can't help if I'm not well-rested," Xavier replied with what Murin was starting to recognize as a unicorn smirk.

"Come on," Murin said, waving his arm. "Let's get out of here. This place gives me the creeps."

"You find out anything worth finding out?"

"I did, yes," Murin replied. "Let's go find Luna. I'll tell you both all about it. I think the three of us are going to be taking a trip up to Briarville."

14.

Early the next morning, Murin, Xavier, and Luna met on the main road in the northernmost part of Edgewood. The sun was just starting to come up over the horizon and there was a chill in the air. Luna and Xavier agreed with Murin that they should go to Briarville and ask Thall about Involore. Both Murin and Luna had been there several times before, though neither of them had ever met Thall. It took the better part of a day to get to Briarville from Edgewood and they had just enough time to get there and back. It was the beginning of the weekend and they had both days off. That gave them just enough time to get to Briarville, find and talk to Thall, and get back to Edgewood before the new week began.

The three of them started walking north as soon as they were together. There were other travelers on the road, mostly traders and adventurers. The road between Edgewood and Briarville was a busy one and considered to be very safe.

The morning went by quickly and uneventfully. With the sun high in the sky, they stopped briefly to have lunch, then continued walking north. It was in the early afternoon that they encountered a single centauride on the side of the road. She was just standing there, looking into the forest.

"What the hell is that thing?" Xavier asked as they got closer to the centauride.

"That's a centauride," Luna answered.

"A what?"

"A female centaur," Murin replied.

"A female what?"

"A centaur has the body of a horse with the head and torso of a human," Luna explained. "They're usually not dangerous unless provoked. I've heard they can be quite friendly, actually."

"I don't..." Xavier said, unable to stop looking at the centauride. His eyes kept going back and forth between her human torso and her backside. "I don't know how I feel about that thing."

"Excuse me," Murin said to the centauride as they got closer to it. "Is something wrong?"

It was obvious to both Murin and Luna that the centauride was having some sort of crisis. She had a worried look on her face and kept gazing out into the forest. Xavier hadn't noticed. He was too busy trying to process what he was looking at. Part of him found the centauride to be an abomination. However, another part of him found the unusual creature to be strangely alluring.

"I can't find my brother," the centauride replied, looking at them briefly before returning her gaze to the forest.

"He's a centaur, I assume?" Murin asked.

"Yes. We live in the forest not too far from here. When I woke up this morning, he was gone. This has never happened before. I'm worried sick. You haven't seen him, have you?"

"I'm afraid not," Luna said. "But we'll let him know that you're looking for him if we run into him."

"Thank you," the centauride replied. "I don't know what to do. I'm so worried."

"I'm sure he's alright. Keep looking. I'm sure he'll turn up eventually." Murin said. He ran his hand down the centauride's back and it seemed to comfort her a little bit. Murin looked at Xavier to see if he was watching. He wanted the unicorn to see how much the centauride liked being touched by him. Xavier was looking alright, but his mind was elsewhere. He was still trying to figure out what to make of the half human, half horse.

"Thanks," the centauride said again.

"Don't we have to keep moving?" Xavier asked, impatiently. "Didn't we get up at the ass-crack of dawn because it takes a long time to get to Briarville?"

"He's right," Murin said. "He's rude, but he's right. We do have to keep going. But, like my friend said, we'll keep an eye out for your brother. And if we see him, we'll let him know you're looking for him. What's his name?"

"My brother's name is Timules. And I'm Kalarpia. Once again, thank you," she replied for a third time.

The three of them continued heading north. Kalarpia kept slowly moving along the side of the road, looking out into the woods. Xavier was happy to get away from her. It wasn't that he didn't like the centauride. But Xavier found himself getting a little aroused when he looked at her from certain angles and it made him uncomfortable. Before long, they were far enough up the road that the centauride was out of sight.

The rest of the walk went by smoothly and they arrived in Briarville that evening. On both sides of the road leading into Briarville, starting about a mile outside of town, thick briar patches made it impossible to veer off the path. Both Luna and Murin had been told stories as kids about children getting stuck in the patches and not being able to get out – ever. Now that they're older, they questioned how true those stories were. But the underlying lesson they never questioned: Stay away from the briar patches.

The three of them walked into town. It was larger than Edgewood and there were lots of people out on the roads and in their yards. None of them paid much attention to Murin, Luna, and Xavier. It wasn't uncommon to see outsiders walking with their horses through town. Murin had a friend who lived in Briarville and they went to go see him first. They wanted to see if he could tell them anything about Thall before they paid him a visit.

"No way," Murin's friend yelled as he opened the door. "What a pleasant surprise!"

"Hey Meldon!" Murin replied. "How've you been?"

"Good, good," Meldon answered. "Let me come outside to talk to you. My father's trying to read."

Murin waved to Meldon's father, who he could see sitting in the living room. Meldon came outside and joined them in the front yard. He was about the same age as Murin and Luna. Like Murin, Meldon was also a farmer. The two of them met when they were young and quickly became friends.

"So, what brings you to Briarville?" Meldon asked.

Murin and Luna explained everything that'd happened to the Briarville farmer. Murin trusted Meldon and knew that he wouldn't say anything to anyone. It took them a little while to convince him that they weren't playing a trick on him, but eventually they did.

"Wow," Meldon said, walking over to Xavier. "So you're really a unicorn, huh? I've only heard about unicorns in stories. Sometimes, I've questioned whether you really exist at all. I guess now I know."

Right before Meldon was about to touch Xavier, Murin grabbed his hand. He could tell that Xavier was about to freak out, just as he had every time Murin tried to touch him.

"He doesn't like to be touched," Murin explained.

"Not by most people, anyway," Luna added with a smirk.

"Unreal," Meldon said, shaking his head – not in disgust but in disbelief. "So, what can *I* do to help?"

"Have you heard anything about Involore or his apprentices visiting Thall?" Luna asked.

"Or have you seen or heard anything about Thall acting differently lately?" Murin added.

"I'm sorry," Meldon answered. "I haven't. But what I *do* know is that Thall is at home right now."

"How do you know that?" Murin asked.

"Because I just saw him not even an hour ago. Thall was at the tavern when I went in to pick up some mutton and ale for dad. He was sitting at a table with someone, talking. While I was waiting at the counter, I overheard part of their conversation. Well, sort of. It was loud in there. But I heard Thall tell the old man that he found what he was looking for – whatever that means. Then he said he was looking forward to going home and relaxing because it had been a long day. By the look of things, it seemed like they were just about done with their meals. I'm sure they are by now, which means Thall should be at home."

"What did the person he was talking to look like?" Luna asked.

"I really didn't get a good look at him. My father always says that it's not polite to stare. Besides, I had no reason to examine him."

"Can you tell us *anything* about him?" Murin asked.

"Well, he was tall. I can tell you that. And he had a long, black beard. Other than that, I can't say.

It's always a bit dark in the tavern and he was wearing a hood. Oh, and he was really old. Did I say that already?"

"Involore," both Murin and Luna said at the same time.

"That was the evil wizard who's planning to kill all the unicorns?" Meldon asked.

"Yup," Murin answered. "That was him. Did you hear them say anything else? Anything at all?"

"Not really. The tavern was loud – as it always is – and it was hard to make out what they were saying. But it did seem like the man in the hood was happy. Out of the corner of my eye, I saw him grin when Thall told him he found what he was looking for. It was kind of a creepy grin. Thall, on the other hand, seemed a bit down. Actually, now that I think about it, Thall *has* been acting a little differently lately."

"How so?" Luna asked.

"He hasn't quite been himself. And it's not just me who thinks so. Several people I've talked to around town have noticed, too. Lately, Thall has seemed sad and preoccupied. He's usually really friendly. He always stops to talk to everybody. I've even talked to him a few times myself. But for the past few weeks, he hasn't really been talking to anyone. And the few people that he *has* talked to all say that he hasn't been himself lately. My dad thinks it's adventurer's depression. He said that explorers like Thall, when they get old, they become sad because they can no longer do what they love. It could be true. My dad is really smart. And Thall barely ever leaves town anymore. He used to always be going here or there, on this quest or that quest. I don't think he's left Briarville once in the past month or two."

"Adventurer's depression, huh?" Murin said. "Maybe. And you're right: Your dad *is* a smart man. He's taught me a lot about farming and life in general. But I have a feeling that Thall's sudden change has something to do with Involore."

"There's only one way to find out," Xavier said. "Let's go see him. Maybe *his* yard will have some decent grass for me to munch on."

"He's a lot different than what I was expecting when you told me that he's a unicorn," Meldon said. "But the whole getting kicked out of the forest thing isn't too hard to believe."

"He's a special unicorn," Luna said, petting Xavier on his side.

They all started walking to Thall's home, Meldon included. He offered to let them spend the night at his house, which they gratefully accepted. Xavier wasn't thrilled about spending the night in *another* stable, but it was really the only option. He couldn't spend the night in the forest, as the woods surrounding the town were filled with briar patches in all directions.

Thall lived a few minutes from Meldon's farm and they were at his front door before long. The sun was starting to set and they could see a freshly-lit candle burning through the side window. Meldon knocked on the door, since he was the only one who Thall would recognize.

"Go away," Thall yelled through the door. "I'm not taking any visitors tonight."

"Please," Meldon yelled back. "It's important. We just need a couple minutes of your time."

Nothing happened for several seconds. Murin, Luna, and Meldon all looked at each other and shrugged their shoulders. Xavier was already walking around Thall's yard, looking for some tasty grass to munch on. Just as Meldon was about to knock again, the door swung wide open. Murin and Luna had heard plenty about Thall, but didn't know what he looked like. Both of them were shocked when they first saw him. He wasn't at all what they were expecting.

"You've got two minutes," Thall said, leaning against the doorway with crossed arms. "What is it?"

15.

Thall stood at only four-feet tall. The sides of his head were shaved but long, brown hair flowed down from the top. His face, arms, hands, and – to a lesser degree – his feet, were an almost-matching shade of brown from years of traveling under the blazing sun. He was wearing a bright-red robe with a pair of matching slippers, made from the fur of several different animals. On his fingers were several gold rings, some with rare jewels on them.

Murin, Luna, and Meldon all looked at each other. Luna and Murin were still trying to get over how different Thall was from what they were expecting, not that they really knew what to expect. Meldon, being the only one who'd met Thall, decided to take the lead and explain why they were there.

"We found out something very disturbing and were hoping you could help us to shed some light on things."

"What? How?"

Again, they looked at each other. This time Murin spoke.

"Why did Involore come to see you?"

Thall didn't answer the question. He eyed Murin up and down first, then Luna before his gaze returned to Meldon. Xavier was on the side of the house, out of view.

"Who are your friends? I've never seen either of these humans before."

Thall was half gnome, half dwarf. Like most dwarves and gnomes, he was short and stocky. While Thall wouldn't have been considered elderly, he was quite old. Both dwarves and gnomes could live for hundreds of years. Thall's youngest son, Vastrel, who was one-quarter dwarf, one-quarter gnome, and one-half elf was nearing his seventieth birthday. Like his father, he grew up to be an adventurer and had left town to go on a quest a few weeks earlier.

"How rude of me," Meldon replied. "This is my good friend, Murin. And this is *his* good friend, Luna. They're from Edgewood."

"I see," Thall replied, his arms still crossed. "And why do you want to know about me and Involore?"

"Because he's planning on doing something really, *really* bad," Luna answered.

"Oh?" Thall asked. "What?"

Once again, Murin, Luna, and Meldon looked at each other. They didn't know if they should tell Thall or not. The thought had crossed each of their minds that it was possible Thall was somehow involved in Involore's evil plan. Though it wasn't discussed beforehand, they all came to the same conclusion, which Murin vocalized.

"We can't say. But if you could just tell us..."

"I've got nothing to say about the nature of me and Involore's arrangement," Thall said and uncrossed his arms. "And it's been two minutes. Your time is up. Good night."

Thall closed the door, hard. Luna and Murin looked at Meldon hoping he could offer some insight into what had just happened.

"That was so strange," he said.

"What?" Murin asked.

"I've never seen Thall like that before," Meldon said. "Like, never. He's usually talkative and friendly. And did you notice the way his expression changed when you mentioned Involore?"

"I sure did," Murin replied. "If I didn't know any better – which I don't, really – I'd think Thall was hiding something."

"I know you never met him before tonight," Meldon said, "but I have. And he's *definitely* hiding something."

"But what?" Luna asked.

"That's what we need to find out," Meldon replied.

"So you'll help us?" Murin asked.

"Of course! Not only will I help you simply because you're my friend, but now I'm curious to know what Thall's hiding. And besides, it's the weekend. I got nothing going on and could use something to do."

"Great!" both Murin and Luna said at the same time.

"So, what are we going to do?" Luna asked.

"We're going to do some serious sleuthing," Meldon replied.

Just as Murin often fantasized about being an adventurer, Meldon had always dreamed of being a rogue. His father taught him to read at a young age, a skill that few farmers ever learned. Meldon loved reading books about burglars breaking into locked rooms filled with treasure, thieves repelling down ropes into otherwise-impenetrable fortresses, spies sneaking up on unsuspecting targets, and other rogue-like activities. Like Murin, Meldon spent much of his free time studying and practicing his secret passion. His friend Reyson was a skilled rogue and had been teaching him the tricks of his trade. While Meldon hadn't exactly mastered any of the rogue skills Reyson was teaching him, he was getting good at a lot of different things. One of those things was spying and Meldon was dying for an opportunity to do it for real.

"Sleuthing?" Luna and Murin asked at the same time.

"Sleuthing," Xavier said, slowly, right after Luna and Murin. "I like that word, too. We should do some brainstorm sleuthing."

"Sorry, Xav," Murin said. "That's not really a thing."

"You have to admit," Xavier replied, "it does sound cool, though."

"It does kind of sound cool," Murin said to Xavier, then turned to face Meldon. "What kind of sleuthing do you have in mind?"

"Let's go back to my farm. You guys must be starving. We'll have something to eat and then," Meldon said, turning to Xavier, "we'll *brainstorm* about the *sleuthing* we'll do."

"I like this dude," Xavier said with a half-smile.

They went back to Meldon's farm and enjoyed a big meal. It was a mild night and they ate outside so Xavier could participate in the conversation. Meldon, eager to use some of his rogue skills, suggested they sneak up to Thall's house and look in his windows. Murin agreed that it was a good idea and volunteered to join his friend on a late-night spy mission. After they finished eating, Meldon got Xavier settled in the stable and got Luna set up in the house with a pillow and blanket. Then, he and Murin left to go spy on Thall.

The sun had long been over the horizon and it was pitch-black outside. It was a cloudy night and there was no moonlight whatsoever. There were torches lit around town, which provided just enough light for the two young men to find their way to Thall's house. They were happy to see that a candle was still burning inside the home of the half gnome, half dwarf.

"Get down," Meldon whispered to Murin, then got down on his belly and started crawling.

"I really don't think that's necessary," Murin replied, speaking softly.

"Shhh!" Meldon insisted. "Be quiet. And do what I say. I'm the one with spy training!"

Murin thought it was a bit silly to be crawling their way to Thall's house. They were still several-hundred feet away and there was no one else around. Even if there had been, it was so dark that it was unlikely they would've been seen. But Murin played along, not wanting to upset his friend. Besides, he could see that Meldon was really enjoying having a chance to put his spy skills to use.

The two young men crawled for several minutes until they got to Thall's house. Slowly, they worked their way over to one of his windows. Meldon and Murin popped up, peeked in, and saw Thall – saw him blowing out the only lit candle in the house.

"Damn," Meldon whispered under his breath.

"We're too late," Murin whispered. "Looks like he's going to bed."

"Yeah it does. No point in sticking around. Let's get out of here."

Meldon started walking along the side of Thall's house back to the street with Murin right behind him. He didn't see that there was a shovel leaning against the side of the house and the wannabe-rogue knocked it over. The shovel fell over and hit a barrel sitting next to Thall's house.

Crash!

It made a loud sound and, immediately after, the boys heard another sound: the sound of Thall's flint and steel. The half gnome, half dwarf heard the crash outside and moved quickly over to the table with the candle he'd just blown out a minute earlier. He knew where everything in the house was and easily found his flint and steel in the dark. After a few attempts, Thall got the candle lit and the boys saw the windows of his house light up.

"Run!" Meldon whisper-yelled.

He took off toward the road with Murin right behind him. The boys ran as fast as they could until they were far away from Thall's house. The seasoned explorer went outside and looked around for a minute before going back in. Thall came to the conclusion that the wind knocked over the shovel and he went back to bed after blowing out the candle.

"Well, that didn't go very well," Murin said, still catching his breath as they walked down the main road. "We didn't learn anything."

"Actually," Meldon said, also breathing heavily, "we did. Thall is known to usually stay up late reading and writing. If he's going to bed this early, it means he probably has to be up early for something in the morning. We should get up early, too, and go back to his house. Maybe we can find something out then."

"I don't know," Murin replied, gradually catching his breath. "Are you suggesting we break into his house when he's not there? I don't think that'd be right."

"We're not breaking in. We're sneaking in, taking a look around, and leaving. It's not like we'll be stealing anything. Just looking for anything that can tell us why he's been associating with that evil wizard."

Murin didn't love the idea but, after a little more convincing from Meldon, he agreed. The boys got back to Meldon's farm and found Luna already asleep. Before long, they were both asleep themselves.

16.

The next morning, Meldon was the first one to wake up. He prepared some food for the others, including Xavier. Like the night before, they all ate together in the backyard.

"This is so freakin' good!" Xavier said in between bites of what Meldon gave him. "What do you call this?"

"That's ham," Meldon answered.

"I don't know what that is," Xavier replied. "Is that some kind of plant or tree or something?"

"No, it's pork," Murin explained.

"Again, no clue what that is."

"It's pig," Luna said. "Ham is cooked pig meat."

Xavier completely froze with his mouth wide open. The ham that he was chewing fell out of it onto the ground.

"Something wrong?" Meldon asked.

"I... I can't..." Xavier tried to say but was having trouble speaking. "Excuse me for a minute."

Xavier walked around the side of the house. Murin, Meldon, and Luna all looked at each other and shrugged their shoulders. None of them knew what was wrong. Eating meat had long been a human – and humanoid, in general – tradition, something that no one questioned. But unicorns don't eat meat. Not only are they not allowed to hurt other living things, but unicorns can't hurt things that once were living – no matter how dead or delicious they may be. When they do, they become violently ill.

Blaaaaaahhhhhh!

"Ewwwwww," Luna yelled.

They heard Xavier vomiting around the corner of the house. He'd eaten quite a bit of ham before realizing what it was and his body was doing everything it could to expel it as quickly as possible.

Blaaahhh! Blaaaaaahhhhhh!

"Should we go check on him?" Meldon asked.

"You guys stay here and enjoy your breakfast," Murin said. "I'll make sure he's okay."

Blaaaaaaaaahhh!

"I think I've lost my appetite," Luna said.

"Hey Xav," Murin said as he walked around the corner of the house. "You okay, buddy?"

Murin stopped as soon as he rounded the corner. Xavier was spewing vomit everywhere. But the sick unicorn wasn't just vomiting – he was projectile vomiting. Xavier had managed to cover the whole side of the house, even getting some on the roof. His vomiting was so violent that it actually tore a few shingles off the side of Meldon's house.

Blaaahhh! Blaaaaaahhh!

Xavier continued vomiting for another minute. Murin stood at the corner of the house, ready to jump behind it if any vomit came his way. Finally, Xavier stopped.

"I think I'm done," he said, looking over at Murin.

"That's good," Murin replied. "I was starting to get worried. I've never seen so much..."

Blaaaaaaaaaaaaaahhh!

Xavier spoke too soon. Just as Murin was in the middle of his sentence, another massive stream of vomit came flying out of Xavier's mouth. The unicorn was looking right at him when it happened and Murin just barely managed to jump out of the way in time, hiding behind the corner of the house. Luna and Meldon both saw him swiftly jump behind the corner, followed by a big blast of vomit which traveled dozens of feet through the air before landing on the ground.

"Okay," Murin heard Xavier say from around the corner of the house. "*Now* I'm done."

"Are you sure this time?" Murin asked, cautiously poking his head around the side of the house.

"Yeah, I'm sure. Totally sure. One-hundred-percent sure. Never been more sure of anything in my life."

Murin slowly started working his way over to Xavier, trying not to step in any unicorn vomit along the way. As Murin approached him, Xavier looked right at him and opened his mouth again. Murin was too far away from the corner of the house to jump behind it, so he did the only thing he could think to do. He looked away, closed his eyes, held his hands over his face, and prepared to be blasted with unicorn puke.

"Ha!" Xavier yelled. "Gotcha! I really am done now. I got it all out – and then some, by the look of it."

"Not funny," Murin replied, lowering his hands, opening his eyes, and slowly turning to face Xavier. He looked around the yard and at the side of the house, checking out the aftermath of what had just happened. There was vomit all over the place. Half-digested grass with chunks of ham in it was everywhere. "And you aren't kidding. I have no idea how you could've possibly puked up so much stuff. Are you feeling better now?"

"Yeah, of course," Xavier replied. "I mean, I don't feel great, but it's hard not to feel better than I did when I was... What did you call it? Puking?"

"Yes, puking."

"Yeah, that was really awful," Xavier continued. "I never want to go through that again. That was freakin' terrifying. I didn't even know that I was capable of puking. It's never happened to me before and I've never seen it happen to any other unicorns, either. Do me a favor?"

"Sure," Murin said. "What?"

"Next time someone tries to feed me a dead animal, warn me first! You should've told me that your friend was feeding me a dead pig. If I'd known that's what it was, I never would've eaten it – even though it was incredibly delicious."

"Sorry," Murin replied. "I didn't know. I just assumed that unicorns could eat meat since horses can."

"Compare me to a horse one more time and see what happens," Xavier replied, only partly joking.

"I know, I know. You're not a horse. And the more I get to know you, the more I realize just how different you are from a horse. But you both..." Murin stopped himself before saying that horses and unicorns looked alike even though, of course, they did. "From now on, I'll let you know exactly what's being offered to you."

"Good," Xavier said.

Both Meldon and Luna were blown away by how much vomit was all over the yard and the house when they came around the corner to see what was going on. Meldon wasn't happy about the shingles that would need to be replaced, but didn't say anything.

After what had just happened, none of them were hungry anymore. They talked for a few minutes about what they were going to do on the other side of the house so they wouldn't have to look at all the vomit. The four of them decided to stakeout Thall's house from down the road. There was a wooded area not too far away where they could wait and watch to see when Thall left the house. Then, when he did, Meldon would use the lock-picking skills he'd learned from his rogue friend so they could go inside and look around. Thall's house was secluded enough that Meldon was confident they could do it without anyone noticing.

They took a series of different roads, Meldon leading the way. He didn't want to walk past Thall's house to get to the stakeout spot, so they went all the way around town. When they got to the spot, Xavier was happy to see some wild grass along with a slow-moving stream. He immediately started chomping away at the grass, but paused and looked over at Murin.

"There's no ham or any other dead animals in the grass in this town, is there?" Xavier asked.

"No Xav," Murin replied with a chuckle, unsure if the unicorn was being serious or not. "There isn't. That's just regular grass. You're good."

Xavier went right back to munching on the grass, occasionally taking breaks to sip from the stream. The other three got comfortable, posting up next to a few trees near where Xavier was. They could clearly see Thall's house from where they were, though they were too far away to see into his windows. Neither Luna nor Murin liked the idea of going into the explorer's home when he wasn't there, but they didn't have a better idea. Meldon, on the other hand, was eager to put his lock-picking skills to use. He'd brought a set of small tools with him that rogue friend had given him.

It wasn't long before they saw Thall leaving his house. Before even thirty minutes had gone by, Meldon spotted Thall come out of the front door. The half gnome, half dwarf hurriedly walked to the road with what looked like a book under his arm.

"He's gone," Meldon said. "You ready?"

"Maybe we should give it a couple of minutes," Murin suggested.

"I say we go now," Meldon replied. "We have no idea where Thall's going or how long until he comes back. The sooner we go, the sooner we can get in and out of there."

"Let's just get this over with," Luna said.

"Fine," Murin agreed, then yelled to Xavier. "Come on, Xav. Time to move."

They cautiously came out of the forest and approached Thall's house, looking around to make sure they weren't seen. No one else was around and it seemed to be safe. They got to the explorer's house and Meldon immediately went to work. He took out his lock-picking tools and began trying to unlock the front door while the others kept watch, Xavier being the only exception. The unicorn wandered around the yard for a minute before finding a comfortable spot to lay down on the side of the house.

"You almost got it?" Murin asked after a couple of minutes.

"I'm working on it," Meldon replied, some frustration apparent in his voice.

A couple more minutes went by and Meldon was still down on his knees, trying to pick open the front door. Murin didn't want to rush his friend but knew how important it was that they get in and out quickly.

"Any luck?" he asked.

"I'm doing the best I can," Meldon shouted, louder than he'd meant to. He calmed his voice and continued, "This isn't as easy as I thought it was going to be. This lock is of higher quality than the ones I've practiced on. I just need another minute."

Another *several* minutes went by. As Meldon's frustration increased, so did Murin's and Luna's.

"I think we should probably call this whole thing off," Murin suggested.

Meldon didn't reply. He just kept trying to pick the lock.

"Come on, Meldon," Luna said. "You did your best. But Murin's right. We should go."

Again, Meldon didn't respond. He just knelt in front of the door, trying to pick the lock. Murin and Luna looked to each other and, unsure of what to do, shrugged their shoulders.

"What's taking so long?" Xavier asked, getting up and coming around the corner.

"Meldon can't pick the lock," Murin answered. "He's tried his best, but it won't budge."

Xavier walked over to Meldon. He was so engaged in trying to pick the lock that he didn't notice the unicorn walking closer until he was right next to him. Xavier leaned down, his face right next to Meldon's. In a deep, loud, and commanding voice, the unicorn spoke a single word.

"Move."

That got Meldon's attention. He figured that if he didn't move on his own, the unicorn was certainly capable of moving him. The defeated wannabe lock picker pulled his tools out of the lock, got up to his feet, and took a few steps back. He, Murin, and Luna all watched Xavier, extremely curious to see what he was going to do. Murin was afraid that the unicorn was planning to kick through the door, just as he had done to the backdoor of his own house. But Xavier didn't turn around. He just tapped his head against the lock and they all heard a surprising – but very welcome – sound.

Click!

"Somebody want to turn the knob?" Xavier asked with a smirk. "Or would you like me to use my hoof to open the door?"

Meldon stepped forward, gently turned the doorknob, and pushed. The door swung wide open.

"What the... How did you..." Meldon asked, hints of confusion, surprise, and frustration in both his face and his voice. "What did you just do?"

"We can worry about that later," Murin said. "Now that the door's open, let's get in and out as quickly as possible."

Meldon, Murin, and Luna went into Thall's house, closing the door behind them. Xavier returned to the side of the house and laid back down in the cool grass. The front room appeared to look the same as it had the night before – what little of it they could see through the door, anyway. There were several books and maps lying around, and many more on shelves around the room. Trinkets of all sorts, from small gems to medium-sized sculptures, also lined the shelves. Meldon worked his way into the back room while the other two continued looking around the living room.

"Hey, check this out," Luna said, calling Murin over to a table in the corner of the living room.

"What is it?" Murin asked.

The second he saw it, he knew what it was. Lying on the table was a map – an extremely detailed map – of the massive forest that Edgewood bordered on. Deep in the forest, much farther than Murin and Luna had ever traveled, two small areas were circled in red ink. In the margin of the map, a few words were scribbled, but none of them were able to read what they said.

"Look what I found!" Meldon said, reentering the living room.

He was holding up a long, thick horn. Both Murin and Luna's eyes widened when they saw it. The possibility that Thall was somehow involved in Involore's evil plan no longer seemed like *just* a possibility – now it seemed probable, if not definite.

"No way," Murin replied. "Is that...?"

"I'm afraid it is," Meldon said. "My father has a book that mentions unicorns and it has some drawings of them. This horn looks exactly like the horns in the books."

"Where was it?" Luna asked.

"It was in the back room," Meldon answered, "hanging on the wall like some kind of trophy."

"This is even worse than I'd imagined," Murin said. "Not only is one of the most powerful wizards in the world planning to destroy the unicorns, he's being helped by one of the most experienced explorers in the world, too. It would be hard enough for us to stop *one* of them. But, *both*? It'll be nearly impossible."

The three of them stood in Thall's living room, incredibly disheartened by what they'd just discovered in his home. Meldon was especially surprised to learn that Thall could be involved in such an evil plan. He'd always seemed so nice and had a reputation for being kind and caring.

Suddenly, they all glanced at each other, but only for a split second. Then, all six of their eyes shot over to the front door when they realized that someone was turning the knob.

"Oh no," Meldon muttered under his breath.

Their eyes darted around the room in a panic, looking for an escape route or somewhere to hide.

Even if there had been somewhere to hide in Thall's house – which there wasn't – it wouldn't have mattered. The front door swung open before any of them had a chance to do anything. They just stood there knowing that they were busted.

17.

Thall immediately saw all three of them but didn't say anything. He walked into the house, locking the door behind him. He was no longer carrying whatever had been under his arm when he'd left the house earlier. Thall took off the light coat he was wearing, hung it up on a hook next to the door, then turned to face the three teens.

"Well?" he asked calmly.

"Well, what?" Meldon asked.

It wasn't that he didn't understand Thall's question. Meldon knew exactly what he was asking. But the young man was so nervous that he couldn't even begin to offer up an explanation. Thall looked Meldon right in the eyes for a couple of seconds before rephrasing the question. This time, he wasn't so calm.

"What in the world are you doing in my house?" the angry half gnome, half dwarf yelled.

"We were... We wanted to... I'm so sorry... I just..."

Meldon tried to answer the question but was way too nervous to say anything that even remotely made sense. The other two were quite nervous as well but not nearly as much. Murin, realizing that nothing coherent was going to come out of his friend's mouth anytime soon, stepped in and spoke.

"We know that you're helping Involore with his evil plan," he said.

"You know nothing!" Thall yelled, his fists clenched.

"We know that you've been meeting with Involore," Luna said. "We know that you're helping him find the unicorns. And we know that you've already killed at least one of them."

Luna pointed to the horn that was still in Meldon's hand. Thall glanced at it briefly, then looked back and forth between Luna, Murin, and Meldon. Nothing was said for several seconds, just long enough that the silence was starting to make everyone uneasy. Then Thall spoke, his voice calm once again.

"Why don't the three of you have a seat," he said, pointing into the back room where there was a table with several chairs. "Let's talk."

The three of them walked to the back room and sat down at the table. Their hearts were all pounding. None of them knew what to expect. Before he sat down, Meldon looked at the backdoor and considered making a run for it, but he couldn't leave Murin and Luna there by themselves. It was him, after all, that had suggested breaking into Thall's house and snooping around.

The seasoned explorer followed the intruders into the back room and joined them at the table. He was used to having human visitors and had several regular-sized chairs. Thall also had a few chairs around the house made for his short stature. He pulled one of them up to the table, climbed up the built in ladder on the side, and sat down. It was several-feet higher than the chairs the others were in and they were all more-or-less at eye level with one another.

"I don't know what you've heard or who you've heard it from," Thall began, "but you obviously know *some*thing."

"So, you admit it?" Murin asked. "You admit you're helping Involore?"

Thall looked down at the empty table. After a short moment of silence, he answered the question.

"Yes."

"I can't believe it," Meldon said. "I can't believe you – of all people – would help Involore to destroy all the unicorns."

Thall glanced up at Meldon with a look of extremely concern on his face.

"*Destroy* all the unicorns?" Thall asked.

"Don't act like you don't know what Meldon's talking about," Murin said. "You just admitted that you were helping Involore."

"Yes, helping him to *find* the unicorns. Not destroy them."

Thall threw his head back, then collapsed into his own hands and started slowly rocking back and forth. He looked like he was almost vibrating, something they weren't sure to be normal for a half gnome, half dwarf. None of them said anything. They just watched Thall rock back and forth with his face in his hairy-palmed hands and listened to him start mumbling.

"No, no, no!" he said, barely audible, his mouth muffled by his hands. "What have I done? I can't believe this. I just want this nightmare to be over. This just keeps getting worse and worse."

"What are you talking about, Thall?" Meldon asked. "What keeps getting worse and worse? What nightmare?"

Thall slowly picked his head up and looked around the table. He had tears in his eyes and was breathing heavily. Again, there was a moment of silence. Finally, the explorer started talking slowly, his voice a bit shaky.

"You kids obviously know *some*thing," Thall said. "But it's clear you don't know *every*thing. You're wrong about me. I'll tell you what: You tell me everything that *you* know and I, in turn, will tell you everything that *I* know."

Murin, Luna, and Meldon whispered among themselves for a minute. The three of them agreed that they should do as Thall suggested. Each of them took turns talking and explained everything they knew to the half dwarf, half gnome. They could tell by his reaction that, not only did he not know about Involore's evil plan to destroy the unicorns, he was just as disturbed by it as they were. After they finished explaining everything to Thall, he kept up his end of the deal and told them everything that *he* knew.

"It's true that I've been helping Involore. He came to me a few weeks ago asking if I knew where in the forest the unicorns lived. My reputation as an explorer is well known and the wizard figured that if anyone knew, it would be me. Well, I didn't know where the unicorns lived, but Involore wouldn't't accept that. He insisted that I knew the forest well enough to find them. While it's true that I *do* know the forest better than almost anyone else, there's a lot of it that I haven't explored. Involore wanted me to draw him a map of the unexplored parts of the forest where the unicorns possibly lived. When I asked him why he wanted to find the unicorns, he refused to answer the question. So, I refused to help him. He became upset and left, slamming my door behind him.

"A week went by and Involore returned. Without saying a word, he walked into my living room and threw *this* down on the table."

Thall dug a small item out of one of his pockets and placed it on the table. It was a rabbit's foot with small rubies and emeralds attached to the paw.

"What is it?" Luna asked, eyeing the item curiously.

"That's Vastrel's lucky charm. He brings it with him everywhere he goes."

"Who's Vastrel?" Murin asked.

"Thall's son," Meldon answered.

"That's right," Thall said. "He'd left a few weeks earlier to go explore a cave in the western mountain range with a couple of other adventurers. Vastrel is already an accomplished explorer and he's still relatively young. He takes after his father – his *proud* father.

"When Involore wantonly tossed my son's lucky rabbit's foot on the table, my heart nearly stopped. With a wicked grin on his face, the wizard told me that if I didn't help him find the unicorns, it wouldn't be a rabbit's foot he'd be throwing on the table – it'd be my son's head. Involore had captured Vastrel and was using him to blackmail me. If I didn't draw him a map and do everything else that he told me to do, he'd kill my son – my *only* son."

"Wow," Meldon said. "I'm so sorry to hear about Vastrel. And I'm sorry for accusing you of being a part of Involore's evil plan."

"It's understandable. If I was in your situation, I probably would've come to the same conclusion, myself."

"So, what happened after that?" Murin asked.

"I drew Involore the map that he wanted, of course. He told me to draw a map of the forest and the parts of the forest where the unicorns *could* be. Now, that's no small task. It's a huge forest – the largest in the known world. But I did the best that I could. I drew him a map with all the unexplored regions of the forest where the unicorns might live. He took the map and left, returning a week later.

"When Involore came back, he demanded I draw him a new map. He brought back the map I'd made him a week earlier and several of the unexplored regions I'd highlighted were crossed out. The wizard told me that the unicorns weren't in those areas and to make a new map. So as requested, I made a new map of the forest. There were still a lot of unexplored areas and I showed him how to get to them as best as I could. As soon as I finished drawing it, he took the map and left.

"A week later, same thing. Involore came back and gave me the map I'd made him a week earlier. Several more areas were crossed out. Again, I made him a new, more-detailed map. When I was done, he took it and left – but not before reminding me that he was holding my poor son as his prisoner. He always reminded me of that fact before leaving, as if I could've forgotten.

"This went on for several more weeks. Then, he came back again just a couple of days ago. Like all the times before, he gave me back the map I'd made him a week earlier. There were only two areas left on that map where the unicorns could possibly live. At Involore's request, I made him a new map. He seemed to be especially interested in one of the areas over the other and insisted I add as much detail as possible to show how to get there. That areas is much deeper in the forest than the other. And when I say deep, I mean *deep*. We're talking miles and miles from the main path. Though I hadn't spent much time that deep in the forest, I did my best to give Involore what he wanted. Once I finished, I gave him the map and he told me that he'd only be needing one more thing from me. Then, he'd release Vastrel."

"What was that thing?" Meldon asked.

"A book," Thall answered. "Weeks earlier, he'd asked me to track down a copy of a rare book for him. As I know you know, Meldon, and perhaps your friends know, too, I've been all over the world. I've made connections all over the place. And I can get my hands on just about anything. Involore wanted me to get him a hard-to-find book, a collection of ancient magic spells. The book is very rare with only a handful of copies known to still exist. But it's a well-known text. I'd learned about the book long before Involore mentioned it, which made me wonder what he could've possibly wanted it for."

"You said it's a book of magic spells, right?" Luna asked. "Involore's a wizard. I don't think it's hard to figure out why he wanted it."

"You don't understand," Thall explained. "It's a book of *ancient* magic spells. Most of the spells are in languages that haven't been spoken in centuries. And of the ones that are in languages still being used today, none of them are castable for one reason or another. That's what I've heard from a number of sources. Nowadays the book is more of a collector's item than a magic book. You're more likely to find it sitting on the shelf of a scholar or a book collector than on that of a modern-day wizard.

"So, I explained all of that to Involore, but he still insisted that I get him the book. I tried to get him to tell me why he wanted it. Or at least give me some kind of hint. But the wizard wouldn't tell me anything. He just told me that I needed to get him the book as soon as possible if I ever wanted to see my son again."

"Were you able to get a copy of the book for Involore?" Murin asked.

"Yes, I was. That's where I just came from, actually."

"From getting the book?" Luna asked.

Before Thall could answer Luna's question, Meldon answered it.

"No. He just got back from *bringing* him the book. We saw you leave the house with what looked like a book under your arm. When you returned, you were empty handed."

"That's right," Thall confirmed. "I managed to get my hands on a copy of the book. Let me tell you: It wasn't easy, even for an experienced trader like myself. But I got the book and just delivered it to Involore along with the final map. We met at the tavern. He thanked me for everything and told me that after he carries out his plan, he'll release my son. Then, he left the tavern walking south down the main road, presumably heading back to Edgewood.

"Before you three showed up and told me about what you'd heard Involore say out in the forest, I had no idea what his plan was. It obviously had something to do with unicorns, but I didn't know what. I never considered that Involore could be planning something so..."

"Sinister," Meldon said.

"Sick," Luna added.

"Twisted," Murin threw in.

"I was going to say evil," Thall said. "But, sinister, sick, and twisted certainly fit, too. If I knew that he was trying to find the unicorns so he could kill them and take their horns, I never would've agreed to help him – even if it meant I'd never see my son again. Speaking of unicorns, where is the one you told me about? Xavier you said his name was, right?"

"That's right," Murin replied. "He's right outside. He should be, anyway."

"Wait a minute," Meldon said as he stood up and walked over to the horn he had found. Before he'd sat down, he put it back on the wall where he'd found it. Meldon took it down once again and held it up facing Thall. "How do you explain *this*?"

"That?" Thall replied. "I picked that up over fifty years ago from a trader in a small town that borders on the Northern Desert. Paid a lot for it – a hundred gold pieces, if I remember correctly. The trader told me that he got it from an adventurer who claimed to have come across a dead unicorn in the forest. He said that the guy, knowing how valuable a unicorn's horn was, cut it off to bring into town and sell.

"When I first saw it, I couldn't take my eyes off the thing. It was unlike anything I'd ever seen before. Of course, there was no way to authenticate it. But I can't imagine what else – other than a unicorn – it could possibly have come from. Whatever it was, I wanted it and haggled with the trader until we agreed on the price. I brought it back to Briarville and have been displaying it on my wall ever since."

"I know someone who might be able to authenticate it," Murin said with a smile.

"Ahhh, the unicorn," Thall replied. "Let's go see him."

18.

They all got up from the table and went outside to see Xavier. He was still lying down on the side of the house sound asleep, snoring. Luna went over to him and gently stroked his head.

"Wake up, Xavier," she said.

The unicorn opened his eyes but didn't pick up his head. He looked at Luna, then at the others who were all looking at him.

"Damn it, Luna," Xavier said. "I was right in the middle of a dream about me and two gorgeous female unicorns playing in a big field of grass. And things were just about to really start heating up."

"I'm sorry," Luna replied. "I always seem to get woken up just as my dreams are getting good, too. But we've got someone we want you to meet. Xavier, meet Thall. He's a legendary explorer who knows the forest where Unicaria is better than anyone."

"It's so nice to meet you!" Thall said, his eyes wide, lips parted. "I can't believe you're real. In all my years, in all my travels, I've never seen an actual unicorn before. I was starting to wonder if you exist at all."

"Well, take a good look because we might be going extinct soon," Xavier replied to Thall, then looked at Murin, finally sitting up. "What's the deal with this guy? Is he helping the wizard? Is he helping us? And what in the world is he? He kind of looks like you, only shorter, fatter, hairier, wrinklier..."

"I'm half gnome, half dwarf," Thall answered, cutting Xavier off mid-list. The unicorn still had another five-or-so differences that he was going to point out. "And I'm not helping Involore – not anymore."

"The real question is: Are you going to help us to *stop* Involore?" Murin asked.

Thall stood up straight and said with conviction, "I'm going to do everything in my power to stop Involore from hurting even a single unicorn. It's my fault that he's going to be able to find them, if he hasn't already. So, to answer your question: Yes, I'm going to help you. I'm prepared to do whatever it takes to stop him."

"What the hell is *that* thing?" Xavier asked, looking at the long horn in Meldon's hand.

"We were hoping that *you* could tell *us*," Thall replied.

"How am I supposed to know what it is?"

"You don't recognize it?" Thall asked. "So, it's not a unicorn horn?"

Xavier got up slowly and casually walked over to Meldon. He leaned down and took a good look at the horn.

"Definitely not," Xavier answered. "I don't know what that thing is but it's definitely not an alicorn."

"You're sure?" Thall asked, disappointed.

Xavier didn't reply. He just gave Thall a look that answered his question. Well, it would've answered his question if he knew how to interpret the unicorn's expression. Fortunately, Murin was getting quite good at reading Xavier's different faces and translated it for Thall.

"Of course he's sure. He's a freakin' unicorn."

"Couldn't have said it better myself," Xavier said and nodded to Murin.

"So, what now?" Luna asked.

"Now," Thall replied, "we recruit some friends of mine. We're going to need all the help we can get. Then, we come up with a plan to stop Involore and save my son."

"Brainstorm?" Xavier asked.

"Brainstorm," Murin answered.

"Hell-to-the-yeah!" the unicorn yelled, then lowered his voice. "Love that word."

Murin and Luna stayed in Briarville for another couple of hours before leaving to head back to Edgewood. Their parents were expecting them back that night so they could resume their duties the following morning. Both of them were incredibly relieved to no longer be alone in their quest to stop Involore from destroying the unicorns. To have such an experienced, well-connected explorer like Thall offering to help made them feel much better about the situation. And knowing that he was recruiting the help of some other seasoned adventurers only increased their relief.

Murin, Luna, and Xavier made plans to meet with Thall just outside of Edgewood three days later. Thall didn't want to meet in the actual village because he didn't want to be seen by Involore or any of his apprentices. After agreeing to help, as soon as they left, Thall went back in the house and began feverishly writing three letters that he'd have sent out immediately. One was to a dwarven warrior Thall had been on countless adventures with. Another to a cunning rogue with more tricks up his sleeves than the average orc could count to. And lastly, he wrote to a powerful wizard who's skills would almost definitely be needed to defeat Involore. Thall knew how powerful Involore was and realized that they'd need all the help they could get. But that's not all the seasoned explorer realized.

Thall understood the true seriousness of Involore's plan. None of the others, not even Xavier, understood the full gravity of the situation. If Involore actually carried through with his plan, it wouldn't just be the end of the unicorns. Those magical creatures didn't simply *represent* all that was good and pure in the world – they were the *source* of it. If Involore was able to destroy all the unicorns, he'd be destroying *all* the good in the world, ushering in an era of unmitigated evil.

It was clear to Thall that Murin, Luna, Meldon, and even Xavier had no clue just how serious things were. He didn't want to make them worry any more than they already were, so he decided to keep it to himself. What wasn't clear to Thall was whether or not Involore fully understood the consequences of what he was planning to do. Involore was incredibly smart. And he was often referred to as an "evil wizard." But Thall wasn't sure if the Involore was *so* evil that he'd be willing to eradicate the world of all that was good for his own personal gain.

After sending out the three letters, Thall went right home and started preparing for what was likely to be an interesting quest. He'd been on adventures all over the world, but had never faced such a dangerous enemy as Involore. With the seriousness of the situation weighing heavily on his shoulders, Thall knew that they had to be successful. Failure was not an option. He prayed that his letters found their intended targets, because he knew that they likely wouldn't be able to defeat Involore without them.

After leaving Thall's house, Murin, Luna, and Xavier went back to Meldon's farm with him. They talked for a while, thanking him for his help with everything. Meldon wished that he could've done more to help them, but Murin assured him that he'd already been of immense assistance. With the long walk back to Edgewood ahead of them, Murin gave his fellow farmer a hug and told him they had to leave. They all said goodbye and Murin, Luna, and Xavier left town, heading south back to Edgewood.

19.

Murin, Luna, and Xavier left Briarville and were making good time walking back to Edgewood – they had to if they wanted to get home before dark. They even passed a few slower-moving travelers on the road. The three of them talked as they walked which helped to pass the time.

"I feel so much better knowing that Thall is going to help us," Murin said.

"I know," Luna agreed. "Me, too. You must be happy as well, huh Xavier?"

"I'll be happy when all this is over," the unicorn said.

Xavier wasn't used to conflict. The events of the previous few days were starting to wear on him. Unicorns usually spent their lives playing and laughing, eating grass, and singing songs – not worrying about evil wizards trying to destroy everyone they knew. He just wanted all the conflict to be over. Unfortunately, a lot more was right around the corner – literally.

The three of them continued down the road. There was one part, about halfway between Briarville and Edgewood, that became windy. With forest on both sides of the road, it was impossible to see what was up ahead. As soon as Murin, Luna, and Xavier came to the curve in the road, two hooded figures jumped out of the woods. Both of them were in mid-chant, about to finish casting a spell on their unsuspecting targets.

"What the..." Murin started saying.

He and Luna froze dead in their tracks. Xavier stopped moving, too. The two spell casters had finished chanting and took off their hoods. It was Evia and Drixius, Involore's wind and earth apprentices. They looked at each other and smiled, seeing Luna, Murin, and Xavier standing there motionless.

"Looks like it worked," Evia said, proudly.

"You three will be coming with us," Drixius said to Murin, Luna, and Xavier.

"Yes, master," Murin and Luna said at the same time.

Xavier didn't reply. He just stood there.

"I don't know if it worked on the horse," Evia said, walking over to Xavier.

She tried to touch him and he took several steps back.

"Easy, big fella," Drixius said.

He walked over to Xavier and reached out to touch what he thought was a horse. His hand just barely grazed Xavier's neck and the unicorn stood up on its hind legs and unleashed a deafening roar.

"Whoa!" Evia yelled with her hands up in the air, taking another step toward Xavier.

Unicorns don't have a fight-or-flight response. They have a flight-or-flight response and Xavier's kicked into high gear. Neither Evia nor Drixius were pure of heart – far from it. The unicorn again kicked his front legs up in the air. As soon as they returned to the ground, he turned around and took off at full speed. Before long, he was down the road and out of sight.

"Forget the horse," Drixius said to Evia. "We got who our master wants to see."

"Did you notice his nose?" Evia asked.

Drixius looked at Murin for a moment, then turned to Evia and replied, "It's not *that* bad. Maybe a little on the big side."

"Not him!" Evia yelled. "The horse! Did you notice the horse's nose?"

"Oh," Drixius replied. "No, I didn't."

"Ugh," Evia said, shaking her head. "Never mind. Let's get these two to the cabin."

"Come on, you two," Drixius said to Murin and Luna. "Follow us."

"Yes, master," they both replied.

The two apprentices began walking down the road toward Edgewood. Both Murin and Luna followed closely behind them taking rigid steps, their unblinking eyes focused straight ahead. Evia and Drixius had cast a compliance spell on them and it worked perfectly. Neither of them had any sort of magical protection and were easy targets. Xavier, on the other hand, was completely resistant to the spell.

Murin and Luna followed the two apprentices for several miles down the road. They passed a couple of other travelers who didn't seem to notice that anything was out of the ordinary. On a long stretch of straight road, Evia stopped.

"Over there," she said, pointing to the woods.

"Good eye," Drixius replied. "I would've walked right past it."

There was a barely-noticeable path going into the woods on the side of the road. Drixius and Evia started walking down it with Murin and Luna right behind them. A minute later, they were deep enough in the woods that they couldn't be seen from the road.

Once Xavier started running, he didn't stop for several minutes. By the time he calmed down, he was several miles away from the others.

"Oh, man," Xavier said. "This isn't good."

The unicorn didn't know what to do. He recognized Drixius and Evia from the time he'd heard Involore talking to them in the forest. Not only did the unicorn recognize their voices, he also recognized their scent. From working in the incense-filled magic shop, their cloaks absorbed a lot of smoke. Xavier knew that Murin and Luna were in trouble and that he couldn't just leave them with the apprentices.

"What am I going to do?" Xavier said to himself. "I have to do something. Wait a minute... Do I? I mean, I don't *have to* do anything." Xavier paused for a moment and rubbed his lips together, lost in thought. Without realizing it, he started tapping one of his front hooves on the ground. The tapping was slow at first, but gradually got faster and faster. Xavier gave the ground one final tap, slamming his hoof so hard into the dirt that it kicked up a small cloud of dust. "Yes I do. I have to do something. I don't *have to* do anything... but I can't do nothing. I have to do *some*thing. I have to... I don't know what I have to do. But I have to... I have to go back."

Xavier started trotting down the road toward Edgewood, quickly picking up speed. Before long, he was galloping as fast as he could. It didn't take him long to get back to where he'd last seen Murin and Luna. He stopped and looked around. They were nowhere to be seen. However, Xavier was still able to smell a faint hint of the apprentice's robes. He could tell that they went south down the road and continued running down it.

After traveling down the road for a few minutes, Xavier lost the scent. He stopped and walked back up the road until he could smell it again. The unicorn followed the scent to a small, barely-worn path on the side of the road going into the woods and cautiously started walking down it.

"Hmmm," Xavier said to himself. "I need to be careful. I should take every precaution I can."

The unicorn enacted his magical ability to walk silently. He continued down the path following his nose, not making a sound. The scent led him deep into the woods and got stronger and stronger until Xavier knew he was getting close.

"They've got to be around here, somewhere," he mumbled.

Sure enough, they were. A minute later, Xavier came to a small cabin in the woods. He slowly approached it, staying as low as possible. He could hear people inside and there was no doubt in his mind: It was Luna, Murin, Drixius, Evia, and maybe a few others. Xavier had spent enough time with Murin and Luna that, when close enough, he could recognize their scent, too. Though it had bothered him at first, he'd mostly gotten used to it. Murin, being a farmer around lots of animals, had a much stronger odor than Luna. Xavier could also easily smell the two apprentices' robes.

Slowly and silently, the unicorn crept up to the cabin – or at least he tried to. When Xavier was about ten-feet away, he was stopped by an invisible barrier.

"What the...?" he whispered.

Xavier cautiously walked around to the other side of the cabin. He tried to approach it and, once again, was stopped by some sort of barrier. The unicorn, using his nose and his hooves, tried to see if the barrier went all the way around the cabin and it did.

It wasn't hard for Xavier to figure out what was happening. He knew that magic could be used to erect all kinds of barriers like the one surrounding Unicaria. Xavier tried to use his own magic to penetrate the barrier, but it was of no use. He couldn't get through.

"Well, this certainly sucks," he said.

Knowing that he wasn't going to be able to get past the invisible barrier, Xavier moved away from the cabin and back into the woods. When he was safely out of sight from the cabin, he stopped to think – and to talk to himself for a minute.

"What the hell am I supposed to do? I'm not meant for this. I'm supposed to be eating grass and chasing rainbows. Maybe I should just go back to wandering around in the forest by myself. No, I can't do that. Those two are trapped in that cabin because of me. I can't walk away from them. But I can't get in to save them, either. Who can I get to help me? I need a wizard or something. Maybe if I go back out to the road and ask someone for help, they'll be able to do something. But Murin and Luna said I shouldn't go around talking to anyone I don't know. What if I ask someone for help and they make things worse? Ahhh, this sucks. This sucks so bad. Maybe Murin's dad can help. Nah, he's a farmer. What's he gonna do, harvest his way to the cabin? Who can I get to help me?"

Xavier stood there in silence, looking up at the sky. Then, his face lit up and he uttered a single word.

"Thall."

20.

Xavier worked his way back to the road and started running at full speed back to Briarville. He passed several travelers along the way, several of them trying to stop what they thought was a runaway horse. None of them were able to even slow the determined unicorn down. He kept running until he got back to Briarville. By the time he arrived there, it was already dark.

Xavier found his way to Thall's house. Fortunately, there weren't many people out and about, and no one tried to stop him. There was no light coming from Thall's windows, so Xavier assumed that he'd already gone to bed. He approached the door and tried using his head to knock on it. Xavier whacked his head against the door several times, but nothing happened.

"I don't have time for this," he said and turned around.

Xavier backed up to Thall's front door. He'd noticed that, usually, whenever a person knocks on someone's door, they knock three times. So, Xavier raised his hoof and kicked Thall's door three times – putting three separate holes in it.

Xavier's head tapping didn't wake Thall up but his kicks certainly did. The explorer jumped out of bed, lit a candle, grabbed a dagger, and ran into the front room. Thall's heart was nearly beating out of his chest and he was ready to defend himself and his property. Then, he saw the three holes in the bottom of his door and a nervous unicorn pacing around out the window.

"What are you doing here, Xavier?" Thall asked, putting down the dagger and opening the door.

"Took... Cabin... Spell... Woods... Apprentices..." Xavier tried to get out all at once, still worked up from everything that had happening.

"Slow down," Thall said in a calming tone. "Tell me what happened, one thing at a time. Where are Murin and Luna?"

"In a cabin in the woods halfway between here and Edgewood," Xavier replied, still speaking quickly.

"Good," Thall said. "Now, why are they there?"

"Because two of Involore's apprentices put a spell on them and made them go there."

"Do you know exactly where the cabin is?"

"Yes. But I couldn't get near it. There's a magical barrier surrounding it. I couldn't get past it. I'm guessing only a wizard would be able to."

Xavier felt a million times better after telling Thall what had happened. Thall, on the other hand, was incredibly concerned. He knew that Murin and Luna were in real trouble and that he had to do something. They were both quiet for a moment while Thall tried to come up with a plan. Xavier quickly became impatient and broke the silence.

"Well?"

"You're right: We *are* going to need a wizard. I sent letters to three skilled adventurers I know to help us: a warrior, a rogue, and a powerful wizard. I explained the dire situation with Involore and the unicorns, requesting they come help us at once."

"Oh, good!" Xavier said, relieved.

"No. Not good," Thall replied. "I just sent the letters today. All three of them are in different towns. It'll take a day for them to get the letters, then another day for them to get here. That might be too late to rescue Murin and Luna. We have to go help them immediately before it's too late."

"Oh," Xavier said, looking down. "Not good."

They stood in silence, once again. This time, the silence only lasted for a few seconds before Thall spoke.

"We really only have one option," he said, leaning out the door, looking down the main road.

"That doesn't sound good," Xavier replied. "Why'd you say it like that? Is it not a good option?"

"No, it's not. But it'll have to do. It's our only hope of saving Murin and Luna."

"What is it?"

"Del."

"What?"

"Not what. *Who*. Erlidel is a wizard – a powerful wizard – who lives on the outskirts of Briarville."

"That's good, right?" Xavier asked. "We need a powerful wizard. Do you not think he'll help us?"

"I don't know. I haven't talked to him in years."

"So, let's go talk to him. What's the problem?"

"Erlidel is a bit, um... crazy," Thall explained. "He almost never leaves his house. No one knows what happened to him. He used to be a well-liked, much-respected wizard. And like I said, a very powerful one. But he gradually got weirder and weirder, saying and doing strange things. Nothing harmful – just odd. Now he mostly keeps to himself. I have no idea if he actually will, but he's the only wizard in Briarville who's powerful enough to help us."

"Well, what are we waiting for?" Xavier asked. "Let's go see him!"

Thall quickly got dressed. He grabbed his dagger, another small sword, and a bag full of gear that he already had packed and ready to go. The seasoned explorer took one last look around his living room to see if there was anything else he needed.

"Don't want to forget *this*!" Thall said, grabbing a map from the table and putting it in his pack.

Again, he looked around. Satisfied that he had everything he needed, Thall put his candle down on the table and blew it out. He joined Xavier outside and shook his head from side to side when he closed his front door and saw the holes in it.

"You should be thankful," Xavier said. "I was going to knock on the window."

"Come on," Thall replied. "Let's go wake up Erlidel."

Much to their surprise, Erlidel was awake – wide awake. As they approached the wizard's home, they could see bright light coming from several windows. For some reason, most wizards seemed to live in old, spooky-looking houses. Erlidel was not most wizards, however, and lived in a modern, well-kempt house. It was on the southern outskirts of Briarville at the end of a long, secluded, dirt path. The house wasn't especially big but it wasn't tiny, either. It was just large enough for the crazy old wizard to live and to pursue his many interests.

Thall and Xavier approached the house with caution. There was no shortage of rumors floating around town about Erlidel. Thall had recently heard that he turned a group of young boys into pumpkins because they'd trespassed on his property. That was just one of many rumors he'd heard about the elderly wizard. Thall didn't actually believe the story. He just assumed it was made up by one of the parents in

Briarville to deter their children from going near the strange wizard's home. Still, he thought it'd be a good idea to be careful as they approached it.

"Looks like someone's inside," Thall whispered, spotting movement through a window.

"No shit," Xavier replied, making no attempt to lower his voice. "You want me to knock on the door?"

"Why don't I do the knocking."

They walked up to the large front door. The doorway was tall enough that Xavier could've comfortably fit through it. Inside they heard talking, which made them think that Erlidel had company. Thall picked up the metal knocker, just barely able to reach it, and hit it against the door three times. The talking coming from inside stopped and all they heard were one pair of footsteps slowly coming toward them.

"What do you want?" a voice yelled through the door.

"Del, it's Thall. Remember me?"

"Thall the Cleric?" the voice asked through the door.

"No, the..."

"Thall the Alchemist?"

"Again, no. If you'd just open up the..."

The door swung wide open. Leaning against the side of the large doorway with his arms crossed was Erlidel. The wizard was tall and lean with long blond hair and a beard to match. He had a smirk on his face, his head tilted slightly to the side.

"Well, well, well," Erlidel said. "If it isn't Thall the Explorer!"

"You knew it was me the whole time?" Thall asked, offering the wizard his hand.

"Of course, I did! Who ever heard of a cleric named Thall? I was just having a little fun. You remember what fun is, don't you, Thall? Most people seem to have less and less of it as they age. Not me. In fact, I've never had as much fun as I'm having right now!"

"I like this guy already," Xavier said.

"Ooohhh," Erlidel hummed. "Who's this? A talking horse? No. No, no, no. This is no talking horse. It's not a horse at all."

"You know what I am?" Xavier asked, surprised.

"Let's look at the facts, as they have presented themselves," Erlidel replied, uncrossing his arms and stepping outside. "You wear no harness. You carry no gear. You talk. And you've got a strange bump on your nose. I know precisely what you are. I've met your kind before."

"You have?" Xavier asked, even more surprised.

"You have?" Thall asked at the same time.

"Oh, yes," Erlidel replied. "You're a pterippus!"

"A what?" Thall asked.

Unlike the half gnome, half dwarf, Xavier knew what a pterippus was – it's a winged unicorn. They were even rarer than regular unicorns and lived separately from them. Though they sometimes would visit Unicaria, it was rumored that pterippi spent most of their time high up in the clouds.

"You're close," Xavier said, impressed with the wizard. "I'm not a pterippus. I *wish* I was a pterippus. That would be freakin' awesome. No, I'm just a regular unicorn. Pterippi are winged unicorns. As you can see, I don't have any wings."

"You're no *regular* unicorn," Erlidel replied. "If you were, you wouldn't be standing at my door. You'd be deep in the forest somewhere, safely hidden away from the wonders – as well as the horrors – of the humanoid world. That's why I assumed you were a pterippus. I've never heard of a unicorn venturing this far from the forest. It looks like your horn's been removed, so I just assumed that your wings had been, too."

Erlidel walked around Xavier as he spoke, examining the unicorn closely. The wizard was careful to not get too close to him. He'd read about how they can only be touched by people with pure hearts and Erlidel knew that any purity he might have had once upon a time was long gone. After walking all the way around Xavier, Erlidel returned to the doorway and leaned against the side of it once again.

"So..." Erlidel asked. "What brings a famous explorer and a unicorn to my doorstep after dark? It must be something interesting and of some urgency if it can't wait until morning. You've certainly got my attention."

"Well, we..." Thall started but was interrupted by Erlidel.

"How rude of me!" the wizard yelled, stepping out of the doorway, pointing into his living room. "Come in! Come in! Sit down. Make yourselves comfortable!"

"Both of us?" Thall asked, looking at Xavier.

"Sure!" Erlidel answered. "Why not? It would be awfully rude of me to invite one of you in but not the other, wouldn't it?"

"It sure as hell would," Xavier replied as he casually strolled into the wizard's home.

21.

Thall and Erlidel had a seat in the wizard's living room. There were several chairs around the room and Erlidel pulled two of them close together for them. Xavier found a comfortable spot nearby and laid down. Erlidel had a round, white rug made out of wool that the unicorn found to be incredibly comfortable. It was the exact same color as Xavier and just large enough for him to lay down on.

"Now that we're all nice and cozy," Erlidel said, "you may continue. Tell me, what brings such unlikely guests to my door at this late hour? You have my full attention."

"What I was going to say before was that we..."

Again, Erlidel interrupted Thall. The wizard hopped up out of his chair and motioned toward the fireplace in the other room. He shouted a single word, which confused both Thall and Xavier.

"Tea!"

"Excuse me?" Thall asked.

"Tea!" Erlidel continued, enthusiastically. "How rude of me to not offer you both a cup of hot tea. I just got a fresh batch of green tea leaves that came all the way from the eastern side of a town at the northernmost part of the Western Plains. If it's not the absolute best tea you've ever had... Well then, I'd like to try whatever tea *is* the best that you've ever had because this tea is the best tea *I've* ever had."

"Del, please," Thall said. "We don't have time for tea. And we don't have time for any more interruptions. Let me tell you why we're here."

After hearing the manic wizard hype up the tea, Xavier did want to try it. But knowing they didn't have any time to waste, he kept his mouth shut.

Besides, he wasn't even sure if unicorns could drink tea.

Erlidel's mood shifted, dramatically. His enthusiasm disappeared and his tone of voice dropped by almost an octave. He slowly sat back down in his chair and looked at Thall. The wizard eyed him for a moment, then his eyes fell to the floor. Once again, Erlidel said a single word.

"Speak."

Thall and Xavier – mostly Thall – took turns explaining to Erlidel everything that'd happened. Gradually, the wizard became more and more interested as the story progressed. By the time they got to the part where the apprentices put a spell on Murin and Luna, Erlidel was literally sitting on the edge of his seat. The wizard leaned forward with his elbows on his knees, fingertips from each hand touching the corresponding digits of the other, his chin lightly resting on top of the tips of his middle fingers. Erlidel's eyes were wide and getting wider with each passing detail. It was obvious to both Thall and Xavier that the wizard was highly interested in their story.

"And that's why we need your help," Thall concluded.

Erlidel slowly got up from his chair. He walked over to the window and looked out, stroking first his beard and then his long, blond hair. Thall and Xavier watched him, curiously. The wizard didn't say a word. He just stood there gazing out into the darkness, lost in thought. At first, Thall and Xavier just figured the wizard needed a moment to think about it. But when several minutes went by and Erlidel didn't answer them, Xavier spoke up.

"Hey!" the unicorn yelled.

Xavier's bassy voice echoed throughout the house, startling both Erlidel and Thall. Even Xavier was a bit surprised by how loud it was. It certainly got the wizard's attention, as intended.

"Yes," Erlidel said, turning around to face the others. "Of course. Of course, yes."

"So you'll help us?" Thall asked.

"Oh, no," the wizard replied. "No, no. No, I don't think so."

"This guy's nuts," Xavier said to Thall. "Let's get out of here. This was a waste of time."

"Just wait a minute, Xavier," Thall replied.

"No, I won't wait a minute," Xavier said, standing up. "All of my family... Everyone I've ever known is going to be killed. And the only two friends I have in the entire smelly-ass world got captured because of me. If we don't go rescue them right now, *they'll* probably be killed, too – if they haven't been already.

"Look," Xavier continued, a little calmer, "we gave this guy a shot. But you weren't kidding when you said he's crazy. This guy's a freakin' nutball. I'm sure he was once the great wizard you say he was, but now he's nothing more than a crazy old man. This dude couldn't cast a fishing rod, let alone any sort of powerful spell. We're not wasting any more of our time with him. He obviously doesn't want to help us. And even if he did, I'm not convinced that he could. He's a weak, washed up, crazy old man who probably can't even remember how to spell the word "spell," let alone actually cast one. I'm getting out of here."

Xavier started walking toward the door. Thall took one look at Erlidel and his heart began to race. The veteran explorer knew that it was never a good idea to insult a powerful wizard. Insulting a powerful *and crazy* wizard – well, that was just begging for trouble.

Erlidel began casting some sort of spell, speaking very rapidly. Though he couldn't use magic himself, Thall had been around plenty of magic users and could often tell what spell was being cast simply by listening to the tone, cadence, and language being used. Whatever Erlidel was casting, it was unlike anything Thall had ever heard before. He didn't even recognize the language it was being cast in. That made him worry even more.

"Erlidel, please," Thall begged.

The wizard didn't acknowledge Thall's plea. He just continued casting his spell. Even Xavier was starting to get worried. He could tell by the look on Thall's face that he thought something bad was about to happen.

Erlidel held his hands high above his head, palms facing the sky. The ground below them began to shake and now both Thall and Xavier's hearts were nearly beating out of their bodies. They saw a flash of light come from outside, then another and another, each one brighter than the last. Thall and Xavier ran over to two different windows, each on different sides of the house, to see what it was. What they saw blew both of their minds.

Meteor after meteor came crashing down from the night sky. At first, it was just one every couple of seconds. But as Erlidel continued casting the spell, the meteors increased in frequency until several were falling from the sky every second. The massive glowing rocks slammed into the ground, shaking the wizard's home like an earthquake. Each meteor landed within a couple-dozen feet of Erlidel's house. Both Thall and Xavier were terrified, expecting one to come smashing through the house at any moment, killing all of them.

Much to their surprise and delight, that moment never came. Erlidel finished the spell and lowered his arms. Within seconds, the meteors stopped. Thall and Xavier, seeing that the meteor shower was apparently over, slowly turned to face Erlidel.

"Who were you saying was crazy and powerless?" the wizard asked, a smug look on his face.

"I definitely take back what I said about you being powerless," Xavier said.

"What does this mean?" Thall asked. "Why the show of force? Does that mean you're actually going to help us or were you just trying to show us that you *could* help us if you wanted to?"

Erlidel once again walked over to the window. He looked outside, but it was no longer pitch black. His yard was littered with the smoldering remains of the otherworldly rocks he'd summoned down from the heavens. This time, the wizard only looked out the window for a brief moment before turning back around. He uttered a single word.

"Okay."

"Okay, what?" Thall asked. "Okay, you'll help?"

"Was that not perfectly clear?" Erlidel asked.

"It was to *me*," Xavier said.

Thall shook his head at Xavier, but was also incredibly relieved to hear that they'd have the wizard's help. Sure, Erlidel was a little crazy. But he was unquestionably the most powerful wizard in Briarville and the only one who could possibly help them.

Xavier and Thall waited in the living room while Erlidel ran around the house getting ready. They could hear the wizard talking to himself – yelling, at times – from the other room while figuring out what to pack. After a few minutes, Erlidel came back into the living room. He still had on the purple robe he was wearing when they'd arrived, plus a pair of sandals on his feet, a small pack on his shoulder, and a long staff in his hand. On each of them, the wizard was wearing several rings and he'd also put on a necklace. A strange silver symbol that neither Xavier nor Thall had ever seen before hung from a thin piece of rope around Erlidel's neck.

"Ready?" Thall asked.

"Ready," the wizard replied to Thall, then turned to Xavier and asked, "Ready?"

"Pffft," the unicorn said. "I've *been* ready."

22.

"What the..." Murin mumbled. "Where are we? What happened?"

The young farmer was sitting in a wooden chair with his hands tied behind his back and his feet secured to the chair's legs. To his right was Luna, also sitting with her hands tied behind her back. They were in a small one-room cabin out in the middle of the woods. It had a couple of windows but both were boarded up, so they didn't know they were in the forest. Neither Murin nor Luna had any memory of how they'd gotten there.

"I wish I could answer those questions," Luna replied. "But all I can do is ask *more* questions. Like, why are we tied up? And who's that?"

Luna was looking at another person tied to a chair on the other side of the room. She could tell that he wasn't human and would soon find out that he's one-quarter dwarf, one-quarter gnome, and one-half elf – an unusual combination of races. The man looked like a taller-than-normal dwarf with pointed ears and fiery, red hair. He was somewhat stocky but mostly muscular. His skin was tan and both Murin and Luna could tell that he was some sort of adventurer by what he was wearing. The man's torso was protected by a thin layer of chain mail armor, his arms and legs covered in leather. On his feet were a pair of well-worn boots made out of animal skin.

"You could just ask me," the man said in response to Luna's question.

"I'm sorry," Luna replied. "That was rude of me. I'm Luna and this is my friend, Murin. Who are you? And do you know how we got here?"

"It's nice to meet you both," the man said. "Though I have to say, I wish we were meeting under different circumstances. My name is Vastrel. And you were brought in by a couple of young wizards. By the look of it, you were both under some sort of mind-control spell."

"Vastrel? That name sounds familiar," Murin said to himself, softly, then looked over at the man and spoke regularly. "Wait a minute. You're Thall's son, aren't you?"

Vastrel looked curiously at Murin for a moment, then at Luna, and finally back to Murin. After a short moment of silence, a smile grew across his face and he answered the question.

"That's right. I'm Vastrel the Adventurer, son of Thall the Explorer. I see my reputation as an adventurer precedes me! That is how you know of me, right? From my already-legendary exploits?"

"Not exactly," Luna replied.

Murin and Luna explained to Vastrel how they'd come to meet his father. They told him about overhearing Involore in the woods, his evil plan to steal all the unicorns' horns, and everything else. The adventurer listened intently, leaning as far forward in his chair as possible. Just as they were wrapping up their story about everything that'd happened, Luna and Murin both noticed Vastrel glancing behind them. Then, they heard something large moving behind their backs.

"Whoa!" Murin yelled when turned his head to see what it was, almost falling over in his chair.

Luna turned her head to look, too, but didn't say anything. She just gasped, her eyes growing incredibly wide. Both of them stared out of the corners of their eyes, heads turned as far as they'd go. Lying on the floor behind them was a centaur on its side with its two front hooves and its two back hooves tied together. It had been asleep and was just waking up.

"Well, well, well," Vastrel said to the centaur. "Look who's finally starting to wake up. You've been asleep for a long time."

"And I'm still tired. I feel like I could go back to sleep for another few hours," the centaur replied, slowly opening his eyes. As they came into focus, he picked his head up an looked at Murin and Luna. "Who are these two humans?"

"I'm Murin and this is my friend, Luna," Murin answered.

"And I bet you're Timules, aren't you?" Luna asked.

"I... How..." the centaur replied. "Yes, I *am* Timules. How did you know my name?"

Murin and Luna explained to Timules how they knew who he was. They told him about how they'd run into his sister, Kalarpia, looking for him along the road going from Edgewood to Briarville.

"She must be worried sick about me," Timules said, looking down. "One minute, I was foraging for berries along the side of the road. The next minute, I was here tied up on the floor with Vastrel."

"How about you, Vastrel?" Murin asked. "How did you get here? And how long have you been here?"

"I was on my way to Edgewood to rendezvous with a few other adventurers," he answered. "We were going to meet there and then start journeying to the Western Mountains. There's a massive cave just south of the mountain range, rumored to be filled with exotic treasures. I never even made it to Edgewood, let alone the cave. As I was walking from Briarville to Edgewood, a trip I'd made without incident countless times before, I was ambushed by two hooded figures.

Next thing I knew, I was here in this room, tied to this chair. I don't remember what happened or how I got here."

"How long have you been here?" Luna asked.

"I've been here for weeks," Vastrel answered. "My centaur friend just arrived a couple days ago."

"Has anyone come by here?" Murin asked. "Has anyone been bringing you food or water?"

"No and yes," Vastrel answered. "No one has come by, aside from a couple days ago when two robed wizards – I assume they were wizards – brought Timules here. Like you, he appeared to be under some sort of spell. They told him to come in, lie down, and go to sleep. He did as they said and then tied him up and left. As for food and water, every few hours a glass of water and a loaf of bread appear a couple inches from my face. I eat and drink what I want, then it disappears a little while later. Same thing's been happening to Timules since he got here – when he's awake, anyway."

"What about, um," Murin started to ask, then paused. He was trying to figure out the most mature way to present the question. "How do you relieve yourself?"

"It's the damnedest thing," Vastrel answered. "I haven't had to go at all since I got here. And neither has the centaur. It's got to be magic, just like the food and water."

"Interesting," Luna said.

"What's *really* interesting is what *you* told *me*," Vastrel said to Murin and Luna. "I've been going crazy trying to figure out why I've been brought here. If everything you said is true, it all makes perfect sense. I'm being held to blackmail my father into helping Involore to find the unicorns. That explains everything."

"Not *every*thing," Timules said. "Why was *I* brought here?"

"Hmmm," Vastrel replied. "That's a good question. I can't imagine what a wizard trying to take over the world might want with some random centaur. There's got to be a reason."

Murin, Luna, Vastrel, and Timules continued talking. They did the best that they could to piece together what was happening. Though there were still a lot of details that they couldn't figure out, all of them knew that Involore and his plan to destroy the unicorns was ultimately why they were there.

A little while later, they heard voices coming from outside. All four of them stopped talking. Timules picked his head up off the ground and the others sat up straight. A minute later, they heard voices *and* movement. The latch to the front door popped up and they all looked over at it just in time to see the door swing wide open.

In walked Involore. The tall wizard was wearing a dark-red robe with glistening jewels around the collar, the cuffs, and around the bottom, which swung just an inch off the ground. In his right hand, a long wooden staff with strange symbols carved into it from top to bottom. Involore's long, black beard was slightly off center, the wind blowing it gently to the side. He had fire in his eyes and a wicked grin on his face.

"Wait out here," Involore said, talking to whoever was behind him.

From where they were sitting, Murin and Luna could see two other robed figures behind Involore. They nodded and the wizard came into the cabin, closing the door behind him. He walked around the room, eyeing each person up and down, the wicked grin never leaving his face. Everyone was eager to hear what he had to say, but no one wanted to be the first to talk. Eventually, Involore stopped in the middle of the room and, looking right at Murin and Luna, spoke.

"You two aren't what I was expecting," he said, his grin finally disappearing.

"Let us go!" Luna blurted out.

"Sure," Involore replied.

"Really?" Luna asked.

"You'll be free to go as soon as my quest is complete – and it almost is. Don't fret, young one. I'm not going to hurt you. I'm not going to hurt either of you. But I can't have you meddling in my affairs now, can I?"

"We're not meddling in anything," Murin argued.

"Oh, but you *have* been meddling!" the wizard said. "You stumbled upon my ingenious plan and I can't have you two running around telling everyone what I'm up to – not that anyone would believe you. Dessa and I had a marvelous laugh when she told me what you told her. I've been a pillar of the community for decades. I even saved Edgewood from certain doom, once upon a time. Dessa didn't believe your little story and I doubt anyone else would, either. Besides our town elder, who else have you told?"

Murin and Luna looked at each other. Though they were both thinking the same thing, Murin answered first.

"No one."

"You know I could cast a truth spell on you, right?" Involore said. "I could have you telling me your deepest, darkest secrets and desires within seconds. But it doesn't matter. Before long, this will all be over."

"You can't hurt the unicorns!" Luna blurted out.

"Ah, yes, it's most unfortunate," Involore replied. "But it's the only way, I'm afraid. If there was any other way... But there isn't. I've studied magic my whole life and harnessing the power of all those alicorns is the only way to create the ultimate potion: the Elixir of Youth. Wizards throughout history have tried and failed to create it, but I will be the first to succeed. And the only way to do that, unfortunately... Well, you two little spies know full well what I have to do."

"I don't think you understand the full repercussions of your actions, wizard," Vastrel said. "If you go through with this, there will be consequences."

"Consequences?" Involore replied. "All actions have consequences. I'll deal with whatever problems arise as they happen."

"For such a smart and powerful wizard," Vastrel said, "you sure are a fool."

Involore didn't reply to Vastrel. He just turned toward him and once again flashed his trademark grin. Then, the wizard turned back to face Murin and Luna.

"Well, as much as I'd like to stick around and chat with a couple of meddling teenagers and an adventurer who will forever be known only as 'Thall's son,' that's not what I came here for," Involore said, walking behind Murin and Luna to where Timules was lying on the floor. The wizard looked down at the centaur and said, "I came here to get *you*."

"What are you going to do with him?" Luna asked, practically yelling. "And what about us three?"

"Don't worry about the centaur," Involore said. "As for the rest of you, you'll be set free when all is said and done. Don't fret. It won't be very long. In just a couple of days, you'll be back shoveling cow manure and you," the wizard said, looking at Luna, "will be back to practicing your cute little healing spells."

Involore used his staff to tap on the door three times, hard. It briefly made Murin think about the time Xavier put a hole in his backdoor. He wondered where his unicorn friend was, but only for a second. The door opened and Murin's attention, just like everyone else's in the room, was focused on the two robed figures who came into the cabin. Once they were in the room, Luna and Murin recognized them. It was Evia and Drixius, Involore's wind and earth apprentices. Little did they know that they were the ones who'd brought them to the cabin. Neither Murin nor Luna had any memory of it happening.

"Cast the spell, then untie him," Involore instructed his apprentices. "He's coming with us."

"Yes, master," the apprentices said at the exact same time.

"You're not going to get away with this!" Vastrel yelled.

Involore casually walked over to Vastrel. He leaned down so their faces were almost touching. Vastrel could feel Involore's long beard brushing lightly against him. The wizard looked Vastrel right in the eyes for several seconds, then whispered in his ear.

"Yes. I am."

The two apprentices cast a compliance spell on the centaur. Once they were confident that it worked, they untied Timules' legs and helped him to his feet. They led the centaur outside, making sure the tall creature didn't hit his head on the doorway.

"Please don't do this," Luna begged Involore.

"Sorry, little girl," the wizard replied. "But it might as well already be done."

Involore walked to the door. When he got to the doorway, he turned around and addressed the remaining prisoners one last time.

"Don't worry. You'll be free soon. And all your needs will be met while you're here. Just ask Thall's son."

"My name is Vastrel the Adventurer!" Vastrel yelled.

"Food and water will be provided for you every few hours," Involore continued, ignoring Vastrel. "You two really should've just minded your own business. Next time you overhear a brilliant wizard plotting an ingenious plan, do yourselves a favor and keep it between the two of you."

Involore turned and walked out the door, closing it behind him. Murin, Luna, and Vastrel could hear them walking off and talking. The voices and footsteps got softer and softer until they were no longer audible.

"What are we going to do now?" Luna asked.

"What *can* we do?" Murin replied. "Sit here and wait or wait here and sit. Those appear to be our only options."

23.

Thall, Xavier, and Erlidel left Briarville and headed south toward Edgewood with Xavier leading the way. The unicorn kept getting ahead of the other two, which he found frustrating. Erlidel was an old man and Thall had short legs, so they could only walk so fast.

"Xavier," Thall yelled, "slow down!"

"Ugh," the unicorn replied and plopped himself down in the middle of the road until the others caught up to him. "I'm traveling with a couple of two-legged turtles."

The whole journey went on like this. Xavier would get ahead of the others, one of them would yell to him, he'd stop until they caught up, and the cycle would repeat. It was dark outside and the road was mostly empty. Aside from a few traders bringing goods from Edgewood to Briarville, they didn't encounter anyone else.

"There," Xavier said, stopping in the middle of the road, looking into the woods.

"Are you sure this is the right spot?" Thall asked. "How can you tell?"

"Am I sure? Of course I'm sure! This is the spot. See that trail leading into the woods?"

Thall didn't see it – not at first. It was the middle of the night and the only light they were using was from the moon. It was almost full and provided just enough light for them to see where they were going on the main road. Xavier had excellent eyesight – all unicorns did – but the other two were old and couldn't see the path leading into the woods until they were right next to it.

"Ah," Thall said. "I see it... I think."

"I can't see anything," Erlidel replied. "I'm going to cast an illumination spell."

"Are you sure that's wise?" Thall asked. "If there's anyone guarding the cabin, we don't want them to see us coming."

"What do you think?" the wizard asked Xavier. "You've seen the cabin. Do you think they have a lookout, someone watching the area around it? Will they see the light coming from the windows?"

"Cast the spell," Xavier replied. "The windows are boarded up and there was no one outside. And even if there was, the path is barely worn and the forest is thick. You two will never make it to the cabin in the dark."

Erlidel nodded and began casting an illumination spell. A minute later, they were surrounded by light. The skilled wizard was able to control how much light there was and kept it dim, only extending out about ten feet in each direction. As soon as he cast the spell, both him and Thall could see the path clearly.

"There it is!" Thall said, pointing to the path.

"No shit," Xavier replied. "I told you."

"How far into the woods is the cabin?" Thall asked. "You said it was pretty deep in the forest, didn't you?"

"Yeah," the unicorn replied. "It is. So lets get moving."

They started down the path, heading into the forest. It was very quiet and each step made a loud sound. Xavier used his magical ability to walk silently, but the footsteps of the other two could be clearly heard. Between the light and the sound, if there was a lookout at the cabin, they would've been seen and heard from a quarter-mile away. Fortunately, the cabin was unguarded and they arrived without incident.

"We're here," Xavier said as they approached the cabin, leading the way.

Thall readied his short sword, just in case. He didn't know what to expect and neither did Erlidel. Xavier led them to the invisible barrier which prevented him from getting to the cabin when he was there before. The wizard walked up to it and first poked the barrier with his finger. Then, he placed the palm of his hand on it and began making circular motions, as if cleaning a window. Erlidel stood still for a few seconds, stroking his long, blond beard, before leaning forward and taking a long, deep breath. Both Thall and Xavier watched the wizard's strange behavior, curiously.

"Yup," Erlidel whispered. "That's a magic barrier alright."

"Yeah, no kidding," Xavier replied, making no attempt to lower his voice. "Can you get rid of it?"

"Shhh," Thall whispered to Xavier. "If someone's guarding Murin and Luna, we don't want them to hear us coming."

"Shhhhhhhhhhhhhhhhhhhhhhhhhhh yourself," Xavier replied, still not lowering his voice. "If someone's in there guarding them, they would've already heard you two coming from a mile away. Were you guys, like, going out of your way to step on every branch you saw? You've both been making tons of noise. And think about it: If there were guards, then why would they need a big protective barrier around the cabin?"

Thall knew that Xavier was right. If there were guards, they would've already known they were there. The half gnome, half dwarf turned his attention from Xavier to Erlidel.

"Can you get rid of it?" he asked the wizard.

"Hmmm," Erlidel replied, stroking his beard. Standing right next to the magical barrier, he turned sideways and bumped it with his hip a couple of times. Then, Erlidel turned another ninety degrees so he was facing away from the barrier. Again, this time using his butt, he bumped it several times. Xavier and Thall just looked at him like he was crazy – because, by most definitions, he was. Erlidel did a few more things that they found strange before he finally answered the question. "Yes, I can. I'm almost certain that I can get rid of this well-constructed wall. Whoever put it up must be quite powerful."

Erlidel took off his pack and placed it on the ground. He began rifling through it until he found what he was looking for: a small glass jar filled with gold-colored powder and a circular-cut emerald the size of a quarter.

"Here," the wizard said to Thall, handing him the emerald. "Hold this up against the magical barrier."

Thall did what Erlidel asked. The wizard opened the jar and poured some of the powder into the palm of his left hand. He stood up and, with his staff in the other hand, began chanting. Xavier started wandering around about a minute into the spell, bored, walking silently around the barrier. Erlidel continued chanting for several minutes. Both Thall and Xavier were starting to worry that maybe the old wizard wasn't going to be able to get rid of it. Neither of them voiced their concerns, though. They just waited patiently. Well, Thall did. Xavier was getting frustrated that the spell was taking so long and began amusing himself however he could.

The unicorn thought it might be fun to put his front hooves up on the invisible barrier, so it would look like he was standing up on just his hind legs. Xavier approached the barrier and tapped it with his nose so he knew exactly where it was. He kicked up his front legs as high as possible, and took a couple of steps forward, expecting his front hooves to land on the barrier. But they didn't land on the barrier – because there was no barrier. Erlidel finished his spell just as Xavier was trying to lean against it.

His hooves came crashing down to the ground, throwing the unicorn off balance. It sent Xavier flying forward, taking several quick steps, trying to regain his balance, but he wasn't able to. The unicorn kept moving forward quickly until he crashed through the cabin door, head first.

"Xavier!" Murin and Luna both yelled when they saw their unicorn friend come busting through the door.

Xavier ended up on the ground in the doorway of the cabin. It was a fairly large doorway, just big enough for him to fit through. He stood up slowly, a little dazed from headbutting the door open. Thall and Erlidel cautiously approached the cabin. When the explorer came through the door and saw who was inside, his face lit up like a candle.

"Son!" Thall yelled.

"Father!" Vastrel exclaimed.

Thall ran over to his son, took a serrated knife out of his pack, and used it to free him from the chair he was tied to. The young adventurer threw his arms around his father and Thall reciprocated. After sharing a long hug with his son, Thall cut the ropes that were tying both Murin and Luna to their chairs.

"Xavier," Luna said, petting the unicorn on the head. "You came back for us. I don't know what to say. I thought we were going to be tied up here until after Involore killed all the unicorns. Never in a million years did I expect you to find help and come rescue us."

"I know," Murin added. "I can't believe it either. I mean, don't get me wrong: I'm happy that you did. But I can't believe you went and got Thall and... Who's this?"

"Jeez," Xavier replied, "You make it sound like I'm totally useless, incapable of doing anything good. I can be helpful – when I want to be. And this guy? This is Erlidel. He's a crazy old wizard from Briarville."

"I'm not *that* old," Erlidel said to Xavier, then turned to Murin and Luna. "Nice to meet you two kids."

"We're not *that* young," Luna replied, trying to be funny. Erlidel didn't seem amused. "And it's nice to meet you, too."

They all talked, catching each other up on everything that'd happened. Erlidel's illumination spell was wearing off just as the sun was coming up over the horizon.

"That spell lasted a long time," Erlidel said. "I'm surprised I didn't have to recast it halfway through our walk. Must be the upcoming holiday."

"I can't believe I didn't think of it sooner," Thall said, his face lighting up once again.

"What?" Murin asked.

"The Day of Magic," Thall replied. "It's four days from now."

"So?" Xavier asked.

"That's it. That's when Involore is going to try to destroy the unicorns. I'm such a fool! I should've already thought of it."

"What's the Day of Magic?" Murin asked.

Thall turned to Erlidel and nodded, indicating that he wanted the wizard to answer the question.

"It's a day when magic is much more powerful than usual," Erlidel answered. "It only comes around once every seven years. The stars, the planets, the moon: They all align in such a way that magic is several times stronger than usual. The effects start several days before the actual holiday and gradually get stronger until they peak at sundown on the Day of Magic. But it's not in four days. It's tomorrow."

24.

"Tomorrow?" Thall asked. "The Day of Magic is tomorrow? How are we supposed to get to the unicorns' part of the forest by then?"

"By leaving right now," Murin said, standing up straight.

"I'm tired," Xavier replied. "Why don't we take a quick ten, maybe twelve-hour nap and then we'll get to it."

"We're all exhausted," Thall said. "But Murin's right. We need to leave right now. We'll head back to the main road and continue south until we get to Edgewood. We have to go into town to get to the path leading east into the forest where the unicorns live. And while we're there, I want to have a little chat with my old friend, Dessa."

"And I'll go talk to my friend, Anora," Luna added. "She's one of Involore's apprentices."

"What are you going to do?" Murin asked Vastrel.

"I'm going to do whatever I can to help you," he replied. "That's what."

"That's my boy," Thall said. "Now let's get going!"

They left the cabin in the woods and headed back to the main road. The sun was now up and they could see just fine. All of them were tired after being up all night. Xavier was especially tired. After running to Briarville and walking back to the cabin, he was ready for a nap. To be fair, though, Xavier was always ready for a nap.

They got to Edgewood a few hours later. Not wanting to waste any time, they all split up right away. Thall headed to his old friend Dessa's house. Luna went to go see her friend, Anora. Vastrel wanted to go to the weapon shop and Murin went with him. That just left Xavier and Erlidel. They hung out in the middle of the village and managed to keep themselves entertained.

"Ha!" Xavier laughed. "That was freakin' awesome! Do it again!"

"Okay, okay," Erlidel replied and pointed at a woman walking down the main road. "Watch this. I'm going to do it to her."

Erlidel began casting a spell, speaking softly. Xavier laid next to him in the grass, his head held up high and his eyes wide with anticipation. A woman was coming down the main road carrying two loaves of bread under her arm and a big jug in her hand. Walking up the road, going in the opposite direction, was a short and stocky dwarf. Just as the two of them passed each other on the road, Erlidel uttered the final words to his spell and snapped his fingers.

"Hey!" the woman yelled.

"What the...?" the dwarven man said.

All of a sudden, the woman was empty handed and the dwarf was holding the items she had been carrying.

"Give me back my stuff!" she screamed.

"I didn't... I don't..."

"Thief!!!" the woman yelled.

"Here! Take it!"

The dwarf nervously handed the woman back her bread and the jug, practically throwing it at her. She snatched it out of his hands and gave him a dirty look before walking off. The man continued on his way with a look of utter confusion on his face. Xavier and Erlidel both laughed like crazy, just far enough away that the man and woman didn't notice them.

"That was great!" Xavier said, still laughing. "You're the first human I've met who really knows how to have fun."

"And you're the first unicorn I've met who knows how to have fun," Erlidel replied.

"How many unicorns have you..." Xavier started asking but cut himself off when he spotted someone coming up the road. "Here comes someone else. Do it again!"

"You're going to love this one," Erlidel replied. "Watch this."

Erlidel kept Xavier entertained – himself, too – with his magic for a while. They stayed in the middle of the village laughing and having a good time. Meanwhile, Vastrel and Murin were at the weapon shop. Murin had been in there plenty of times before and knew Tundrot, the owner. He liked to go in and look at all the expensive weapons. Sometimes, when Tundrot was in a good mood and not too busy, he'd even let Murin hold some of them.

"May I?" Murin asked, pointing to a short sword hanging on the wall.

"Yeah," Tundrot answered. "Go ahead, Murin."

Murin took the short sword down off the wall. Vastrel was walking around the shop, examining the impressive collection of weapons. He saw Murin take the sword down out of the corner of his eye and watched him swing it around a little bit. Impressed, the adventurer turned to face Murin.

"I thought you were a farmer?" Vastrel asked.

"I am," Murin answered.

"I've never met a farmer who knew how to use a short sword like that before," Vastrel said.

"I have a friend who is training to be a warrior. He's been showing me how to use a sword when we have time. I accept that my fate is to be a farmer like my father and his father before him. But I've always dreamed of being an adventurer, like you. You're lucky that your father was an explorer."

"My father wanted me to be a map maker," Vastrel replied. "He thought the life of an adventurer was too dangerous."

"So, what happened?"

"I realized that, as much as I loved and respected my father, it was up to me how I wanted to live my life. I knew that I'd never be happy copying maps all day. I didn't want to be someone who made maps. I wanted to be someone who explored them. So against my father's wishes, as soon as I was grown up, I started going on adventures. Naturally, my father wasn't happy at first. But eventually, over time, he came to respect my decision. Well, maybe not respect. But he realized that I wasn't going to change and came to at least accept it."

"So, you're saying I should disobey my father's wishes and become an adventurer?" Murin asked.

"What I'm saying is that you should follow your heart. If you love farming, then be a farmer. But it sounds to me like your heart yearns for something else. Perhaps you could figure out a way to be a farmer *and* an adventurer. Look at my father, for example. He's known as an explorer, but he's also a map maker, a gem expert, an adventurer, a scholar, a diplomat, and about ten other things."

"You've given me a lot to think about, Vastrel," Murin said with a smile. "Thank you."

"You're welcome," Vastrel said, then turned to Tundrot and pointed at a weapon hanging on the wall in front of him, just out of reach. "I'll take this warhammer right here."

Neither Involore nor his apprentices took any of Vastrel's stuff when they ambushed him and brought him to the cabin in the woods. However, after they cast the compliance spell on him, Vastrel had dropped his warhammer somewhere along the way to the cabin.

"Excellent choice!" Tundrot replied.

The store owner came eagerly running out from behind the counter, bringing a stepping stool with him. He climbed up it, took the warhammer off the wall, and handed it to Vastrel. Tundrot then went back behind the counter, leaving the stool where it was.

"Just the warhammer?" Tundrot asked Vastrel. "I have a wonderful selection of knives and daggers. You never know when a hidden dagger in your boot is going to come in handy."

Vastrel looked down at his boots, then looked back up at Tundrot. He opened his mouth as if to speak, but didn't. His gaze left Tundrot once again, this time looking over at Murin for a moment. The young man was still cautiously swinging the sword around the large store. Vastrel looked back at Tundrot and finally answered him.

"You're right. You never *do* know when you're going to need an extra weapon. In addition to the warhammer, I'll take that knife right there," Vastrel said, pointing to a knife on a shelf behind the counter. "And Murin will take the short sword he's holding."

"What?" Murin asked. He stopped swinging the sword and looked over at Vastrel and Tundrot.

"We have no idea what we're going to face out there in the forest," Vastrel told Murin. "The better we're armed, the more likely we are to be successful."

"As much as I like this short sword," Murin said, looking down, "I can't afford it."

Vastrel dug through his pack, taking out a medium-sized pouch filled with coins. He plopped it down on the counter and Tundrot's face lit up like a fireball spell. Murin's eyes also widened when he heard the heavy pouch land on the counter.

"How much for the hammer, the knife, and the sword?" Vastrel asked.

"Well, let's see," Tundrot said. "The warhammer is fifteen gold pieces. The short sword is twelve gold. And the knife is two gold and five silver. But I'll sell it all to you for only twenty-eight gold pieces."

"I'll tell you what," Vastrel countered. "You throw in another knife and I'll give you thirty gold."

"Thirty gold for *two* knives, the warhammer, and the short sword..." Tundrot said, thinking out loud. After a brief pause, he looked up at Vastrel, smiled, held his hand out over the counter and replied, "Deal!"

Vastrel shook the store owner's hand. The smile on Murin's face was even bigger than the smile on Tundrot's. Vastrel took thirty gold pieces out of his pouch and counted it on the counter with the store owner. Then, Murin and Vastrel thanked Tundrot, said goodbye, and went to go meet up with the others.

"Thank you for the sword, Vastrel," Murin said as they were walking back to the village center. "I don't know what to say. Just so you know, I have no way of paying you back."

"Sword *and* knife," Vastrel corrected.

"Huh?"

Vastrel handed one of the knives that he'd bought to Murin. The young man's face lit up once again.

"Anytime someone is trying to sell you something, you should be suspicious," Vastrel said to

Murin. "The weapon store owner was just trying to make more money, but he did have a point. You never *do* know when you're going to need an extra weapon. That's why I got a knife for myself and also one for you. Tuck it away in your boot. Hopefully, neither of us will need to use them. Oh, and don't worry about the gold. Consider them both a gift for letting me join you on what is likely to turn out to be the adventure of a lifetime."

"Well, thank you," Murin replied. "Thank you so, so much."

The young man stopped briefly to tuck the knife into his boot and Vastrel did the same with his. They continued walking up the road until they met up with the others. The whole time, Murin's hand was on the hilt of his brand-new short sword. It came with a cheap-but-sufficient scabbard, which the young man wore with pride. For a few minutes, between the sword, the adventurer walking next to him, and the quest he was about to go on, Murin forgot that he was a farmer. He actually felt like an adventurer himself and that put a huge smile on his face. But, just as Murin was getting to the rendezvous point in the middle of the village, a familiar voice brought his thoughts crashing back to reality.

"Murin!"

25.

"Oh no," Murin said under his breath, then turned around quickly. His smile instantly vanished. "Father, I was going to..."

"You were going to what?" Mr. Fieldstone yelled. "You were supposed to be back from Briarville yesterday. Do you know how worried we've been? Your mother didn't sleep a wink last night."

"I'm sorry," Murin replied. "It's just that..."

"I don't want to hear it. Get back to the farm and take care of your responsibilities. Your brothers and sisters are doing *your* work because you're not there. And what are you doing with that weapon? I don't want that thing anywhere near my property. Get rid of it."

"I'm sorry, father, but..."

"I just told you that I don't want to hear about how sorry you are. Now lose the sword and march your ass back to our farm."

"I can't do that," Murin said, unable to make eye contact with his father.

"You can't do *what*?" his father asked, crossing his arms.

Thall, Xavier, Erlidel, and Luna saw Murin's father yelling at him. They had all met back at the rendezvous point and were waiting for Murin and Vastrel. Luna grabbed Thall's arm and started walking toward Murin, pulling the half gnome, half dwarf with her.

"Come with me," she said to him as they walked.

"What about us?" Erlidel asked, referring to Xavier and himself.

"Just stay put for a minute," Luna yelled.

Murin tried to explain to his father everything that had happened and everything that would soon happen if he and the others didn't intervene. It wasn't going so well. Murin was always a bit anxious around his dad. But at that moment, he was more anxious than he'd ever been before and was struggling to form complete, coherent sentences.

"And Dessa, too... All the unicorns... We have to go... The wizard's going to do it... Involore... We must stop it... And then the apprentices..."

"Hi, Mr. Fieldstone," Luna said, interrupting Murin, as she approached him and his dad.

"Luna, this isn't really a good..."

"I'd like you to meet someone," she continued, interrupting him. "Mr. Fieldstone, I'd like you to meet Thall the Explorer. He's going to explain to you why Murin didn't come home yesterday and why he's not going to be home for the next several days, at least."

"Hi," Thall said, offering Murin's dad his hand. "You've raised quite a mature and intelligent young man. I don't know if you know who I am..."

"Of course I do!" Mr. Fieldstone replied, shaking Thall's hand, firmly. "Everyone knows who you are. The question is: How do you know my son? And what is Luna talking about, 'being gone for the next several days?'"

Thall looked up at Luna, then Murin. They both knew why he was looking at them and answered the question before he even had to ask it.

"Tell him everything," Murin said.

And that's exactly what Thall did. The famous explorer explained everything that'd happened to Murin's father. It took a few minutes, Thall and Mr. Fieldstone going back and forth but, eventually they came to an agreement.

"I'm trusting you to look after my son," Murin's father said to Thall. "Your reputation is legendary and there's no doubt in my mind that you will succeed in your mission. Speaking of which, I know I'm just a farmer, but is there anything I can do to help?"

"Thank you, kind sir," Thall replied. "I'll do everything I can to make sure your son stays safe. And actually, there *is* something you can do to help us."

"Name it."

"We could use a few horses to help us get out into the forest faster. Do you have five horses we can borrow?"

"We've only got four horses on the farm right now," Mr. Fieldstone replied. "But you're welcome to borrow them. They're all trained and very mild mannered."

"We'll take them," Thall said. "Thank you."

"And you," Mr. Fieldstone said to his son. "I'm still not happy about you going on this quest. I think you and Luna should leave it to the trained adventurers. But you are an adult now and I have to let you make your own decisions. Is there anything I can do to make you change your mind?"

"I'm sorry, father," Murin replied, making eye contact briefly. "But I'm going."

"Then all I can say is: Safe journey. You listen to everything Thall the Explorer says to you. And when you get back, we need to sit down and have a long talk."

"Okay," Murin replied, finally making lasting eye contact. "Thank you, father. I will."

Mr. Fieldstone wrapped his arms around his son, giving Murin a long, firm hug. Then, he turned and walked off, heading back to the farm to get the horses ready. Once he left, Xavier and Erlidel came over and joined them all.

"What did Dessa have to say?" Vastrel asked his dad.

"Nothing," Thall replied. "Nothing at all because she wasn't home. There was a note on her door that said she'd be out of town for a few days."

"That's an awfully strange coincidence," Murin said, then turned toward Luna. "How about you? Did you go to Anora's house? Was she home?"

"Nope," Luna replied. "Same thing as Dessa. Except with Anora, it wasn't a note. It was her mother who told me she'd be out of town for the next few days. And guess who she's with?"

"Involore?"

"Yup. Involore. Anora's mom said she'd be out of town with him working on her studies but didn't know where they were going."

"Well, *we* know where they're going," Murin said. "Let's go get the horses from my farm and then we'll head out into the woods."

"How are we going to fit five people on four horses?" Thall asked as they started walking.

"There's only one way that I can think of," Luna replied, petting Xavier who was walking next to her.

"I know you're not suggesting what I think you think you're suggesting," the unicorn replied.

"It won't be so bad," Luna replied. "I'm not that heavy. It'll be fine."

Xavier didn't reply. He just kept walking along with the others. Luna could tell that the unicorn didn't like the idea of having her ride on his back, but was happy he wasn't putting up a fight.

They got to the farm and found Mr. Fieldstone in the stable with two of Murin's siblings getting the horses ready. One of the horses was Lily, the one that Xavier had let out of the stable his first night in Edgewood. As soon as Lily saw the unicorn, she unleashed a loud roar.

"Easy, girl," Murin's dad said, petting Lily on the head.

"Well, that was rude," Xavier said. "Somebody needs to teach that horse some manners."

Murin looked at Xavier and shook his head. It suddenly occurred to him that Xavier could've used the same magical ability to have opened Lily's gate as he'd used to open Thall's door. For a second, Murin wanted to question the unicorn about it. But he thought it would be best to just let it go for now.

"So, you really are a unicorn, huh?" Murin's dad asked after hearing Xavier speak.

He took a couple of steps toward Xavier and reached out to pet him on his side. Just in time, Luna grabbed Mr. Fieldstone's hand.

"He's a unicorn who doesn't like being touched by most people," Luna replied, then let go of his arm. "Don't take it personally."

"Yeah," Murin parroted, shooting Xavier a somewhat-dirty look. "Don't take it personally."

Mr. Fieldstone stepped away from Xavier and went back to getting the horses ready. Murin helped him and his siblings. Before long, they were ready to go. All the horses had been fed and were wearing saddles. Murin grabbed an extra saddle, handed it to Luna, and she walked over to Xavier.

"What the hell do you think you're doing with that thing?" the unicorn asked.

"It'll make it easier to ride you," Luna replied. "Trust me. It'll be better for you and it'll be better for me."

"Nope."

"What do you mean, 'Nope?'" Luna asked.

"I mean you're not putting that thing on my back. You're lucky I'm going to let you ride me at all. I'm not a freakin' horse. I'm a unicorn, remember? I don't know how I can make that any clearer. I'm not meant to be ridden. I'm meant to roam freely without some girl bouncing up and down on top of me. No saddle."

"But..."

Xavier stomped one of his front hooves and puffed a massive gust of wind out of his nostrils. Luna knew exactly what the gesture meant and immediately stopped trying to get Xavier to agree with her. She knew it was pointless and put the saddle back where it was.

"All right," Thall said. "Let's get going. We're at least a half day behind Involore. We've got a lot of ground to cover. A lot of catching up to do."

They thanked Mr. Fieldstone for the horses once again. He helped everyone get on them and said goodbye. Xavier gave Luna a hard time for a minute but eventually knelt down so she could get on top of him.

They rode off down the main road in Edgewood, heading toward the trail leading into the forest to the east. The group caught the attention of everyone who was out and about. Anyone who was on the road got out of the way for them, watching them quickly disappear, leaving a trail of dust in their wake. They knew that they'd need to hurry if they wanted to catch Involore in time.

Before long, the group was out of Edgewood and in the forest. They made great time for the first few hours that they were in the woods. Riding single file, they blazed down the path. There weren't many people out in the forest. But the ones who were could hear the group clip-clopping loudly down the path and got out of their way with plenty of time to spare.

Murin and Luna had both spent plenty of time out in the forest. The main path was considered to be reasonably safe and they had both traveled pretty far down it without any problems. But after a few hours of traveling on horseback, the group was farther down the main path than Murin or Luna had ever been. And a little while after that, they left the main path to head northeast up a different one.

With Thall in the lead, he kept his map handy, slowing down and consulting it every so often. He led the group up a narrow path, surrounded by thick forest on both sides. The seasoned explorer warned the others to stay on their guard. He explained to them that they were entering a part of the forest that was known to be filled with all kinds of dangerous monsters.

"As long as we stick together," Thall said, "we should be alright. Most monsters won't attack a group like ours. Stay close."

"*Most* monsters won't attack a group like ours," Vastrel replied, patting the warhammer at his side. "But *some* will. And we'll crush them like the scum that they are."

"Yeah, we will," Murin said, patting the hilt of his short sword, his voice a little shaky.

From the safety of Edgewood, Murin loved to fantasize about battling with monsters. But being out in a dangerous part of the forest where he might actually run into them, the thought of fighting one terrified Murin. He did his best to remain calm because he didn't want to look weak, especially in front of Vastrel, who he looked up to. Luna was quite scared, too, but didn't say anything. She just kept her eyes focused to the front, trying not to let her imagination get the best of her.

They continued up the path. It wasn't nearly as wide or as worn as the main path and they could only travel at a fraction of the speed that they had been moving at. Still, being on horseback allowed them to travel faster than they would've been able to otherwise.

All of a sudden, Thall stopped. The others all stopped behind him.

"What is it?" Vastrel whispered.

"Did any of you hear that?" Thall asked.

"No."

"What?"

"Nope."

"Hear what?"

"I don't hear anything," Xavier said. "But something smells absolutely freakin' disgusting."

The group stayed put for a few seconds and kept quiet to see if they could hear anything. At the same exact time, they all looked to their right when they heard something in the woods. Then, their heads all turned to the left when they heard rustling in the woods on the other side of the path. Everyone's attention was piqued, but Murin and Luna were overflowing with anxiety. Their hearts were beating like a hummingbird's and felt like they were going to burst out of their chests.

"Narg!" they heard someone – or something – yell from the woods to the left, just in front of them.

All at once, four monsters jumped out of the woods, ambushing the group. Two were in front of them and two behind, blocking any chance of escape. Without hesitation, Erlidel began casting a spell and both Thall and his son pulled out their weapons. The hardened adventurers had been through plenty of similar situations and knew just what to do. Murin and Luna, on the other hand, were frozen solid. They were so scared that neither of them moved. And Xavier was as close to having a panic attack as any unicorn could be. His flight-or-flight response was kicking in hard but he had nowhere to go. Like Murin and Luna, he froze and just stood there on the narrow path, blocked in at both ends.

"Let's do this!" Vastrel yelled and hopped down from his horse, warhammer in hand.

26.

Blocking the path stood four orcs – two in the front and two in the back. They were ugly creatures and, as Xavier had already pointed out, had a very distinct odor to them. Both Murin and Luna knew what orcs were but had never actually seen one. They stayed up on their rides, as did Erlidel. Both Thall and Vastrel jumped down from their horses and prepared for battle.

"Targ alga!" yelled the biggest orc, seemingly the leader of the group.

All four orcs were carrying weapons. Two of them had rusty daggers, one had a rusty short sword, and the last had a small battle axe – also rusty. A couple of the orcs were wearing armor, if you could call it that. One was wearing a leather helmet with a ripped tunic and a pair of way-too-tight shorts. Another had rusty gauntlets on with baggie pants and no shirt. The last two were just wearing tattered clothing, likely stolen from other groups they'd ambushed in the past.

As soon as the lead orc spoke, the others raised their weapons to attack. Little did they know, they had ambushed a group of skilled adventurers – well, three skilled adventurers, two inexperienced young adults, and a unicorn, to be precise. But those three skilled adventurers made quick work of the unlucky orcs.

"Die, orc!" Vastrel yelled.

He raised his new warhammer overhead and brought it crashing down on one of the orcs in front. It smashed right into the orc's shoulder, causing it to drop its dagger. Thall, like his son, raised his weapon and attacked the other orc in the front. But before he had a chance to swing his short sword, the orc he was going to attack sliced at him first. Thall took a step back, but the orc's short sword slashed him in the arm. The famous explorer immediately countered, swinging his own short sword at the orc. Not only was it a direct hit, Thall managed to chop the orc's head clean off. It fell to the ground and rolled a few feet down the path.

Murin, Luna, and Xavier were all blown away by what they were seeing – especially Xavier. The unicorn had never seen anything nearly as violent in his entire life. It was so disturbing to him that he was actually shaking and Luna could feel it from on top of him. With nowhere to go, his shaking got even worse when an orc approached him and Luna.

"Ahhhhhhhhh!" she screamed.

The orc wearing a leather helmet grabbed Luna by the leg and was trying to pull her down from Xavier. With a closed fist she hammer-punched the orc on the top of the head several times but it didn't seem to phase him. What *did* phase him was when Erlidel finished his spell a moment later.

The crazy wizard leaned back on his horse, so far back that he could see behind himself. He pointed his fingers at the two orcs in the back, including the one tugging at Luna's leg. The second Erlidel finished casting his spell, a bolt of lightening fired out of his fingers, each bolt striking one of the orcs in the middle of its chest. Both of them went flying back several feet, landing in the woods. Each had a massive hole in the middle of their chests with smoke coming out of it. Luna breathed a huge sigh of relief when she saw her would-be attacker dead on the ground.

The only remaining orc had managed to pick up its dropped dagger and held it out in front of itself. Vastrel could see fear in its eyes and that made him smile. The orc saw how quickly its friends had been killed and knew that it was next. With them being on horseback – or unicornback, in Luna's case – the orc knew it had no chance of escaping.

It lunged at Vastrel, trying to stab him in the neck. He narrowly escaped, dodging out of the way at the last second. Vastrel had his warhammer raised high, waiting to strike. Again, the orc took another stab at the experienced adventurer. This time, Vastrel easily moved out of the way. Still, he held his hammer high, waiting for the perfect opportunity to do some real damage. That opportunity came when the orc took one final stab at Vastrel.

"Garg!" the orc yelled, lunging forward, trying to stab Vastrel in the face.

The orc telegraphed its attack a second before it lunged forward, something that Vastrel picked up on. He noticed that the first two times it lunged at him, the orc pivoted slightly to the side first. When Vastrel saw him pivot that third time, he knew another stab attempt was imminent and acted accordingly. The moment the orc pivoted, so did Vastrel. He took a wide step to the side just as the orc lunged at him and swung his warhammer as hard as he could.

Crunch!

The sound of metal smashing bone echoed throughout the forest. Vastrel's powerful blow caved in the orc's head, sending it straight down to the ground. Just to be sure that the orc was dead, Vastrel raised his warhammer overhead one last time and sent it crashing down on the lifeless orc's head. Again it made the same sound, a sound that Murin, Luna, and Xavier would not soon forget.

Crunch!

For several seconds, no one said anything. Murin, Luna, and Xavier were all still quite shaken up. Thall and Vastrel searched the orcs, taking the few copper pieces and one silver they found. They threw the orcs' weapons into the woods and dragged their corpses to the side of the road. The two orcs that Erlidel has zapped were already in the woods, still smoldering. The last thing to be removed from the path was the severed orc's head. Vastrel picked it up by its hair, swung it around around a couple of times, then let go, sending it flying into the woods.

"I can see you still got it, father," Vastrel said to Thall. "You took that orc's head clean off with one swing."

"Lucky shot," Thall replied.

"Nonsense," his son said. "And you know it."

Thall smirked, then walked over to Murin and Luna, who were still on the backs of their rides.

"You two alright?" he asked, then looked at Xavier. "You *three*, I should say?"

"I'm okay," Murin said, his heart rate finally starting to slow down.

"Luna?" Thall asked.

"Just a little shaken up from that orc trying to grab me. But I'm fine," she said, then noticed the cut on Thall's arm. "But you're not. Let me heal that for you."

"It's nothing, really."

"Please. I've been studying to be a healer for years and this is a good opportunity to put what I've learned into practice."

Thall agreed to let Luna heal him. He helped her down off Xavier and she began casting a basic healing spell. She was so shaken up by what had just happened that it took her a little longer than usual to remember all the words. But she managed to cast the spell, laid her hands on Thall's arm, and the gash that the orc's rusty short sword had put in it instantly disappeared.

"Excellent work! Thank you, Luna," Thall said. Then after helping her back up onto Xavier's back, he asked the unicorn, "You okay, Xavier?"

"I'm all good," the unicorn replied. Thall could clearly see that Xavier wasn't all good, but didn't say anything. Xavier was still shaking a little bit and Thall recognized a look in his eyes that he'd seen many times before – the look of someone who'd just witnessed their first episode of violence. "But we should get going. As if those ugly things didn't smell bad enough before, the two that the wizard zapped now smell even worse. If I have to keep smelling them, there's a good chance I'm going to vomit. And I'm pretty sure no one wants that."

"No, we don't," Murin said.

"Definitely not," Luna agreed.

"Okay then," Thall said, walking back to his horse in the front. "If everyone's all set, let's keep moving."

They continued heading up the path, single file. Most of them traveled in silence for a while, all except Murin and Xavier. Murin's horse was walking in front of Xavier and he had his head turned so he could talk to the unicorn.

"How are you really doing, Xav?" Murin asked.

The unicorn was about to tell Murin the same thing that he'd told Thall: that he was fine. But the truth was, he wasn't fine. Xavier had never even seen two people get into a fist fight before, let alone a battle resulting in four deaths. Violence didn't exist in Unicaria. He was used to peace and harmony, fun and games – not violent ambushes and evil wizards planning world domination. Life outside of the unicorn community was really starting to take its toll on Xavier and, in that moment, he decided to just be honest with Murin. That young man was the closest thing to a friend that Xavier had and he was starting to trust him.

"That was the worst experience of my life," the unicorn replied. "I've never been so scared before."

"I know, buddy," Murin replied. "Me, too. I've been fantasizing about getting into a battle with monsters since I was a little kid. But as soon as those orcs jumped out, I froze. I couldn't move. I felt like I was paralyzed. It was almost like I wasn't even here, like I was just watching everything happen in slow motion from far away. Some adventurer I am. Maybe my father's been right all along. Maybe I'm not cut out to be an adventurer. Maybe I should just accept the fact that I'm a farmer and will always be a farmer."

"If you're not cut out to be an adventurer, I don't know who the hell would be," Xavier said.

"What do you mean, Xav?"

"Take this with a grain of sand..."

"Salt," Murin corrected.

"What?" Xavier asked.

"Salt. The saying is 'Take it with a grain of salt.'"

"Oh, right. I'm still learning all your stupid human sayings, most of which don't make any sense at all," Xavier said, then started over. "Take this with a grain of *salt*, since I've only been around humans and other humanoids for a few days. But from what I've seen and from what I've heard, you seem like you'd make an excellent adventurer. You went way out of your way to help me, for one. When we heard about Involore's evil plan, your instinct was to take action and alert your village's elder. You like to explore... You've got many talents... There are a lot of things that would make you a good adventurer."

"Thanks," Murin replied, speaking slowly, really surprised by what Xavier was saying. "But you saw what happened back there. I didn't get down to even try to help defeat the orcs."

"So what? Vastrel, Thall, and Erlidel took care of those smelly things. You didn't need to help. But you gained some much-needed experience. Now you know what it's like to be ambushed, to see real battle. Next time, when something like that happens, you won't be as shaken up. I just hope I'm not around to see it. I never want to go through anything like that ever again."

"If I didn't know any better, I'd think you were trying to make me feel better."

"Well, don't get used to it. And besides, I'm just being honest."

"Thanks, Xav," Murin replied.

The rest of the day went by without incident and they continued up the path until it was starting to get dark. All of them were extremely tired and eager to settle down for the night so they could get some sleep. Off in the distance, they could hear running water and the sound of waves crashing against rocks. Before long, they came to a large wooden bridge going over a wide river. The slow-moving river emptied out into a massive salt-water lake that was just a little ways up the path.

27.

One by one, they crossed the bridge. First was Thall, followed by Vastrel, Erlidel, and Murin. Luna and Xavier were in the back. Everyone was exhausted, too tired to appreciate the view from the middle of the bridge. They all kept their eyes to the front for the most part. The bridge was long, wide, and sturdy. It had clearly been there for some time, but was still in good condition.

"What was that?" Xavier asked.

As Xavier and Luna were crossing the bridge, something in the water caught the unicorn's eye. The others kept moving forward, but Xavier stopped right in the middle of the bridge.

"What was what?" Luna asked, looking in the water.

"I... I thought I saw something," Xavier replied, walking over to the edge of the bridge, looking down over the side. "I guess not."

"It's probably just your mind playing tricks on you," Luna replied. "You're tired. We all are."

"Yeah," Xavier said. "Maybe."

The unicorn shrugged it off and continued crossing the bridge. After taking a few step, Xavier stopped again, violently turning his head to the side.

"There!" he yelled, getting not just Luna's attention, but the attention of the others. "You didn't just see that?"

"See what?" Luna asked. "What did you see?"

"It was some kind of unicorn fish," Xavier replied.

"Huh?" Luna asked, confused.

"A huge fish with a big horn just popped out of the water for a second, then went back under. You really didn't see that? It was huge!"

"I didn't see anything," Luna replied. "Let's just keep going. We're all tired and need sleep."

"I didn't imagine it," Xavier said, puffing a gust of air from his nostrils. "I'm telling you. I know what I saw."

The unicorn again walked over to the side of the bridge, now almost all the way across it. Both Luna and Xavier kept their eyes on the water but didn't see anything. The others came over, too, and looked out into the water. They stayed there for several minutes, gazing into the river. None of them saw anything out of the ordinary.

"Come on, Xavier," Luna said, petting the unicorn's head. "Let's keep going."

"I swear I saw I big fish with a horn," Xavier replied. "You believe me... Don't you?"

"Sure. I believe you."

Luna didn't believe him and Xavier knew it, but the unicorn was too tired to press the issue further. They all continued walking up the path, which ran along the river until it emptied out into a massive saltwater lake. With the sun on the horizon, it seemed like the perfect place to break camp for the night. Small waves crashed upon the sandy shore and everyone got off their horses, securing them nearby. They all looked out over the water, which went as far as the eye could see.

After checking out the area, everyone unpacked their stuff and got set up for the night. They got a fire going and before long the sun was over the horizon. Xavier was the first to fall asleep. He curled up in a ball halfway between the fire and the water. The sound of the crashing waves soothed him and, within minutes of closing his eyes, Xavier was out cold. Erlidel was the next to fall asleep after eating some jerky he had in his pack. Murin and Luna were both tired, but sat near the water talking among themselves for a while. That just left Thall and his son who sat next to the fire talking quietly.

"We're here," Thall said, taking out his map, laying it on the ground, and pointing to the area where the river met the lake. "This is an ideal place to stay tonight. Then, at the first sign of daylight, we'll pack up and keep going."

"Where are the unicorns?" Vastrel asked.

"Either here or here," Thall replied, first pointing to two different spots on the map, then just one. "But I'm almost positive they're here. That's where Involore is heading. I'm sure of it."

"Let's hope you're right," Vastrel said. "There's no room for error. We don't know how far behind them we are."

"Hopefully, taking the horses helped us to close in on them at least a little bit. Because if we don't stop them..."

"I know," Vastrel replied. "Believe me, I do. I thought about it a lot while we were traveling. It'll usher in an era of unmitigated evil. What I *don't* know is *how* Involore is going to get to the unicorns and kill them all."

"I've been thinking about that," Thall replied. "The last thing I gave to Involore was an ancient magical text. Most of it is outdated incantations and useless rituals. But there was one part that I found interesting."

"Which part?"

"I copied it down on a piece of parchment," Thall said while digging through his pack, taking out a small, crumpled up piece of parchment. "Ah, here it is."

Thall flattened out the parchment and laid it on the ground in front of the fire for his son. They both read it to themselves, silently. It read:

In a land of purity, wholesomeness, and good
In a land hidden deep within the wood
A single drop of blood so pure
Will slay more souls than a sword ever could

A drop will do, but better is two
One drop red, one drop blue
A beating heart turned bleeding heart
Must stop to bid thine souls adieu

"What does it mean?" Vastrel asked his father.

"Involore wants to kill all the unicorns so he can take their alicorns to harness their power. I think this rhyme is about just that. To kill all the unicorns, he needs to sacrifice someone who is pure of heart. In other words, someone who has never intentionally harmed anyone else. It sounds to me that if someone pure gets killed in that part of the forest, it'll destroy all the unicorns."

Vastrel didn't reply. He just gave his dad a confused look.

"You don't think that's what it means?" Thall asked.

"I have no idea what it means. I suppose it could mean that."

"I looked through the entire magic book. That's the only part that Involore could've possibly been interested in. The rest was outdated nonsense."

"That still doesn't tell us how Involore is going to get to the unicorns," Vastrel said. "Their part of the forest is said to be protected by powerful elemental magic. Any idea how someone could break through?"

"No clue," Thall replied. "But Involore obviously knows how to – or at least he thinks he does. Tomorrow, on the Day of Magic, his spells are going to be much more powerful than usual. He's been planning this for months."

"Tomorrow's going to be an eventful day," Vastrel said, putting his hand on his father's shoulder. "We need our rest – especially you, old man. Why don't you get comfortable. I'll take first watch."

Thall agreed and gave his son a long hug before finding a good spot in the sand to lay down on. The half gnome, half dwarf took off his boots and got cozy, falling asleep within a minute of closing his eyes. Vastrel sat by the fire getting lost in though, but still keeping an ear and an eye out for trouble. Murin and Luna were both still sitting near the water, talking.

"That was really cool back there," Murin said. "What you did, I mean."

"What do you mean, what *I* did?" Luna asked.

"Healing Thall like that. I've never seen you actually use your healing powers. You're so lucky to be doing what you've always wanted to do. I remember you as a little girl saying that you were going to grow up to be a healer just like your dad was. And now, look at you."

"What about you? You've always dreamed of being an adventurer. And now here *you* are on the adventure of a lifetime."

"But once it's over, it's over," Murin said, looking out over the water. "After this adventure is over, it's back to the farm for me. You get to keep studying and practicing the healing arts. All I'll be doing is planting seeds and shoveling manure."

"If that's what you want to do..."

"You know it's not what I *want* to do," Murin replied, looking over at Luna. "It's what I *have* to do. It's my destiny. My father's a farmer and his father was a farmer. Guess what *his* father was?"

"A farmer?" Luna guessed.

"A shepherd, but close enough. You get my point. I'm a farmer, not an adventurer."

"Says who? If you want to be an adventurer, be one. No one's stopping you. We're not little kids anymore, Murin. We can do whatever we want to."

"But what about my father? I don't want him to be disappointed in me. And what about the farm? My siblings will need my help once my parents are too old to work anymore."

"Your father might be a little mad, but he'll get over it. And the farm won't fall apart without you. I mean, yeah, you do a lot there. And you're better with the animals than any of your siblings. But they'd find a way to make it work without you."

"Okay," Murin said. "Maybe that's all true. But there's an even bigger problem: I'm a lousy adventurer. When we got attacked by those orcs back there, I was too scared to even get down from my horse's back. I just froze up. Not very adventurer-like."

"You weren't the only one," Luna replied. "I was terrified, too. But I feel like you're just making excuses."

"What do you mean?"

"What I mean is that you just gave me a bunch of reasons why you can't be an adventurer. But they're not *good* reasons. They're all things that you could overcome. You're forgetting the most important reason why you *should* become an adventurer."

"Which is what?" Murin asked.

"It's what you've always wanted!" Luna said, whisper-yelling, not wanting to wake the others. "It's your dream, Mur! It's what you've always wanted. Even after putting in a full day on the farm, you muster up the energy to practice the warrior skills your friend's been teaching you. So you froze up your first time in battle. So what? Adventurers aren't born. They're created. You have the potential to be a great adventurer. But you need to believe in yourself. You need to trust that you can do it."

"Thank you, Luna," Murin replied with a smile.

"We both need to get some sleep," Luna said without returning Murin's smile. "If we keep talking, I'm going to start getting angry because we've talked about this a million times before. You know how I feel. And you know what you need to do. You need to make a decision and stick to it."

"I know. You're right. Good night, Luna."

"Night."

Murin leaned over and gave his friend a long hug. They sat in silence for a few minutes looking out over the water, Luna resting her head on Murin's shoulder. He thought about everything she'd said and knew, deep down, that she was right. The only thing stopping Murin from becoming an adventurer was himself. He *was* an adult now and could decide his own fate. But Murin was scared and rightly so. The life of an adventurer could be a tumultuous one, but it was his dream since childhood.

Murin and Luna got up and walked a little closer to the fire. They curled up in the sand and within minutes of closing their eyes, they both fell asleep. Everyone slept through the night, Vastrel, Thall, and Erlidel taking turns keeping watch. It was an uneventful night and everyone slept well, especially with the soothing sound of crashing waves and running water in the background.

28.

Cock-a-doodle-dooooooooo!!!

Everyone woke up immediately, sitting up and looking around. It was still mostly dark outside, the very first sign of light just starting to appear on the horizon.

"What the hell was that godawful sound?" Xavier asked.

"It sounded like a rooster," Murin replied. "But there aren't any out here... I don't think."

Murin was right. There weren't any roosters within several miles of their location. Erlidel, who took the final overnight watch, used his magic to wake the others by recreating the sound of a rooster. The only difference was that Erlidel's spell was several times louder than an actual rooster – about five times louder. Everyone looked around, trying to spot the rooster responsible for waking them up. Of course, they didn't find one. What they did find was Erlidel laughing like a maniac, sitting on a stump near the fire.

"Damn it, wizard," Vastrel said, realizing that the rooster sound was Erlidel's doing. "You could've cast a more pleasant-sounding spell to wake us all up."

"I could've, sure," the wizard replied. "But it wouldn't have had the same effect. I wanted to wake you all up quickly and I did. We've got a big day ahead of us. No time to waste. Although to be honest, I didn't intend for it to be *that* loud. I forgot that today is the Day of Magic. It must've increased the strength of the spell."

"Del's right," Thall agreed, rubbing his eyes. "We *do* have a big day ahead of us. Let's have a quick meal, then we'll pack our stuff and get moving."

Everyone got up and headed in different directions so they could relieve themselves. Most of them headed toward the woods, but Xavier walked over to the water.

"Holy shit!" the unicorn yelled. "Holy freakin' shitblast! Guys, look! Get over here, quickly! I told you I wasn't making it up!"

Most of them were still in the middle of doing what they were doing. As soon as each of them finished, they walked over to where Xavier was standing. Before long, everyone was standing around in a half-circle on the beach. In the middle of them laid a strange creature that none of them had ever seen or even heard of before – all but one of them.

"I shouldn't have doubted you, Xavier," Luna said. "What is that thing?"

Vastrel shrugged his shoulders. Murin's facial expression told Luna that he didn't know. Xavier obviously didn't know, either. Even Thall, in all his travels, had never seen such a strange beast.

"That?" Erlidel replied. "That right there is a narwhal. And by the look of it, a dead one. It must've washed up onto the shore overnight."

"You've encountered these strange creatures before?" Thall asked.

"Oh, yes," Erlidel answered. "But never anywhere around here. The only time I've ever seen them was when I went on an adventure to the easternmost of the Southwestern Islands in the Northern Sea. There are tons of them up there. I don't know what this one's doing this far south, though. I just assumed they only lived in icy waters. It must've migrated down here for some reason. Fisherman used to catch them and take their horns. They'd bring the horns back to land and sell them to gullible fools, telling them that they were unicorn horns. You'd have to be an idiot to think that a narwhal horn is actually an alicorn!"

Erlidel pointed at the narwhal's horn and laughed. Thall, feeling foolish, looked down at the ground. He realized that the horn in his home that he'd paid a hundred gold for wasn't from a unicorn, but rather it was merely the horn of a dead sea animal. Both Luna and Murin looked over at him but his gaze remained averted. Xavier was still looking down at the horned sea creature. It was large and looked like a dolphin or a whale – two creatures that they *were* all aware of – with a long horn sticking out of its face. And Erlidel's assessment was correct: It was a dead narwhal. Its lifeless body laid there motionless in the sand, the tide having gone out hours earlier.

"I have, I don't know, a million questions," Xavier said, looking up at Erlidel. "What are these things? I know there are flying unicorns."

"Yes, pterippi," Erlidel replied.

"Right," Xavier said. "Are these things some sort of underwater unicorns that can swim? Can they talk? Do they have magical abilities?"

"Oh, I don't think so," Erlidel replied. "I think they're just regular animals with horns, like deer or moose. They only difference is that narwhals live underwater and only have one horn. But I think they have a lot more in common with with that fish right there than they do with you or any of us."

Erlidel pointed to another dead sea creature that had washed up on the shore: a small fish. They all stood around the dead narwhal for a minute, getting a good look at the unusual creature. Thall examined its horn and came to the conclusion that the horn hanging on the wall in his house had indeed, in all likelihood, come from a narwhal.

"Can we eat this thing?" Luna asked. "I'm really hungry."

"That's probably not a good idea," Murin answered. "We don't know how it died. It may have just washed up onto the beach and got stuck here. In that case, we probably could eat it. But it also may have died from disease, died out in the ocean, and then floated to the shore. On the farm, if an animal dies from disease, we don't eat it cause we could get sick, too. I think the same thing applies here."

"I agree," Thall said. "Murin's right. It probably would be safe to eat but since we don't know how it died, I think it's best to just leave it here."

Everyone agreed. They returned to the campfire and ate some of the food they'd brought with them, which consisted mostly of various types of jerky and fruit. As soon as they were done, everyone packed up their stuff and got ready to get back on the trail. Thall laid his map on the ground and they all gathered around it.

"We're here," Thall said, pointing at the map. "And we need to get to here."

"What's that other area that's circled?" Erlidel asked.

Thall explained to Erlidel about how he'd made a series of maps for Involore. He told the wizard that Involore seemed much more interested in one area over the other and that he was sure it was where Involore was going.

"Hmmm," Erlidel hummed with suspicion. "Let's hope you're right."

All packed up, they readied their horses and prepared to continue heading to the part of the forest where the unicorns were. Xavier walked over to the dead narwhal to take one last look. He found it to be fascinating.

"What a weird creature you are," Xavier said, leaning down toward the narwhal. "I have to admit: That is a nice horn. Not as nice as mine used to be, mind you. I wonder if other narwhals have horns as nice as yours or if yours is nicer than most of the others. In the unicorn community, my alicorn is considered to be among the absolute..."

"Xavier!" Luna yelled, walking over to the unicorn. "Stop talking to that dead... I forgot its name. What's that thing called, again?"

"That is a narwhal," Erlidel answered from atop his horse. "Well, it *was* a narwhal. Now it's a dead narwhal."

"Stop talking to that narwhal and bend down so I can get on top of you," Luna continued.

"Say please," Xavier said with a smirk.

"Ugh," Luna replied. "Please."

Xavier bent down and Luna hopped on top of him. They joined the others and off they rode, continuing up the path. It lead along the lake for a while before branching off in a different direction. Once again, they were surrounded by trees on both sides of the path. Not surprisingly, they didn't run into anyone else out there. They were far from any of the main paths that connected the towns on the sides of the forest, like Edgewood.

They continued down the path for several hours into the afternoon, riding single file with Thall in the lead. The ride was uneventful and they covered a lot of ground. Thall realized that they were approaching the unexplored part of the forest that was circled on the map. He kept it handy with part of the map poking out of the top of his bag. The explorer reached behind himself and grabbed it. As he rode,

Thall opened the map and looked at it. A concerned look grew across his face and he slowed his horse.

"This can't be," Thall said.

"What?" Vastrel asked.

"According to the map," Thall explained, "we're already in the unexplored part of the forest. And we have been for a little while now."

"Xav, does any of this look familiar?" Murin asked.

"Nope," Xavier replied. "Not at all. This definitely isn't where the unicorns live."

"How can you tell?" Thall asked.

"Well," Xavier replied, "for one, there are no paths in, around, or leading directly to Unicaria, like the one we're currently on. That alone is a dead giveaway."

"No, no, no!" Thall said and stopped his horse, the others stopping behind him. "This can't be right. I was certain... There's no way that... This has to be the... Involore said that..."

"Involore said?" Vastrel repeated, almost yelling. "You picked this spot over the other one because of something Involore said? The evil wizard who's trying to usher in a new error of unending evil? You listened to *him*?"

Murin and Luna looked at each other but didn't say anything. They did, however, silently mouth the phrase "Usher in a new error of unending evil?" at the same exact time while staring at each other with worried looks. Neither of them fully understood just how dire their situation truly was – but they were starting to.

"I... But he... I thought..." Thall tried to say, then got down off his horse and started over, speaking much slower. "I've doomed us all."

"If the unicorns aren't here, then they must be in the other circled area on the map," Vastrel said, getting down off his horse and walking over to his father. "Let's get moving!"

"You don't understand," Thall said, holding open the map for his son and the others to see. "We're *here*. The other circled part of the forest is *here*. The only way to get there is to go back the way we came and go all the way around *here*. By the time we get there, it'll be way too late. In all likelihood, the damage will already be done by then."

"If I had to guess – and I do because I don't actually know – I'd guess that Involore is going to make his move right around sunset," Erlidel said. "That's when magic will be at its strongest, the peak of this wonderful day."

"Let's assume that's true," Murin said. "Let's assume Involore is going to do what he's going to do when the sun starts going down. Can we make it there in time?"

"No way," Thall answered without hesitation. "There's no way we can cover that much ground by sundown."

Luna hopped down from Xavier's back. Murin and Erlidel came down off their horses, too, so everyone was on the ground. They all gathered around Thall, who was still holding the map. Xavier was the only exception. He wandered off the path, looking for some grass to munch on.

"I can't believe I was wrong," Thall said. "I thought for sure that this was the right place. That damned wizard tricked me. He must've suspected that I was onto him and intentionally deceived me. I'm so angry at myself. And I'm so sorry. So, *so* sorry."

"It's not your fault," Murin said, trying to make him feel better. "You did what you thought was the right..."

"That doesn't matter!" Thall yelled, flailing his arms wildly. "I wasn't right. I was wrong! I was a fool. And now we're all going to suffer unspeakably because of me."

"What do you mean by that?" Luna asked. "*We're* going to suffer?"

Thall did his best to collect himself. He rolled up the map, put it under his arm, and turned to face Luna and Murin. After swallowing hard and taking a deep breath, Thall explained just how serious the situation was.

"They aren't just horned horses that live hidden in the forest. They're not just pretty animals that can talk and use magic. Unicorns represent all that is good in the world. Actually, they more than represent it – they *are* it. Without them, only evil would exist. Unicorns are the source of all that is good. All that is pure. All that is right and just. To destroy them like Involore is planning to do means that there will be no more good in the world. No more justice. No more virtue. It'll all be gone the second the unicorns are destroyed. And it's all my fault."

Murin and Luna both wanted to tell Thall that it wasn't his fault, but neither of them did. The gravity of the situation hit them both like a ton of bricks and they were speechless. While Thall was talking to Murin and Luna, his son grabbed the map from under his arm. Vastrel unrolled it and was looking at it with Erlidel. They were talking among themselves, double checking to make sure Thall was right about how long it would take to get to the other circled part of the forest. Luna saw them out of the corner of her eye and became hopeful that maybe they'd figured out how to get there by sundown. Her hope was soon crushed.

"Yeah," Vastrel said, holding up the map for all to see, "father's right. There's no way we can get there before sundown. It's just not possible. We'd have to take *this* path back for several hours, then take *this* path for another several hours. We'd be lucky if we got there by midnight."

"Can you use magic?" Murin asked Erlidel. "It *is* the Day of Magic, after all. Can you use your magic to transport us there? I know wizards can disappear and magically reappear elsewhere."

"I've already thought of that," Erlidel replied. "First of all, I *could* cast a teleport spell on myself. I've done it many, many times. But it only works on me. Well, it only works on one person, I should say. And even then, it uses a lot of my magical energy. Like, *a lot*, a lot. It's a powerful spell. There's no way I could teleport all of us. One or maybe even two of us, since it's the Day of Magic. But then I'd be completely useless. It would use all my magical energy and I'd need at least a day to recover before I could cast anything more powerful than a basic sleep spell."

"That's no good," Thall said. "We'd need you to be able to use your magic against Involore. It looks like this is the end of the road for us. I'm so terribly sorry for dooming us all."

No one said anything for several minutes. They secured their horses along the narrow path, then wandered off in different directions. Luna and Murin ended up sitting down on a couple of stumps in the woods, not too far from where the horses were. Thall walked off by himself, his head down the entire time. Vastrel started walking in that direction but Erlidel advised him to give his father a few minutes to himself and the adventurer agreed. Then, Erlidel wandered off into the woods by himself.

29.

"I had no idea this was so serious," Murin said, looking over at Luna. "I mean, I knew it was serious. But not the-whole-world-is-going-to-turn-evil serious."

"I know," Luna replied. "Me either. I thought it was bad enough that Involore's planning to kill all the unicorns. But turning the whole world into one giant ball of evil is something different altogether."

"I'm not even sure if I fully understand what that means," Murin said. "But I have to imagine it won't be fun."

"Well, whatever it means, I guess we'll find out soon enough."

Luna held out her hand and Murin took it into his. They sat there on the tree stumps in silence, holding hands. Their minds wandered, thinking about how different things would be with no good in the world, only evil.

Meanwhile, Thall paced around the forest also lost in thought. He blamed himself for what Involore was about to do to the world he'd spent his life traveling and mapping. The explorer thought about the elves in West Emeralion and the good people in the mining town of Rhanaldia. He thought about the gnomes on Ellicia Island and the fisherman in the Port of Lucindale. And of course he thought of the good people of Briarville, the town he'd called home for several decades. Thall continued to pace around with his head down, thinking about how much suffering everyone he'd ever known was about to experience.

Vastrel, still holding onto his father's map, looked it over one more time. And once again, he agreed with Thall's original assessment. There was simply no way to cover the distance they needed to before sundown.

Erlidel was the only one who wasn't incredibly depressed, thinking about the horrible fate the world was about to experience. He was actually in a good mood, having fun. The old wizard found a patch of beautiful green and gold flowers. He sat down next to them and played a game he'd enjoyed since childhood.

"The world is going to turn evil and we're all going to die," Erlidel said, plucking a petal from the flower he was holding and letting it fall to the ground. Next to him were a pile of flower petals and a few petalless stems. "The world is *not* going to turn evil and we're *not* all going to die. The world is going to..."

The wizard sat there with a big, goofy smile on his face, plucking petal after petal. He found comfort in the game, juvenile as it was. It had been many years since the last time Erlidel played it, which made him enjoy it even more.

The first time he played the petal-plucking game, he was just a young wizard around Murin and Luna's age. A friend told him about it one afternoon when they were talking about a young woman Erlidel was interested in. At first, he thought it was stupid. But Erlidel went along with his friend's suggestion, picked up a flower, and plucked it one petal at a time. As young Erlidel plucked the final petal, he uttered the words, "She loves me." Sure enough, she did.

Ever since that first time playing the petal-plucking game, whenever Erlidel played it, the last petal he plucked had always been right. Though Erlidel was well aware that the world was full of strange, supernatural forces, he also valued logic and rationality. Even though he'd played the game several times over the years and each time it was right, he chocked it up to nothing more than chance. Still, he enjoyed playing the game and it helped to take his mind off the terrible fate the world was about to behold.

"The world is going to turn evil and we're all going to die," Erlidel said, picking up a new flower and plucking a petal, the big, stupid grin still on his face. "The world is *not* going to..."

After a few minutes, everyone found their way back to the horses. Erlidel brought a couple of flowers with him and was still playing his game, plucking away. The only one who wasn't there was Xavier.

"Hey, Xav!" Murin yelled, cupping his hands around his mouth. "Come back to the horses. Xavier!"

A few seconds went by and there was no sign of the unicorn. Murin and several others started yelling his name, facing in all directions.

"Xavier!!!"

"Why are you yelling?" the unicorn asked calmly, silently emerging out from the woods. "I'm right here."

Everyone shook their heads – everyone except Erlidel. He was still talking quietly to himself, plucking away at his flowers. Xavier silently came out of the woods and stood facing the rest of the group.

"Where'd you go?" Murin asked. "I was starting to get worried about you."

"I was looking for some grass to eat. Sadly, I didn't find any. What I *did* find was a knot in a tree that looks just like an eyeball. *Just* like an eyeball. It's eerie. It's almost like it follows me around wherever I go, like it's looking at me."

"That's great," Vastrel said, rolling his eyes. "Let's start heading back to Edgewood."

"You don't understand," Xavier stated. "I've seen that eyeball before."

"What do you mean?" Murin asked. "When?"

"I passed it after being kicked out by the elders. I know exactly where we are now. I can get us to Unicaria. We don't have to go back the way we came."

"You're sure?" Murin asked, a cautious smile starting to appear on his face.

"Of course I'm sure," Xavier replied, stomping one of his front hooves. "If I wasn't sure, I would've said that I wasn't sure. Did I say I wasn't sure?"

Murin exhaled and replied, "No."

"There's no way," Thall said, taking the map from Vastrel and opening it. "The only way to get there is to take this path back the way we came and then go up the path that branches off from it. If we go through the woods like you're suggesting, we'll be forced to stop *here*. And if we try to go *this* way, we'll be stopped *here*. There are massive rock cliffs blocking our path if we go one way and an impassible river if we try to go the other."

For the first time, Xavier looked at the map. He'd never learned how to read a map but was smart enough to somewhat understand what he was looking at.

"Your map's wrong," Xavier said.

"Impossible!" Thall yelled, his face getting a bit red.

"Impossible, indeed," Vastrel agreed. "My father's the best map maker in the world. And that's not just *my* opinion. His map-making skills are known by everyone. That's why Involore went to *him* instead of one of the many other less-skilled map makers out there."

"The map's wrong," Xavier said once again.

"What specifically is wrong with it, Xav?" Murin asked.

"Here," Xavier replied, forgetting for a second that his alicorn was gone and trying to use it to point at the map. He sighed, then used his nose to point to where the rock ledges and river were. "There are no rocks or rivers here."

"There most certainly are!" Thall argued, throwing up his arms. "I saw them with my own two eyes. Touched them with my own two hands!"

"I'm sure you did," Xavier replied. "Your map's still wrong."

"How dare you..." Thall screamed but Murin cut him off.

"Xavier," Murin said to the unicorn while holding up a finger to Thall. The explorer's face was now beet red, but he stopped talking. "What do you mean you're sure he saw the rocks and water but the map's wrong? Are you saying that if we went there right now, we wouldn't see those things?"

"Oh, I'm sure we'd *see* them," Xavier replied. "But they're not actually there. I mean, they are, but they're not. Before they took my alicorn, I'd never seen them before. But after being kicked out, as soon as I left Unicaria, when I turned around, they were there."

"What are you saying?" Thall asked. "That they're some sort of illusion?"

"Not exactly," Xavier replied. "They're really there. But it's all created by magic. Involore has somehow figured out how to get through it. So by the time we get there, maybe it'll all be gone and we can get through, too."

"Do you think we can get there before sundown?" Luna asked.

"Maybe if we left right now and moved quickly," Xavier replied, then nodded his head toward the horses. "These smelly idiots won't make it, though. The forest gets thick in some parts. You'll have to leave them here."

"Are you sure you're not just saying that because you want to get away from the way they smell?" Murin asked.

"No, they really won't make it. But getting away from their stench *will* be nice."

"I can't just leave them out in the middle of the forest," Murin said.

"Ohhh!" Luna exclaimed, practically jumping off the ground. "I know a spell!"

"What kind of spell?" Murin asked. "How is a healing spell going to help?"

"I've told you a thousand times, I can cast more than..." Luna yelled, then paused, took a deep breath, and lowered her voice. "I can cast a return spell. Well, four of them. They're used for situations exactly like this. They make your horse, mule, or other animal return home, going back the way it came."

"We're really far from home. You think it'll actually work?"

"Since it's the Day of Magic, I think there's a really good chance that it will," Luna replied. "Besides, it's either that or we leave them here defenseless in the middle of the forest."

"Okay. Do it," Murin said, then went one by one petting his horses. "Have a safe trip home."

"Well, what are we waiting for?" Thall asked, taking his gear down from his horse. "Let's get going!"

Everyone grabbed their gear. After making sure they had everything, Luna cast the return spell. One at a time, the horses turned and started galloping back the way they had all come from.

Now on foot, they started walking into the woods with Xavier in the lead. The last to join them was Erlidel. He was down to his last flower and plucked the final petal from it as he followed them into the woods.

"...going to die," Erlidel said, then pulled the final petal and let it fall to the ground. "The world is..."

30.

They all marched into the forest on foot with Xavier leading the way. A few minutes into the walk, he pointed out the eyeball-like knot in the tree he'd told them about.

"Oh wow," Murin said. "It really does look like an eye."

"Just wait," Xavier replied. "Watch. It looks like it's following you."

Sure enough, Xavier was right. It *did* look like it was watching them. The knot was about fifteen feet up and appeared to follow the group.

"That's freaky," Luna said.

"Yeah, it is," Murin agreed.

Before long, the knot was out of view. They continued through the forest for the next couple of hours. For the most part, they traveled in silence. None of them could stop thinking about what was going to happen to their world if they didn't stop Involore. Their minds would all start thinking about something else soon, though, when a more immediate threat reared its head.

"Look!" Vastrel said, pointing to their left.

Off in the distance through the woods they could see several humanoid figures on the top of a small hill. Vastrel, Thall, Xavier, and Erlidel all instantly recognized what they were: hobgoblins.

"I don't think they've seen us, yet," Thall whispered. "We need to be as quiet as possible. If there are enough of them, they'll attack us. Especially if they consider this part of the forest their home. If they think we're trespassers, they'll definitely attack."

"I hate hobgoblins," Vastrel whispered. "I hate those things with all my heart."

"I'll cast a silence spell," Erlidel whispered. "Everybody stay put for a minute. And stay low."

Everyone crouched down and Erlidel began casting a silence spell. It was one of the first spells he learned as a young wizard and could recite it quickly and with ease. They kept their eyes on the hobgoblins off in the distance while the spell was being cast. The monsters were far enough away that they couldn't really hear them, but they could see them well enough. It soon became clear that it was a large group of hobgoblins. Erlidel came to the end of the spell but, right as he was reciting the final words, Xavier unleashed a loud sneeze.

"Achoooooooooooo!"

"Xavier!" Murin whispered.

"Sorry," the unicorn replied. "I fought it off as long as I could. I've been needing to sneeze ever since we crouched down. Man, I feel a million times better now, though, so it's all good."

It wasn't all good. Xavier's sneeze was so loud that it sent all the birds in nearby trees flying away. It was also loud enough to catch the attention of the hobgoblins off in the distance. All at once, they turned to face the group.

"Do you think they see us?" Xavier asked.

The hobgoblins all looked to their leader. It raised a hand high overhead, then threw it down violently, pointing toward the crouching group. The hobgoblins, all at once, reached down to grab their weapons and started charging toward them.

"Yup," Thall replied. "They see us alright."

"Ready your weapons," Vastrel yelled, standing up and grabbing his warhammer. "Prepare for battle!"

Everyone stood up quickly. Thall took out his short sword and Erlidel began casting a spell. Murin, too, took out his short sword. His hands were shaking like crazy and he could barely get it out of its scabbard. He held it out in front of himself, his heart pounding. Luna and Xavier, both unarmed, stood behind the others. Their hearts were also beating hard and fast.

It didn't take the first group of hobgoblins very long to close the gap between them and the adventurers. The hobgoblins were tall and lean with green skin that had an orange tinge to it. All of them were wearing armor and carrying weapons. There were twelve hobgoblins in all: eleven regular hobgoblins and one leader who's weapon and armor were clearly of a higher grade than the others. Like regular goblins, they had big, pointed ears, sunken eyes, and bald heads. However, they were much taller, much smarter, and much more dangerous.

Vastrel, Thall, and Erlidel knew that hobgoblins weren't particularly dangerous by themselves but since they often attacked in groups, were not to be taken lightly. There were twice as many hobgoblins as there were of them. The seasoned members of the group knew that they should be able to defeat the hobgoblins, but it wouldn't be easy. Murin, Luna, and Xavier didn't know what to expect and that terrified all three of them.

"Arrrggghhh!" the first hobgoblin to close in on the group yelled as it raised its rusty short sword.

"Arrrggghhh!" each hobgoblin behind him yelled as they approached the group.

The hobgoblins didn't waste any time before attacking. As soon as they reached the group, they started swinging and stabbing away. Vastrel and Thall took several steps forward as the hobgoblins were approaching. They raised their weapons high overhead and the second the first hobgoblins were in range, they attacked.

"Die!" Vastrel yelled as he swung his warhammer down on the first hobgoblin to reach him.

Vastrel got his wish. His warhammer came crashing down on the hobgoblin's head, caving in its skull, sending it straight to the ground. Right behind the first hobgoblin was another and it swung its rusty short sword at Vastrel before he had a chance to defend himself. The sword connected with Vastrel's shoulder. Fortunately, his chain mail armor absorbed most of the blow and it didn't break the skin.

His father, standing next to him, also engaged the enemy. Thall swung his short sword at the first hobgoblin to approach him. His blade connected right above the elbow, slicing its weapon-holding arm right off. The hobgoblin screamed out in pain, holding its arm with the other hand. The hobgoblin's heart was beating fast and hard after running through the woods, which caused blood to squirt out of its arm hard and fast.

Next to him was another hobgoblin and it attacked Thall with its dagger. The monster stabbed at Thall, hitting him in the shoulder. The sharp point pierced the skin, going in about an inch. Thall didn't even flinch. The veteran explorer had been in countless battles and his experience showed. The hobgoblin quickly pulled its dagger back and blood began to trickle out of the wound.

Murin stood several feet behind Thall and Vastrel, frozen in fear. He had his short sword raised, barely able to hold it, his hands were shaking so badly. Next to him was Erlidel, still casting an attack spell. Luna and Xavier stayed several feet behind them where it was safe – for the moment.

The next group of hobgoblins were fast approaching. Vastrel raised his warhammer over his head once again and sent it down with fury at the one who'd slashed his shoulder. Two for two, he killed the monster with one blow.

Crunch!

Vastrel's warhammer smashed the hobgoblin right in the face and he heard the familiar sound of bone being crushed. The blow caved in the monster's face and it immediately fell to the ground right next to the other one Vastrel had killed. As he was pulling his warhammer up, getting ready to swing again, another one stabbed Vastrel with a rusty dagger. It hit him in the hand, going almost all the way through. Like his father, Vastrel took the hit like a champ. Though it hurt quite badly, the seasoned adventurer didn't make a sound.

Thall was surrounded by three hobgoblins. The one who's arm he'd lopped off went running back the way it had come from, screaming the whole time. The first one attacked, swinging its rusty short sword at the half dwarf, half gnome. Thall just barely managed to dodge out of the way. He wasn't so lucky with the next attack. As Thall jumped out of the way of the first attack, it gave one of the other hobgoblins an opening. Being the smart creatures that they were, it saw the opening and took a shot. The hobgoblin lunged at Thall with its dagger, hitting him in the belly. He was only wearing a thin layer of leather armor and the dagger went right through it. This time, Thall did make a sound.

"Ughhh," he moaned as the hobgoblin pulled the dagger out of the wound.

Thall looked the hobgoblin right in the eyes and swung his short sword with all his might. The hobgoblin was much taller than Thall and he had to swing his sword up at the monster. The razor-sharp blade slashed the hobgoblin's neck and blood immediately started pouring out of it. The monster dropped its dagger and held its neck with both hands, but it didn't make much of a difference. Within seconds the hobgoblin fell to the ground. The third hobgoblin surrounding Thall had a whip and took a crack at him. It hit Thall on the top of one of his hands, slicing it open.

Murin still stood there motionless, watching the action. His eyes were focused on Thall and Vastrel, and he didn't notice that a hobgoblin had managed to get around them. It was approaching Xavier and Luna. Xavier's flight-or-flight response kicked right in and he silently darted off into the woods. Luna stood there terrified as the hobgoblin approached her with its short sword raised and a menacing smile on its face.

"Ahhhhhh!" Luna screamed.

Vastrel and Thall didn't even turn their heads. They had their hands full with the hobgoblins attacking them. Likewise, Erlidel was too busy reciting the end of his attack spell to look. Murin *did* look. Luna's voice snapped him out of his frozen state and he turned to see why she was screaming. When he saw the hobgoblin getting ready to attack his best friend, Murin finally snapped into action.

"Luna!" Murin yelled.

He moved quickly over to where she was, raising his short sword high overhead. Just as the hobgoblin was about to swing *its* short sword at Luna, Murin swung *his* at the hobgoblin. The sword slashed down at the hobgoblin's head, slicing through the well-worn leather helmet it was wearing. The blow also slashed through the hobgoblin's skin and blood started tricking down its forehead and onto its face.

The monster stumbled around, slightly dazed from the hit and slightly blinded from the blood. As it did, the hobgoblin did its best to wipe the blood out of its eyes.

"Again, Murin!" Luna shouted. "Hit it again while it can't see!"

Murin followed his friend's advice and swung his short sword once again. This time, he wound up and swung the sword with all his might at the hobgoblin's neck. The blade connected and severed the monster's head – almost. Murin's sword went about three-quarters-of-the-way through. The hobgoblin fell to the ground and landed with the back of its head touching the middle of its back, right between its shoulder blades. Blood squirted out of its neck for a few seconds, then stopped.

Murin and Luna's eyes met. Luna flashed a quick smile and he did the same. Then, Murin turned around, saw a hobgoblin approaching Erlidel, and ran over to defend the wizard.

Vastrel and Thall were still going at it with several hobgoblins. Every time they killed one, another one would approach them. Vastrel swung his warhammer at one directly in front of him but missed. The heavy weapon crashed down, leaving a dent in the ground. The hobgoblin countered, slashing Vastrel's leg with its rusty short sword.

Thall was now surrounded by four hobgoblins. They towered over him, taking turns attacking. The first one lunged at him with a dagger, piercing his upper leg. The hobgoblin with the whip took another crack at Thall, but this time it missed. Another one slashed at Thall with its short sword, slicing him in the chest, right through his armor. Thall had been hit several times and was really starting to feel it. He swung his sword wildly at the hobgoblin that had just stabbed him with its dagger. Thall's sword connected, but just barely. It slashed the hobgoblin across its chest but didn't do any serious damage.

The fourth hobgoblin surrounding Thall had a rusty battle axe. Just as Thall was attacking one of the other hobgoblins, it swung the axe at him. The edge of the sharp weapon connected with Thall's neck and blood started pouring out of it, turning the explorer's front all red.

"No!" Vastrel yelled, seeing it happen out of the corner of his eye. "Father!"

Thall clutched at his neck and fell to his knees. The surrounding hobgoblins stood over him and repeatedly attacked the defenseless explorer. Within seconds, Thall collapsed to the ground.

"Noooooooooo!" Vastrel screamed.

Neglecting the hobgoblins that he'd been battling with, Vastrel stepped over to the ones that had just killed his father. With fire in his eyes, he started violently swinging his warhammer over and over again, going berserk on them. The first swing hit one of the hobgoblins in the head and killed it instantly, sending it straight to the ground. Its corpse landed right on top of Thall's. Vastrel, full of rage, swung again and hit another hobgoblin in the chest. It didn't kill it, but it did break several of its ribs.

Meanwhile, Murin was engaged with the hobgoblin that was going to attack Erlidel. His spell was nearly complete and Murin held off the hobgoblin long enough for the wizard to finish casting it. Murin swung his short sword at the monster and nearly slashed it across the face, but it jumped back just in time. It countered, lunging at Murin with a dagger. He was able to move out of the way and raised his sword to attack again. But before

Murin would get the chance to take another swing, Erlidel finished casting his spell.

The booming sound of thunder filled the air. Even though the rest of the sky was mostly clear, a dark cloud suddenly appeared over the battlefront. Several bolts of lightening came zapping down from the sky, each one hitting a different hobgoblin. They were all instantly killed – all but one. The hobgoblin leader somehow managed to survive the strike, but just barely. While all of his peers fell to the ground, some with smoke coming off their smoldering corpses, the leader fell to his knees and dropped his sword.

Vastrel casually walked over to the hobgoblin leader, swinging his warhammer along the way, almost playfully. The hobgoblin was in somewhat of a daze from being hit by lightening, but was lucid enough to understand what was about to happen. It raised its hands above its head in a futile attempt to defend itself as Vastrel approached. The hardened adventurer raised his warhammer high above his head and uttered a few words before bringing it down with all his might.

"This is for you, father."

Smash!!!

The blow caved in the hobgoblin's skull and it fell to the ground. Vastrel walked over to his father, dropped his warhammer, then picked up the corpse of the hobgoblin that had fallen on top of him. Holding the corpse in front of him, Vastrel spit right in its face, then wantonly tossed it out of the way.

Vastrel stood above his dead father for several seconds, looking down at him. He held his emotions in for as long as he could, then fell to his knees and began crying. His tears flowed freely, dripping off his face onto his father's body. The others looked on in silence, knowing there was nothing they could say or do to make Vastrel feel better. After a couple of minutes, the adventurer pulled himself together, stopped crying, and gave his father one last hug. Using two fingers, he shut Thall's eyelids, then kissed him on the forehead.

"Goodbye, father," Vastrel said. "Goodbye."

31.

Everyone looked around at the aftermath of what had just happened. The ground was littered with twelve hobgoblin corpses in addition to Thall's. For a couple of minutes, no one said anything. They all needed to catch their breath and calm down after the heated battle. Taking turns, one by one, each of them knelt down next to Thall and quietly said goodbye to the famous explorer. Vastrel stood over his father's body as they did, happy that they each took the time to do so.

"Are all the herbgerblins dead?" Xavier asked, emerging from the woods.

"Hobgoblins," Murin corrected. "And yes, they're all dead. Unfortunately, so is Thall."

Xavier was unaccustomed to being around death. No one that he'd ever been close to had died before. The only one in Xavier's family that he was aware had died was his grandfather. But he'd passed away before Xavier was born. The unicorn cautiously approached Thall's corpse, being careful not to step on any of the dead hobgoblins.

"He's really gone?" Xavier asked. "Like, for good?"

"Yes," Vastrel replied. "Father's with his ancestors now – *our* ancestors. He died triumphantly in the heat of battle... battling with these good-for-nothing hob-" Vastrel said, kicking one of the dead monsters right in the face, "-goblins."

Xavier stood over Thall's corpse. He leaned down and said a few final words to him.

"You were a good dude," the unicorn said. "Sorry about kicking a hole in your door."

"That was *my* door!" Murin corrected.

"I kicked a hole in *his* door, too," Xavier replied.

"Of course you did," Murin said, shaking his head, then turned to Vastrel. "I'm sorry about your father. He *was* a good dude. Normally, I'd never suggest leaving him here but, given the circumstances..."

"I know," Vastrel replied before Murin finished his sentence. "We need to keep moving. And we don't have time to bury my father. But let's at least move him so he's not surrounded by a bunch of worthless hobgoblins. Help me carry him over there."

"Sure," Murin agreed.

They picked the deceased explorer's body up and carried it off into the woods away from the dead hobgoblins. Vastrel wanted to come back for it after their quest was over, so he placed it next to a large oak tree that would be easy to find. Vastrel, one last time, knelt down next to his father and gave him a kiss on the forehead.

"I'll come back for you, father. Mark my words."

Everyone gathered up their belongings and got ready to continue onward. Vastrel went through Thall's pack and took the map and some other supplies. He also took the food that Thall was carrying and divvied it up among the group. Luna offered to heal Vastrel's wounds and he agreed. While she did, Erlidel went around to all the corpses, searching them for any valuables they might've been carrying. Aside from a few silver and copper pieces, he found nothing worth taking.

After having a quick look at the map to regain their bearings, the group continued heading toward the unicorns' part of the forest. Once again, Xavier took the lead, followed by Vastrel and Erlidel behind him. Murin and Luna brought up the rear, walking side by side. For the first few minutes, everyone walked in silence. Then, Murin and Luna started talking to each other and so did Erlidel and Vastrel.

"How do you feel right now?" Luna asked Murin.

"I feel a lot of things," he replied. "Sad, mostly."

"I don't mean about Thall. We're all sad about that. I mean about actually being in a real battle. How do you feel about slaying that hobgoblin?"

"I don't know. I haven't really thought about it, yet. It hasn't sunken in."

"Well, I think you did great. You were incredibly brave. You saved my life, Murin. Thank you. Thank you for that."

"You're very welcome," Murin replied.

Though he tried not to show it, Murin was quite proud of himself. He just didn't want to seem like he was happy after Thall's tragic death. But Luna's words meant a lot to him. Even though he did freeze up at first, Murin snapped into action when it mattered most. For the first time in his life, Murin felt that maybe – just maybe – he *would* actually make a good adventurer.

Luna and Murin continued to talk as they walked. Meanwhile, Erlidel and Vastrel were having a conversation of their own.

"He was very proud of you, you know," Erlidel said.

Vastrel looked over at Erlidel, unsure what the wizard was talking about.

"Your father, I mean," Erlidel continued. "He talked about you all the time."

Vastrel didn't reply. He just looked over at the wizard again and flashed the most convincing smile he could muster.

"I remember when you left to go on your very first adventure," Erlidel went on. "I'd never seen your dad so proud about anything as long as I'd known him. And we go way back."

"Nonsense," Vastrel replied. "I appreciate what you're trying to do, old man. I do. But lying to me about my father isn't going to make me feel any better. He was furious that I wanted to become an adventurer. He wanted me to stay in Briarville, to live my life as a humble map maker."

"It's you who's spurting nonsense," Erlidel said. "Thall was honored that you wanted to follow in his footsteps and explore the world. But he knew firsthand how hard the life of an adventurer could be. He knew the sacrifices you'd have to make. That's why he tried to convince you to be a map maker. Because to be an adventurer, you have to want it. You have to *really* want it. And you did. In spite of his efforts to convince you otherwise, you stayed true to your desire, your thirst for adventure."

"So, you're telling me that my father actually *wanted* me to be an adventurer?"

"The only thing your father wanted you to be, Vastrel, was happy. And the fact that exploring and adventuring brought you happiness, well, that made *him* happy. You have the same love of exploration that he did. He couldn't have been more proud. I'm sure he still would've been proud of you if you had decided to just make maps. It's a noble profession. But I can't imagine him being any happier than he was with the way you turned out."

Vastrel put his hand on the wizard's shoulder for a moment as they walked. He looked over at him and flashed a genuine smile.

"Thank you," Vastrel said. "Thank you for your kind words on this most tragic of days."

Erlidel nodded. They continued following Xavier through the forest, moving as quickly as possible. The unexpected battle with the hobgoblins ate up some much-needed travel time and they were doing their best to make up for it.

After traveling all afternoon and into the evening, they were nearing the circled part of the map. The sun was approaching the horizon quickly. Off in the distance to their left, they could see massive cliffs of sheer rock just as Thall's map predicted. As they continued onward, they heard running water coming from up ahead. Before long, the group came to a massive river.

"Here we are," Xavier said. "Unicaria is just on the other side of the river."

They all stopped and looked around. The river was very wide and moving quickly. There was no sign of a bridge or any other way to get across.

"Looks like my father was right all along," Vastrel said. "Looks like we can't get there by going this way. I guess this is the end of the road."

Erlidel approached the river. He got down on his hands and knees, crawling over to it. The wizard first stuck a single finger in the water, then his whole hand. Slowly, he crawled back a few feet and sat up straight, taking off his pack. He dug out a small glass jar of silver-colored powder, opened it and poured a little bit into his palm. After reciting a couple of phrases, Erlidel blew the powder out of his hand. The gentle breeze guided it straight into the water. As the powder hit the water, its color changed from silver to a glittery red.

"Looks like the unicorn's right," Erlidel said. "This is the work of magic – powerful elemental magic."

"Can you use *your* magic to get through it?" Vastrel asked.

"I'm good," Erlidel replied. "But I'm not *that* good. There's no way."

"Then this really is the end of the road," Vastrel said, pointing at the horizon. "The sun is about to go down. Involore's probably already gotten through this strange magical barrier and is killing all the unicorns as we speak."

No one spoke for several minutes. Everyone took off their packs and had a seat near the river's edge. After everything they'd been through, after they'd come so far, all of them felt incredibly defeated. The thought that Involore was so close and about to do something so evil, yet they were unable to reach him, weighed heavily on all their minds.

32.

They all sat near the river looking over at the horizon. The sun was no longer nearing the horizon – it was now halfway over it. Xavier drank compulsively from the river, doing whatever he could to take his mind off what was likely happening to his fellow unicorns. Just the thought of it almost brought him to tears. Murin and Luna felt bad for Xavier – Murin, especially. He could tell just by looking at Xavier that he was having a hard time. The unicorn would glance up at the horizon, then slurp down several mouthfuls of water. Glance at the horizon, then slurp. Horizon. Slurp. Horizon. Slurp. Over and over again.

"It's going to be dark soon," Vastrel said and stood up, finally breaking the silence. "We should set up camp and then start heading back to Edgewood first thing in the morning."

Everyone agreed, but no one spoke. They all just nodded their heads and got up. The sun was now almost entirely over the horizon. They all started unpacking their stuff to get ready for the night. Xavier continued to drink from the river, looking up every so often.

"Um... Hey," he said, glancing up. "Guys?"

"What is it, Xav?" Murin asked.

"You know those massive walls of rock over there?"

"Yeah," Vastrel answered. "What about them?"

"They're not there anymore," Xavier replied. "Look."

Sure enough, the rock cliff was gone. Where it had been, there was nothing but forest. They all stood there trying to figure out what it meant. Erlidel was starting to piece together in his mind what was happening.

"Hey, unicorn," Erlidel said.

"What, old crazy wizard man?" Xavier replied.

"Rocks and a river block the entrance to the unicorns' part of the forest on this side. Does something else block it on the other?"

"Uh huh. What, I don't know."

"I bet *I* do," Erlidel replied. "Involore's been training his four apprentices to be elemental wizards, one for each element: fire, wind, water, and earth. I think the unicorns use elemental magic to protect their home. This side is protected by water. Over there is – or I should say, *was* – protected by earth. I bet the other two sides are protected by something fire and wind related."

"Yeah," Xavier said. "Come to think of it, that sounds right. I remember hearing something about the Council of Elders using elemental magic for this or that."

Vastrel took out his father's map. He laid it down on the ground and everyone gathered around it. Sure enough, there was a small-but-active volcano on the other side of the circled area. And there was something scribbled on the map where the forth side of the circled area was.

"What does it say?" Erlidel asked. "I can't read your father's handwriting. I never could. Great map maker. Terrible handwriting."

"It says," Vastrel replied, looking closely at the map, "mini hurricanes and violent, impassible winds – I think."

"Ha!" Erlidel yelled. "So, I was right! Which means..."

Before the wizard could finish his thought, right before everyone's eyes, the loud and fast moving river disappeared. Suddenly, where the river had been, there was nothing but forest. The sound of running water was replaced mostly by silence – but only for a minute.

"Aaaaaahhhhhhhhh!"

Everyone stopped what they were doing and picked their heads up. Coming from the forest up ahead, they heard a woman screaming.

"Did you hear that?" Murin asked.

"Yeah," Luna replied. "What was that? It sounded like someone screaming."

A few seconds later, they heard more yelling coming from the forest.

"What are you doing? No! No!!! Stop!"

Everyone gathered up their gear as quickly as possible and started running toward the screams. They ran through the dense forest where the river had been just a minute earlier. The forest was thick and they couldn't see very far up ahead. Vastrel was in the lead, with Murin and Erlidel right behind him. Luna and Xavier followed closely behind them.

"Please! Why are you doing this to me!"

The screams got louder and louder as they worked their way through the dense forest. After a few minutes of weaving through the woods, they came to an opening. There was a large, mostly-open field filled with tall, wild grass. There were some trees scattered around, but not many. Xavier instantly recognized where he was: home. The unicorn had spent countless hours in that field, eating and playing in the grass. Xavier stopped as soon as he got to the field and inhaled deeply. Then, he had himself a quick snack.

They all stopped when they got to the field, but only for a second. On the other side, a few hundred feet away, they saw Involore and his four apprentices. They also saw what looked like a dead horse lying on the ground near them.

Vastrel, after stopping for just a second, started running toward them with his warhammer in hand. Murin, Erlidel, and Luna followed closely behind him. Xavier had a few more bites of wild grass and then followed everyone else but, unlike them, he didn't run. Xavier casually strolled his way over, stopping several times for another mouthful of grass here and there.

As they got closer to Involore and could make out what he was doing, they were shocked by what they saw. Involore and three of his apprentices were standing next to a large oak tree that appeared to have fallen over. It didn't fall over on it's own, though. Involore used his magic to chop the tree down so it was lying on its side and could be used as a makeshift table. And lying on the horizontal tree was Anora. Her hands and feet were already tied with rope and the other apprentices were tying her body to the tree. Everyone realized that it was Anora who had been screaming, but she wouldn't be for much longer. After the apprentices finished tying her to the fallen tree, Drixius took a piece of cloth and used it as a gag, stuffing it into Anora's mouth.

Lying on the ground not too far away, they saw another familiar face. It was Timules, the centaur that Involore had captured. The poor half man, half horse was lying there moaning, unable to get up. All four of his hooves had been removed. To get through the four elemental barriers surrounding the unicorns' part of the forest, each apprentice had to cast an elemental spell. And for their spells to work, they each required a freshly-severed centaur's hoof.

The apprentices finished securing Anora to the tree despite her best efforts to get away, just as Vastrel and the others approached them.

"It's over, Involore," Vastrel yelled, still catching his breath. "This ends now."

"Don't worry," the evil wizard replied. "It's *almost* over. I just have one more thing to do."

Involore pulled out a dagger that was hidden under his cloak, but it wasn't just any ordinary dagger. The hilt was encrusted with precious gems and the blade was made with the finest metals the world had to offer. It was obvious to everyone what he was about to do. The wizard was planning on sacrificing his water apprentice, Anora. She served *two* purposes in his plan. First, she used her elemental magic along with the other apprentices to gain access to the unicorns. And now, since she was pure of heart, Involore was going to sacrifice her. He'd figured out that sacrificing someone pure of heart on the unicorns' land would destroy all of them instantly.

From studying ancient texts, Involore gradually pieced together a way to get to the unicorns and destroy them all at once. The mystical creatures represented everything that was good in the world, everything that was pure of body, mind, and soul. To sacrifice someone who was pure in the unicorns' land, Involore realized, would instantly suck the life force out of all them. Purity among unicorns was universal, but rare in humanoids. To find and sacrifice such a person within the boundaries of Unicaria would taint the pristine land and put an end to all the unicorns. And that would allow Involore to collect their alicorns so he could harness the awesome magical power they were thought to contain.

Vastrel raised his warhammer and, following his lead, Murin raised his short sword. Anora glanced over at the group with a look of absolute terror. Her eyes met Luna's and they became glassy, tears forming in the corners. Involore flashed a wicked smile, then pointed at the group with the dagger in his hand.

"Attack!" he commanded his apprentices. "Kill them all."

"Yes master," Drixius and Evia replied.

Galan didn't say anything. He did, however, do what his master told him to. The three apprentices stood in front of the fallen tree and all began casting spells. Vastrel raised his warhammer high overhead and started running straight toward Involore. He planned on running right past the apprentices and attacking Involore directly but right before he got to them, he slammed face first into an invisible wall. Drixius cast a quick barrier spell and finished it just in time for Vastrel to run right into it. Both Vastrel's body and head smacked into the wall, nearly knocking him out. The adventurer fell backward on his butt, dropping his warhammer.

Erlidel got to work right away and started casting a spell. Murin, after seeing what had just happened to Vastrel, cautiously approached Drixius. The earth apprentice had already started casting another spell. Murin raised his short sword and swung at the apprentice, but not as hard as he could've, which was smart. The sword slammed into the same invisible wall that Vastrel had run into. Had Murin swung the sword as hard as he could've, it would've really hurt him when it hit the wall. But it still didn't feel good and nearly caused Murin to drop his sword.

Off in the distance, coming out of the thick forest but staying along the edge of the clearing, a number of unicorns started to emerge. Involore saw them out of the corner of his eye and the wicked smile on his face grew even larger. The unicorns gathered to see what was happening and watched from a safe distance. Most of them had no idea what was going on, but some of the elders knew all too well what the evil wizard was trying to do. They also knew that, since unicorns aren't allowed to hurt anyone, all they could do was watch from a distance and hope for the best.

Erlidel finished casting his spell. He'd originally started casting an offensive spell, but abandoned it to cast something that would remove the wall Drixius had put up. It worked. Vastrel grabbed his warhammer and stood up but was still a little dazed. He took a wild swing at Galan, but the fire apprentice was easily able to move out of the way. Galan was in the middle of casting a fireball spell and took aim at Vastrel. He pointed his finger at the adventurer, uttered the final words of the spell, and a giant fireball came flying out of his finger. It went soaring through the air – just not in the direction that Galan wanted it to. The large ball of fire shot out of his finger at a ninety-degree angle, going sideways. It flew across the open field and slammed into a tree at the edge of the forest. The tree burst into flames, the bark catching on fire.

"Damn it!" Galan yelled.

Immediately after Galan cast his fireball spell, Evia finished casting her spell. She pointed at Vastrel as she spoke its final words. Evia's aim turned out to be much better than Galan's. Out of her finger a massive gust of wind formed, spinning around furiously, creating a mini tornado. As soon as it was fully formed, the tornado went straight for Vastrel. He turned and ran as fast as he could, but the tornado easily caught up to him. It swept Vastrel off his feet, sending him flying through the air in one direction, his warhammer flying off in another. Vastrel's body slammed down to the ground over a hundred feet from where it was picked up, instantly knocking him out. Evia smiled, mimicking the evil grin she'd seen on her master's face countless times before.

Murin lunged at Drixius with his short sword. The earth apprentice was focused on the spell he was almost done casting and didn't have time to defend himself. Murin's sword pierced right through the apprentice's cloak, deep into his abdomen. It instantly put an end to Drixius' spell. A minute later, it put an end to the apprentice's life. Murin pulled his sword out of Drixius just as violently as he'd stabbed it into him and blood started pouring out of the wound. The earth apprentice fell to his knees, pressing the palms of both hands against the wound to try to slow the bleeding. In spite of his best efforts, blood flowed freely out of the wound. Before long, Drixius took his last breath and collapsed to the ground.

Xavier had managed to work his way over to where everyone else was. He and Luna stayed back a little ways, far behind Murin and Erlidel. Both Luna and Xavier were terrified, watching everything that was happening. They both looked over at Involore at the same time and their terror turned into extreme panic.

Involore was standing next to Anora who was tied to the fallen tree. In one hand, he was holding the jeweled dagger. In the other, Involore was holding a long piece of parchment, reading from it. Anora's eyes were wide, tears running down the sides of her face. She tried to free herself, wiggling around as much as possible, but it was of no use. Involore read the final words from the parchment, then dropped it.

He immediately started reciting another spell in an ancient tongue that none of them, not even Erlidel, recognized. As he did, Involore took a step closer to Anora so he was standing over her. With both hands, he raised the dagger high overhead.

33.

Dozens and dozens of unicorns had gathered around the edges of the open, grassy area. Several of them looked away, not wanting to see what was about to happen. Xavier's eyes were focused on the blade in Involore's hand. His heart was beating faster than it ever had before and a million thoughts ran through his head at the same time. For a split second, Xavier's eyes abandoned the dagger and looked around. Vastrel was halfway across the field lying on the ground. Murin was too far away from Involore to get to him before he plunged the dagger into Anora. And Erlidel was in the middle of casting a spell aimed at Evia.

Xavier wished that he could attack Involore. He wished that unicorns were allowed, at least in instances like this, to harm others. Xavier was just close enough that, if he darted at Involore as fast as he could, he might be able to get to him just in time to knock him down. But Xavier couldn't do it. He might have been a bad unicorn – at least according to some – but he was still a unicorn and could not harm others, regardless of the circumstances.

"No!" Luna yelled as she watched Involore raise the dagger above his head, wrapping his fingers tightly around the hilt.

The evil wizard chanted the final words to the long, complicated spell he was casting. The only thing left that he had to do was plunge the dagger into Anora's pure heart and it would destroy all the unicorns instantly. Involore's trademark evil smile appeared on his face once again. He held the dagger tightly, took a deep breath, and prepared to plunge it into Anora's chest.

Xavier could see all the other unicorns gathered in the distance. He thought about his parents, siblings, other relatives, and friends. Though they were too far away for him to see any of their faces, they were all watching. Brina, Civia, and the other elders were watching, too. All eyes were on Involore – well, *most* were. Xavier's little sister, Ebelle, was one of the unicorns with their heads turned. She couldn't bear to watch Involore plunge the dagger into Anora's heart.

The wicked grin still plastered across his face and the dagger high above his head, Involore pulled it back another couple of inches and prepared to stab it into Anora's chest. With all his strength, the evil wizard slammed the dagger deep into the heart – but it wasn't Anora's heart that Involore plunged the long, jewel-encrusted dagger into.

Just as Involore's arm started to move, Xavier darted at him as fast as he could. The unicorn bolted at the evil wizard, running faster than he ever had before. The dagger came screaming down at Anora but before it hit its intended target, Xavier leapt over her and the tree she was tied to. The long, sharp blade stabbed deeply into the unicorn's side, piercing his heart. Xavier went crashing down to the ground, the dagger lodged firmly into his side, all the way to the hilt.

"Xavier!" Murin screamed. "No!!!!"

A second later, Erlidel came to the end of his spell and took aim at Evia. A massive burst of water launched at the wind apprentice, freezing her solid the second it hit her. Erlidel waved his hand and uttered a few more words and a giant boulder appeared above Evia's frozen body. The crazy old wizard made a fist and swung his hand down. Immediately after, the massive rock fell on Evia, shattering her frozen body into a million pieces.

Dozens of "Ooohs," "Aahhs," and other gasps came from the unicorns off in the distance. None of them had ever seen anything even remotely as violent before. Many started talking among themselves but were still paying close attention to what was happening in the field.

"No!" Involore screamed, then looked over at Murin, Luna, and Erlidel. "You're going to pay for this!"

"It's over, Involore," Murin replied. "You're finished."

"Oh, but that's where you're wrong. It's *you* who's finished!" the evil wizard replied, then turned to Galan, pointing at Murin. "Attack him!"

Galan didn't want to attack Murin. He was one of the only people who'd ever been nice to him. Still, the fire apprentice didn't want to disappoint his master. Galan began casting a spell, taking aim at Murin.

Meanwhile, Involore noticed that Erlidel was casting a spell, no doubt aimed at him. The evil wizard began casting a spell of his own, taking aim at Erlidel. Luna ran over to Xavier to cast a healing spell on him. Though she did her best, Luna was unable to heal the unicorn. The dagger's blade had pierced deeply into his chest, penetrating his heart. Xavier just lied there, motionless, eyes closed.

Galan finished his spell and took aim at Murin. He pointed his finger and a fireball came flying out. It would've hit Murin, had he been standing about twenty feet to the right. Murin was ready to jump out of the way, but he didn't have to move at all.

"You don't have to do this, Galan," Murin said.

Galan looked over at Involore. He was in the middle of casting a powerful offensive spell on Erlidel and couldn't stop to tell Galan to continue attacking. Involore did, however, shoot his fire apprentice a look that delivered the message just fine.

"I'm sorry, Murin," Galan mumbled and began casting another fireball spell.

Erlidel came to the end of his spell just as Involore came to the end of his. The sky began to crackle and a second later, booming thunder was heard all around. It terrified all the onlooking unicorns, as they'd never seen such severe weather in their beloved part of the forest. Several meteors came screaming through the sky, aimed right at Involore. The first few missed, but the last one hit. The meteor hit the evil wizard right in his chest, sending him flying back ten feet. It knocked the wind out of him and burned a hole in his cloak but a few seconds later, Involore was back on his feet.

At the same time, a single bolt of lightening came crashing down from the sky, hitting Erlidel in the middle of his back. He went flying ten feet forward, landing on his chest. Like Involore, Erlidel had the wind knocked out of him and his robe slightly burned, but quickly got back up to his feet. Immediately, the two wizards each began casting another spell.

A moment later, Galan finished casting his. Like before, he took aim at Murin and shot a fireball out of his finger. This time, it shot about ten feet to Murin's right. Like before, he didn't even need to try to move out of the way.

"I don't want to have to hurt you, Galan," Murin said. "Stop. Please, stop!"

"I'm sorry," Galan replied and began casting another spell.

Involore and Erlidel were both coming to the end of their spells. Once again, they took aim at each other as they chanted the final words. A mountain lion appeared out of nowhere in front of Involore and immediately started attacking him. At the same time, a series of fireballs came flying down out of the sky at Erlidel. Several of them hit, knocking the wizard to the ground. His now-tattered cloak was on fire and he rolled around, extinguishing the flames. Erlidel managed to get back up to his feet, slowly.

The mountain lion that Erlidel had conjured swung its razor-sharp claws at Involore, scratching him across the face and chest, tearing up *his* now-tattered robe. It pounced on top of him, knocking the evil wizard to the ground. Involore began casting a quick defensive spell as the vicious animal bit into his arm and once again took a swipe at his face. He finished the spell and the mountain lion instantly turned to dust. Some of it blew away in the breeze, but most of it just fell to the ground, leaving a grey circle. Involore slowly got up, leaving a silhouette of himself in the dust on the ground. Bloody and bruised, he got back up to his feet and began casting another spell.

Galan cast yet another fireball spell at Murin and once again, he missed. This time, his aim was a little better – he only missed Murin by about five feet. It came close enough that Murin stepped to the side. This time, he didn't say anything. Murin was starting to accept that he was going to have to attack Galan.

The wizards were almost done casting their next round of spells. Both of them were hurt badly, but managed to finish them. They both knew that the other was close to death, so they each cast a quick and easy offensive spell. A series of fireballs flew out of Erlidel's fingers, several of them striking Involore in the chest, knocking him to the ground. Above Erlidel, a bunch of heavy rocks appeared and soon started falling. Several of them hit, knocking him down. This time, Erlidel didn't get up.

"Erlidel!" Murin yelled.

"No!" Luna screamed.

Involore, after lying on the ground for several seconds, very slowly got back up to his feet. He was bruised and bloody, his cloak torn and burned to pieces. Still, his trademark grin reappeared on his face when he saw that he'd put an end to Erlidel. Involore turned to Galan.

"You still haven't finished him?" he asked. "You really are useless. It's really not that hard. You cast the spell, you point, and you shoot. It's that simple. I've never met such an idiot before. I'll give you one more chance. If you don't hit him this time, I'm going to show you both how a fireball spell is cast."

Galan swallowed hard. He was so nervous that he was shaking. Murin still felt bad for Galan, even though he was trying to kill him.

"You shouldn't talk to him like that," Murin said to Involore. "He's not an idiot."

Galan didn't know what to do. He'd never had anyone stick up for him before. The confused apprentice looked at Murin, then over at Involore. For the first time, he saw Involore in a weakened state. Galan knew that Involore was badly hurt. It was obvious to anyone who looked at him. The fire apprentice glanced down at the ground, then up at Murin and began casting another fireball spell.

Murin readied his sword and prepared to attack. Involore rubbed his bloody fingers together, the wicked grin still on his face. Luna and all the unicorns looked on, their eyes wide.

Galan came to the end of his spell. Murin was ready to try to dodge the attack if it came close to him. Galan missed Murin by the largest margin yet – but this time, he wasn't aiming at Murin.

At the last second, Galan turned and pointed at his master. The evil grin on Involore's face turned into a look of mild amusement. He didn't think that Galan would even come close to hitting him.

"You can do this," Murin said. "I believe in you, Galan."

Out of Galan's finger, fireball after fireball came firing out. Each one was a direct hit, landing dead in the center of Involore's chest. They sent him flying back, landing on the ground. A couple of the fireballs had caught what remained of Involore's robe on fire and he laid on the ground burning, motionless. The flames eventually extinguished, as did the evil wizard's life.

"I'm not an idiot," Galan mumbled.

"No you're not," Murin said, sheathing his short sword, walking over to Galan, and putting his hand on his shoulder. "You did good – really good. I'm proud of you."

Galan smiled. He'd never felt such satisfaction in his entire life. Everyone else breathed a sigh of relief. It was over. It was finally over.

Luna ran over to Anora, who was still tied to the tree. Murin threw her the boot knife that Vastrel had bought for him and she used it to free Anora. Vastrel, a hundred feet away, was just starting to regain consciousness. He slowly got up and worked his way back to where all the action had been, picking up his warhammer along the way.

After congratulating Galan on a fireball spell well cast, Murin approached Xavier's body. There was no question about it: the unicorn was dead. Xavier laid there in a pool of blood, motionless. Murin knelt down beside him and started tearing up.

"I'm so sorry, Xav," Murin said, doing his best not to cry. "I'm so, so sorry. I'm going to miss you so much."

34.

Two dead wizards, two dead apprentices, and a dead unicorn laid in the middle of the field. Cautiously, now that the action seemed to be over, some of the unicorns started walking over to get a closer look. Luna had freed Anora and they both walked over to where Xavier and Murin were. After finding his warhammer, Vastrel came over and joined them. Galan, still processing everything that had just happened, sat down on the fallen tree that Anora had been tied to.

"I'm so sorry, Mur," Luna said. "I know how much you liked Xavier."

"My condolences as well," Vastrel added.

Anora and Luna walked over to Xavier and knelt down next to Murin. Like Murin, they both started tearing up. Several unicorns circled around them, including Xavier's family and all the elders.

"He sacrificed himself for me," Anora said. "That was the most selfless act I've ever seen."

"He sacrificed himself for all of us," Murin replied, barely able to speak he was so choked up. "Xavier was a good unicorn. Maybe not by *their* standards," he said, looking up at some of the unicorns that had gathered. "But by *my* standards, he was a good unicorn."

"He was a *great* unicorn," Anora added.

Several of the unicorns started crying. They might not have all been crazy about Xavier, but none of them wanted to see him die. His little sister, especially, was sobbing like crazy.

"Isn't there anything you can do to bring him back?" Luna asked, looking at some of the gathering unicorns.

"Sadly, there's nothing we can do," Brina replied. "We have many magical gifts, but revival isn't one of them."

Murin did his best to hold back his tears. Luna and Anora, both leaning over Xavier, made no attempt to do so and began crying. At the exact same time, a single tear dripped from each of their faces and landed on Xavier. They continued crying, each of them running their fingers over the unicorn's side. Suddenly, Luna's eyes widened and she looked over at Anora.

"Did you just feel that?" Luna asked.

"Feel what?" Anora replied.

Luna put both her palms on Xavier's side. Barely – just barely – she could feel a faint heartbeat. Luna grabbed Anora's hands and put them on Xavier's side where hers had just been. Anora didn't react for several seconds. Then, her face lit up, too.

"I feel it!" she said.

Murin, Vastrel, and several onlooking unicorns all asked at the same time:

"What?"

"You feel what?"

"What is it?"

"What are you feeling?"

Luna was about to answer them but, right before she had the chance, Xavier opened his eyes. Just about every unicorn that saw Xavier's eyes open gasped. Then, word of what happened quickly spread around the group to those on the other side who weren't able to see. Xavier's sister was one of the unicorns who couldn't see his face from where she was standing.

"What is it," Ebelle asked. "What happened?"

"Xavier opened his eyes," another unicorn told her.

Ebelle didn't reply. She just started crying even harder, but she wasn't the only one. Tears were already flowing like rivers from many of the unicorns before and now started they pouring out like waterfalls.

A minute after Xavier opened his eyes, he groaned, picked his head up, and glanced over at his side. Then, he looked over and saw Murin, Luna, and Anora next to him.

"Hey, Murin," Xavier said, coughing. "You want to do me a quick favor?"

"Anything," Murin replied. "What?"

"You want to pull that massive dagger out of my side? It really freakin' hurts."

"Of course, Xav!" Murin replied.

Murin got up off the ground. He stood over Xavier, positioning himself so he'd be able to pull out the long dagger.

"Wait!" Luna said and ran over to them. "Let me start casting a healing spell so when you pull out the blade, it doesn't kill him all over again."

"What do you mean kill me *again*?" Xavier asked.

"I'll explain it to you later," Murin replied. "Although I'm not exactly sure what happened myself, to be honest."

Xavier didn't reply. He put his head back down on the ground and his eyelids closed about three-quarters of the way.

"Ready?" Murin asked Luna.

"Ready," she replied. "Go!"

Murin wrapped his fingers around the hilt of the dagger and tried to pull it out. It didn't budge. Luna was on her knees next to Xavier, casting a healing spell. Murin, making sure his feet were planted firmly on the ground, with all his might started pulling the dagger out of Xavier's side. He pulled it all the way out and tossed it wantonly on the ground. Vastrel, a moment later, went over and picked up the jewel-encrusted dagger.

Blood started pooling out of the wound in Xavier's side. The unicorn's eyes were now completely shut once again. Everyone else's eyes were the exact opposite: wide open. No one made a sound – no one except Luna, casting her healing spell. She chanted the final words and placed her hands on Xavier's wound. Right before everyone's eyes, the blood stopped flowing out of it and the wound closed.

"Come on, Xav," Murin said. "Open your eyes."

"Come on, Xavier!" Ebelle yelled.

The next few seconds felt like hours for everyone standing around Xavier. He laid there motionless, eyes closed. Then, Xavier turned his head so he was looking straight up at the sky. He opened his mouth and projectile vomited up all the blood that had gathered in his throat and lungs.

Blaaaaaaaaaaaaahhh!!!

The blood went flying high up in the air. A lot of it had gathered in Xavier's large lungs and it all came out at once. Blood flew dozens of feet up into the air, then rained down on everyone. Even Galan, sitting far away from them, caught a few drops of unicorn blood on his cloak. Normally, everyone there would've been mad at Xavier for vomiting blood on them. But given the circumstances, every one of them was thrilled because they knew it meant he was alive.

"That a boy, Xav!" Murin yelled, a big smile on his face. "Get it all out!"

"I'm pretty sure I already did," Xavier said looking right at Murin, his face only a couple of feet away. "Wait a minute..."

Xavier opened his mouth and made a gagging sound, looking Murin right in the eyes. Murin knew that he couldn't move out of the way in time, so he just closed his eyes and got ready to get a face full of blood.

"Ahhh, just messing with you!" Xavier said and laughed, coughing a little bit.

Murin didn't shake his head this time. He just smiled. Luna leaned down and kissed Xavier on the top of the head.

"Move," Xavier said.

"What, buddy?" Murin asked.

Xavier rolled over, almost knocking Murin and Anora over in the process. The unicorn stood up on his hooves and turned his head side to side, stretching his neck. As soon as Xavier got up to his feet, everyone cheered.

"Yes!"

"All right!"

"Woo hoo hoooo!"

"Yay Xavier!"

"Way to go!"

Xavier approached Murin. He stood in front of him for a few seconds without saying anything. Then, the unicorn leaned down slightly, putting his face right next to Murin's.

"Go ahead," Xavier said.

"What?" Murin asked.

"Go ahead and pet me – just this once."

"Really?"

"Do it before I change my mind."

Murin very cautiously put his hand on the top of Xavier's head. He ran it down his neck and all the way down his back. Xavier didn't flinch – not on the outside, anyway. The other unicorns looked on in disbelief. To be touched by someone who wasn't pure of heart was torturous for a unicorn. They couldn't believe that Xavier was able to stay still while Murin touched him. On the inside, he was freaking out. Every instinct in his body was telling him to run away. Xavier's flight-or-flight response was kicking into high gear. But he didn't move. He let Murin pet him and it put a huge smile on the young man's face.

"Thank you, Xavier," he said. "Thank you so, so much. It means a lot to me. I hope it wasn't too bad for you."

"Nah, it was fiiiiiiine," Xavier replied.

It wasn't fine. But Xavier managed to stay still and it made Murin happy. Several unicorns approached Xavier and the others.

"Xavier!" his sister said, coming over to him, rubbing the side of her face against the side of his. "I missed you soooooooooo much! It's so good to see you! You look so strange without your alicorn. Did you miss me? Did you miss any of us?"

"Maybe a little bit," Xavier replied, tilting his head to the side.

Next, Xavier's parents came over to him. They, too, rubbed the sides of their faces against his and told him that they missed him. Then, his brother did the same.

"I missed you, Xavier," Astra, his old friend said, coming up to him and rubbing the side of her face against his. "As annoying and rude as you can be sometimes, I missed you. A lot."

Brina, Civia, and the other elders gathered together privately while Xavier caught up with his friends and family. The nine members of the Council of Elders got together in a circle and discussed the events that had just taken place.

"I don't know if that's a good idea," one of them said.

"I think we should," another elder said.

"I do, too."

"But what about..."

The Council of Elders talked for several minutes. Then, they all walked over to Xavier with Brina in the lead. The other unicorns that were talking to Xavier saw the Council of Elders coming over and all stepped back. Brina walked right up to Xavier. He didn't say anything. Xavier just waited for her to say something to him.

"Well, Xavier," Brina said, "this has been an interesting turn of events, to say the least."

She paused, giving Xavier a chance to speak. He didn't say a word.

"What we just witnessed was nothing short of miraculous," Brina continued. "You displayed a level of selflessness we've never seen before. Had you not sacrificed yourself, as soon as the wizard's blade pierced that lovely young woman's pure heart, we all would've been killed – every single one of us. You saved us, Xavier. You saved all of us."

"Not alone, I didn't," he replied.

"No, I suppose not," Brina said, looking around at Murin, Luna, Anora, and Vastrel, then down at Erlidel's corpse. "You *and* your friends saved us. We couldn't be more thankful. So, thank you – all of you."

"Your welcome."

"No problem."

"Welcome."

"Myself," Brina said, "along with the other elders, have met to decide your fate once again."

She paused once more giving Xavier a chance to reply. He didn't say anything.

"We've decided to allow you back into Unicaria."

Several of the other unicorns gasped, but Xavier maintained his composure. After a few seconds, everyone got quiet again.

"Your display of heroic selflessness saved us – in addition to everything your humanoid friends contributed. You showed us that you're not a bad unicorn, Xavier. You're an unusual unicorn, for sure... You're a little different than the rest of us... But you are, deep down, a good unicorn. We were wrong to exile you from our home – from *your* home. Please accept our sincerest apology. Welcome back, Xavier."

"What about my alicorn?" Xavier asked.

The Council of Elders gathered around Xavier in a circle. One by one, starting with Brina, each of them tapped their alicorn to the unicorn to their right. After going all the way around the circle, the last unicorn tapped Brina's alicorn. She took a couple of steps forward, leaned down, and tapped her alicorn against Xavier's head.

Again everyone gasped, especially Xavier's non-unicorn friends. They'd never seen him with his magnificent alicorn, which was now back on his head in all its glory. A big, goofy smile appeared on Xavier's face as he looked up and saw it between his eyes. The happy unicorn uttered a single word.

"Sweet."

"Welcome home, Xavier," Brina said.

"You know what I just realized?" Luna said.

"What?" Murin asked.

"If Xavier had never been kicked out of here in the first place, he never would've been able to save all of you," Luna said, then looked right at Brina. "Did you know that all this would happen? Is that why you exiled him in the first place? Because you somehow knew that it was the only way to save the unicorns?"

"I assure you, we knew nothing of this before today," Brina replied. "And even if we did, do you really think we would've sent Xavier, of all unicorns, to be the one to save us?"

"I suppose not," Luna said. "So, I guess it was just fate then, huh?"

"That's one way to look at it," Brina replied.

"I have a question," Luna said, stepping closer to Brina and the other elders.

Brina didn't reply. She just looked at Luna, curiously.

"I'm sorry..." Luna said. "Is something wrong?"

"No, *I'm* sorry," Brina replied. "It's been many, *many* years since I've seen a human, especially up close. Ask your question and I'll answer it as best as I can."

"Xavier was dead," Luna said. "I'm sure of it. But then, when me and Anora were next to him crying, he came back to life. Why did that happen? *How* did it happen?"

Brina turned to some of the other elders. In the unicorns' language, they talked among themselves for a moment. Then, Brina turned back to face Luna and answered her question.

"We're not completely sure ourselves," she explained. "But, we have a theory."

"I'd love to hear it," Luna said.

"There are ancient stories about the tears of pure humans being able to heal injured unicorns. When the tears from you and your friend landed on Xavier, it must've brought him back to life. I've only heard stories about unicorns being healed, never revived. But, since magic is at its strongest today and since there were tears from *two* of you, it must've been powerful enough to bring Xavier back."

"That makes sense... I guess," Luna said, then turned to Xavier. "That just leaves one question: What are you going to do, Xavier?"

"I'm going to go drink some water from the stream just on the other side of those trees over there. All I can taste is blood. Although honestly, it's really not that bad. It *is* unicorn blood, after all. But still, I want to get the taste out of my mouth."

"No," Luna said, laughing. "I don't mean right now. I mean in general. Are you going to stay here? Are you going to come back to Edgewood with us? You're more than welcome to come back with us if you want to."

Xavier looked at Luna and Murin for a moment, then over at some of the other unicorns. He hadn't had time to think about what he wanted to do. On the one hand, it was good to be back in Unicaria. But Xavier couldn't forget that they'd kicked him out. And he'd really grown to like Murin, Luna, and some of the others that he'd met in civilization, though he didn't really care for village life. Xavier thought about it for a minute, but it didn't take him very long to figure out where he really wanted to be.

"I think I'll be staying here," Xavier answered. "This is where I belong."

Even though Xavier gave Murin and Luna the answer they were expecting to hear, it still made them sad. They'd really grown quite fond of the unicorn over the short period of time they'd known him.

"We understand," Murin replied and smiled.

"We'll let you say goodbye," Brina said to Murin and the others. "We need to get to work on creating a new magical barrier to protect our land."

"You may want to talk to *him* before you do," Murin said, pointing over at Galan. "He can tell you exactly – well, maybe not *exactly* – but he can at least tell you a little bit about how he, Involore, and the other apprentices got through this time. Maybe that can help you build a better, even-more impenetrable barrier."

"Good idea," Brina agreed. "Thank you."

Brina instructed all the unicorns to leave the field except for the Council of Elders. They walked over to Galan and asked him a bunch of questions while Murin, Luna, Anora, and Vastrel said goodbye to Xavier.

35.

Standing together in the field, Murin, Luna, Anora, and Vastrel took turns saying goodbye to the now-horned unicorn.

"Had you not gone to get my father when you did, I'd probably still be tied up in that cabin in the woods," Vastrel said to Xavier. "For that, I'm forever grateful. If there's anything you ever need, don't hesitate to ask. I'll be in Briarville in my father's house – when I'm not out adventuring."

"I can't imagine what I'd ever need from a dwarven-elven-gnome or whatever you are," Xavier replied. "But I'll keep that in mind."

"Take care of yourself, unicorn," Vastrel said.

Xavier nodded to Vastrel and he nodded back. Then, Vastrel walked off and had a seat at the edge of the forest.

"You saved my life," Anora said to Xavier. "I'm forever in your debt. I just wish I'd had the chance to get to know you."

"Glad I could be of service," Xavier replied. "You should probably stop helping evil wizards, though – just sayin'."

"I will," Anora replied, cracking a smile. "Take care, Xavier."

"Later."

Anora walked off, joining Vastrel at the edge of the forest.

"I didn't really like you at first," Luna said to Xavier. "I thought you were rude, abrasive, and abhorrent."

"Gee, thanks," Xavier replied.

"Let me finish!" Luna said. "But over time, as I got to know you, you've really grown on me. I'm actually going to miss you, Xavier. You really are a good unicorn."

"Well, don't go around telling that to too many people. I have a reputation to maintain."

"Take care and be well, Xavier," Luna said, laughing.

"You, too."

Luna nodded and smiled at Xavier. He did the same. Luna ran her fingers through Xavier's hair one last time, then started walking toward Vastrel and Anora. She wanted to give Murin a moment alone with Xavier to say goodbye. He'd spent the most time with the unicorn. As Luna was walking, out of the corner of her eye, she saw Timules move – just a little bit – off in the distance.

Quickly, Luna ran over to the injured centaur. The whole time, she'd assumed that he was dead because he hadn't been moving at all.

"You poor thing!" Luna said to Timules. "Let me see if I can help you."

The centaur didn't reply. He was in too much pain to say or do much of anything. Luna got down on her hands and knees next to him and began casting a healing spell. She wasn't sure if it was going to work, since all four of his hooves had been cut off and were nowhere to be found. Fortunately for the centaur, Luna's spell *did* work.

"Cool," Luna said under her breath as Timules' hooves appeared right before her eyes. "It actually worked."

"It *actually* worked?" Timules said. "You didn't think it would?"

"I wasn't sure if it would or not to be honest," Luna replied. "Maybe it did cause it's the Day of Magic."

"It doesn't really matter now, does it?" Timules said, slowly standing up on his brand new hooves. "Thank you. Thank you. Thank you!"

"One thank you is enough," Luna said and smiled.

Both Luna and Timules walked over to join Vastrel and Anora. Meanwhile, Murin and Xavier were saying goodbye.

"I'm really going to miss you, Xav," Murin said.

Xavier didn't reply. Murin noticed that the unicorn's eyes were starting to get a little glassy.

"Are you... Are you tearing up?" Murin asked.

"Don't be absurd," Xavier replied, doing all he could to hold back his emotions. "Unicorns don't cry."

"I just saw like fifty unicorns crying a few minutes ago!" Murin yelled.

"Okay, fine. You got me. Unicorns cry. But *this* unicorn doesn't."

"Uh huh," Murin replied, tearing up again himself. "Will I ever see you again? Can I come visit you? Will *you* come visit *me*?"

"Unicorns usually don't hang out with humans or other humanoids," Xavier said.

"There's nothing *usual* about you, Xav," Murin replied, half-laughing, trying to hold back his tears.

"That's fair, I suppose," Xavier replied, half-laughing himself. "Maybe I'll come visit you someday."

"I'd love that. I really, really hope that you do."

"And what about *you*? What are *you* going to do?" Xavier asked.

"What do you mean?"

"Are you going to accept your 'destiny,'" Xavier said, using one of his front hooves to make an air quote, "and live out the rest of your years as a farmer? Or are you going to use the balls that you appear to have grown during this adventure and tell your father that the farming life isn't for you?"

"I haven't decided yet, if I'm being honest. What do you think I should do?"

"I think you should do what everyone should do – whatever the hell you want to. It's *your* life. Live it however you want to. If you were cool with shoveling shit all day, every day, I'd say stick with being a farmer. It seems like a safe way to live. But I think we both know you yearn for something more. You've always wanted to be an adventurer. Now that you've been on an actual adventure, do you still feel that way?"

"I'll be honest. Adventuring, in reality, is a lot different than I'd thought it would be. It's not all dragon slaying and damsel rescuing like I'd imagined. But these past few days have been the most rewarding of my life. So, to answer your question, I've never been more afraid to be an adventurer – yet, I've never wanted it more."

"Then it sounds like you already know what you want to do," Xavier said and smiled.

"I guess you're right," Murin replied and smiled back. "I just hope my father isn't too disappointed. Well, Xav, I guess this is goodbye – for now, at least. Please do come visit me. Anytime you want. Really."

"I just might do that," Xavier said, then leaned down and pressed the side of his face against Murin's – but only for a second. "Goodbye, Murin. I'm going to go bother Astra for a while."

"Goodbye, Xav," Murin replied. "Take care. I'll miss you."

Murin turned and started walking to go join the others. The Council of Elders had finished questioning Galan and he walked over to Luna, Anora, Timules, and Vastrel. Murin did his best to hold back his tears, but a few managed to sneak out. The same was true for Xavier. The only difference was that a *lot* of tears fell from his eyes into the grass as he walked away. Both of them managed to pull it together quickly and regain control of their emotions before anyone saw them. Murin wiped the tears from his face as he approached Luna, Anora, Vastrel, Timules, and Galan.

"Are we ready to get going?" Murin asked.

"Can I go back to Edgewood with you guys?" Galan asked. "I don't want to go back by myself."

"You're more than welcome to join us," Murin replied. "But it's going to take us a long time to get back. We're not taking any of the main paths for most of the way. We have to go back through the dense forest so we can find Thall and give him a proper burial."

"Thall the Explorer?" Galan asked. "He's dead?"

"Unfortunately, yes. He is," Vastrel replied. "He was my father. He died triumphantly in the heat of battle."

"Oh," Galan said. "I'm sorry to hear that."

"And I've been thinking," Vastrel said to Murin and Luna. "Why don't the four of you go back together. Find your way back to a main path. Once you get there, find a good spot to camp for the night. Then in the morning, follow the main path all the way back to Edgewood. You should be fine. And if you run into any trouble, I know you can handle yourselves. I'm going to go back the way we came. I need to give my father a proper burial. But there's no reason we all need to."

"What about Timules?" Luna asked.

"He can come with me," Vastrel replied. "I'll make sure he gets home safely on my way back to Briarville."

Timules nodded in agreement.

"You sure?" Murin asked. "We're all in this together. We'll help you if you want us to."

"You're going to make a great adventurer, Murin," Vastrel replied. "You already *are* a great adventurer, albeit an inexperienced one. A true adventurer always puts the party's needs above their own. But I'll be fine burying him on my own. You guys just get back to Edgewood safely."

"Okay," Murin replied and smiled. "Thank you for everything, Vastrel. You've inspired me more than I could ever put into words."

Vastrel nodded at Murin. Then, he offered him his hand and they exchanged a long, firm handshake. Vastrel said goodbye to Galan, Anora, and Luna before addressing Murin one last time.

"Keep practicing with that short sword. I may call on you to join me on an adventure someday and I'll need you to be as experienced as possible."

"I hope you do," Murin replied and smiled. "Goodbye, Vastrel. Please say goodbye to your father for me one last time, too, as he leaves this realm to go into the next. And thank him. None of this would've been possible if it wasn't for him."

Vastrel almost smiled. He put his hand on Murin's shoulder for a second and nodded. Then, he turned and started walking off back the way they'd originally come from with the centaur at his side.

"Ready?" Murin asked Luna, Anora, and Galan.

"Ready," they all replied at the same time.

The four of them started walking through the woods until they came to a barely-noticeable path. They followed it for quite a while until it connected with another slightly-more-worn trail. Galan cast an illumination spell – successfully on the third attempt – to help them see since it was dark outside. A short while into their journey home, they ran into someone they all knew. But never in a million years would they have expected to see her out in the middle of the forest late at night.

36.

"Dessa?" Murin asked. "What are you doing way out here in the forest?"

Sitting on a tree stump just a few feet off the thin path was Dessa, Edgewood's leader and eldest citizen. Standing next to her was a man wearing chain mail armor with a sheathed long sword at his side. She ignored Murin's question and looked right at Galan.

"Where's Involore?" she asked, angrily. Then, Dessa looked at Anora. "And what are *you* doing here? Where are all the alicorns? If Involore ran off with them without me..."

"Anora, what is she talking about?" Luna asked the now *former* water apprentice.

"Dessa and Involore were in on this together," Anora answered. "In fact, I think it might have been *her* who put him up to it in the first place."

Murin and Luna looked at each other. Neither of them could believe what they were hearing.

"Where's Involore?" Dessa asked again, standing up and taking a couple of steps toward Galan.

"He's finished," Murin replied, answering for Galan. "And now so are you."

"What's he talking about?" Dessa asked, still looking at Galan. "Where are my alicorns?"

"They're safely on the heads of the unicorns they rightfully belong to," Luna said.

Dessa stood still for a moment, fire in her elven eyes. She looked from Galan to Anora, Anora to Murin, Murin to Luna, back to Galan, then over to her guard. He was standing at attention, his hand on the hilt of his still-sheathed sword. But it wouldn't stay sheathed for very long.

"Kill them," Dessa ordered, taking a few steps backward. "Kill all four of them."

Without hesitation, the guard pulled out his long sword and raised it high above his head. Murin immediately unsheathed his short sword and prepared for battle. He was exhausted from everything that'd happened, but mustered up the energy to defend himself and the others. Galan took a few steps backward and began casting an offensive spell. Anora did the same.

Murin stepped forward to protect the others, his sword raised high overhead. The guard, both taller and more muscular than Murin, approached him with an utterly emotionless face. As soon as he was close enough to attack, he did. The guard swung his sword down at Murin's head. Murin raised his short sword to block the attack and successfully managed to do so. Murin countered, swinging his short sword at the guard. The blade connected with the guard's side, but his chain mail armor prevented it from slicing him.

"Come on, Murin!" Luna cheered.

The guard attacked Murin again. He lunged at Murin and the tip of his sword pierced Murin's shoulder, but just barely. Blood trickled out of the wound but didn't slow him down. Murin attacked again, lunging at the guard. The tip of his blade hit the guard in the center of his abdomen. His armor stopped the blade from breaking the skin but it did knock the wind out of him.

"Stop screwing around and kill them!" Dessa yelled. "They're barely grown ups. You should easily be able to defeat them!"

Galan finished reciting his spell. He pointed at the guard and three fireballs came flying out of his finger. They almost hit him, but not quite. Each fireball screamed past the guard's head, hitting the tree right behind where Dessa was standing. As the fireballs hit, they burst into flames and she had to dodge out of the way to avoid getting hit by burning bark falling from the tree.

"Watch it, you idiot!" she yelled.

When the fireballs whizzed past the guard's head, they distracted him for a second. Murin saw an opportunity to attack and took it. He swung his short sword as hard as he could, slashing the guard's arm. Only his torso and crotch were protected by armor. Blood began dripping from the guard's arm and his focus returned to Murin. He swung his long sword once again.

Cling!

Murin raised his sword to defend himself and their swords slammed against each other. They each pushed as hard as they could, their blades locked together. Being much larger than Murin, the guard was able to slowly push his short sword down. Then, the guard kicked Murin in the chest and he fell to the ground, landing on his back.

The guard stood over Murin and held his long sword in front of him, the tip facing down, preparing to pierce it through Murin's chest. Luna watched from only a few feet away, terrified. Galan was busy casting another spell and Anora was still reciting her first.

"No!" Luna yelled.

Luna remembered that she was still carrying the knife that Murin had let her borrow to free Anora from the tree she was tied to. Luna quickly took it out of her pocket and ran up behind the guard.

"Arrrgggghhh," he yelled as she slashed his neck.

The guard, now holding his long sword with one hand, used his other to put pressure on his neck.

Luna didn't sever a major artery, but she did cut the guard deeply enough that he felt it. Blood trickled out, slowly. When he realized that the wound wasn't serious, both of his hands returned to his sword.

Murin was getting up to his feet, but not quickly enough. The guard had a chance to attack before Murin was able to defend himself. Again, the guard raised his sword. Luna saw what was happening and feared that her effort to stop the guard from killing Murin might have been in vain. She knew that she wouldn't be able to attack him from behind again. Now he was watching her out of the corner of his eye. The guard's sword started moving toward Murin's neck. He swung it as hard as he could, strong enough that it would've taken Murin's head clean off, had it connected. But, fortunately for Murin, it didn't.

Anora couldn't have finished casting her spell at a better time. A massive blast of icy water came out of her fingertips, aimed right at the guard. As soon as it hit him, both him and his sword turned to ice. The rigid guard toppled over onto the ground, landing on his side.

"Smash him, Murin," Anora said. "Before he unfreezes."

Murin didn't waste any time. Now back up to his feet, Murin raised his sword high overhead and slammed it down on the frozen guard, shattering him into a million pieces. Ice chips flew off in all directions and Murin raised his sword once again. With the guard out of the the way, he turned toward Dessa. She was standing in front of the tree that Galan's fireballs had hit, holding a medium-sized pack.

"You're going to have to come with us," Murin said, breathing heavily.

"Oh?" Dessa replied. "And why in the world would I want to do that?"

"Because we need to bring you back to our village so the good people of Edgewood can decide what to do with you."

"There's nothing *good* about those simple-minded fools," Dessa replied. "After they hear you meddling kids tell your story of what happened – what you *think* happened – I'll be hanged."

"You should've thought of that before you conspired to destroy the unicorns," Luna said. "And for what? So you could have a little more power? You're already in charge of our entire village."

"An entire village," Dessa parroted. "An entire village? With even just a few of those alicorns, I could've taken control of the entire continent. With all of them, I could've taken over the entire world. I would've been unstoppable."

"*You* could've taken over the entire world?" Anora asked. "*You* would've been unstoppable? What about Involore? I thought you two were partners in all this."

"What about that washed-up wizard? He was nothing more than a pawn, just like you – just like all of you. As soon as I got my hands on those alicorns, you wizard wannabees and your washed-up master would've simply vanished... just like I'm about to do."

"I'm sorry, but you're not going anywhere," Murin said and slowly started approaching Dessa.

Galan never stopped casting his second fireball spell. He continued while Murin, Luna, and Anora were talking to Dessa. After reciting the final words, he pointed at her and several fireballs came blasting out of his finger.

This time, Galan's aim was spot on. Fireball after fireball launched straight at Dessa. None of them hit her – but they would've, had she still been there. Right after she mentioned vanishing, Dessa pulled a small potion out of her pack. She popped it open and chugged the bright-green liquid in a few quick gulps. As soon as she finished drinking it, right before everyone's eyes, Dessa disappeared. The fireballs that Galan launched went right through where she'd been standing and slammed into the same tree the others had. It sent pieces of flying bark in all directions. A fiery chunk of bark came straight at Murin's face, but he batted it out of the way with his sword.

"Where'd she go?" Murin asked.

"If that potion was what I think it was," Anora replied, "she could be anywhere."

"What do you mean?" Luna asked.

"I'm pretty sure that was a teleport potion. It certainly looked like one – same color and size, anyway. They're made for emergency situations. What they do is make you instantly disappear and then randomly reappear somewhere else."

"How random are we talking?" Murin asked.

"Like, *really* random," Anora explained. "Dessa could literally be anywhere. I've never used a teleport potion myself, but I've read about them. They're rarely used, but often carried by adventurers – and evil village elders, apparently. They work fast and they work well, ideal for getting out of dangerous situations when normal means of escape aren't possible. But the trade off is that you can't control where you end up. You,whatever you're wearing, and whatever you're holding just randomly relocate to somewhere else."

"Like, anywhere in the world?" Luna asked.

"I think I remember reading that it sends you to a random location on the same continent. But, in Dessa's case, it might as well be anywhere. This continent is the largest in the world by far, from what I understand. She could be in Rhanaldia, the Port of Lucindale, East *or* West Emeralion – anywhere."

"I wonder where she ended up," Galan asked.

"I doubt we'll ever know. Dessa knows that she can never return to Edgewood. After we tell everyone about what happened, they'll want to see her head on a pike. It would be suicide for her to go anywhere near Edgewood or any of the other nearby towns."

"Well then," Galan said, "I guess we'll never know."

They searched the area for anything that might be of value. When Dessa vanished, her pack and the clothing she was wearing disappeared with her. However, there was another large sack sitting next to the tree stump Dessa was sitting on when they first saw her. Anora opened it and a big smile appeared on her face when she saw what was inside.

"Guys, look!"

She held the bag open for the others to see. It was filled with fresh fruit, bread, several types of preserved meat, and two full waterskins.

"Awesome!"

"Yes!"

"We'll be eating good tonight!"

In addition to the food-filled sack, they also found a handful of gold, silver, and copper pieces. The divided them up evenly among the group. Luna healed the wounds Murin had sustained from the guard and they got ready to continue traveling down the narrow path. Anora cast another illumination spell so they could see, everyone grabbed their gear, and they resumed walking.

After a while, they got to where the narrow trail met the main path going through the forest. Just as Vastrel had suggested they do, the group found a good spot a little off the path to make camp for the night. After surveying the area to make sure it was safe, they put their stuff down, built a campfire, got comfortable, and broke out the sack full of food they were all dying to start eating. They were all so hungry that, for the first several minutes, none of them said a single word. They just stuffed their faces, enjoying every bite and every sip of what was in the sack. But after a little while, they all started talking and laughing.

"Here's to Thall and Erlidel," Murin said, raising one of the waterskins that they'd found in the sack. "If it wasn't for them, we never would've been able to accomplish what we did. They sacrificed themselves for us, for the cause, so that we could succeed. Here's to Thall and Erlidel!"

"Here, here!" everyone cheered, raising whatever was in their hand at the time.

The group continued to talk and laugh, but only for a little while. They were all absolutely exhausted after everything they'd been through. Shortly after they finished eating, all but one of them fell right asleep. Murin stayed up to take first watch and they switched off every couple of hours during the night. It went by uneventfully and everyone slept better than any of them had in days.

37.

The next morning, they got up, finished the little bit of food that was left, packed their belongings, and started heading back to Edgewood. They traveled as quickly as possible and made excellent time, stopping infrequently. There were plenty of other travelers on the main path but, aside from saying hi, they didn't stop to talk to any of them. Eventually, they safely got home.

"What are we going to do now that we're back?" Galan asked as they walked into the town. "We have to tell somebody about what happened, but who? With Dessa gone, who's in charge of the village now?"

"That's a good question," Murin replied. "But it's one that I'm not even going to think about until tomorrow. I'm going home. The only people I'm telling anything to tonight are my family."

"I feel the same way," Anora replied. "My mother must be worried sick about me."

"I wonder if my mother even noticed that I was gone," Luna said, looking down.

"So, we'll all just go home right now," Galan concluded. "Got it."

They stopped near the center of the village. There weren't many people out and about, but the few who were all took notice of them. No one approached the group, but they could tell that they were being watched.

"Well," Murin said, "it's been quite the adventure. Thank you all for being a part of it. What we accomplished is nothing short of miraculous. Each one of us played our part and worked together to defeat what may have been the greatest threat our world's ever faced."

The others nodded and smiled. They all hugged and talked for another minute before going in different directions.

"You want to walk with me since we're going the same way?" Anora asked Luna.

"Sure!" she replied.

Galan turned to Murin and opened his mouth. But before he spoke, Murin already knew what he was going to ask.

"We can walk together, too, Galan," Murin said. "Come on."

The girls walked off in one direction, the boys in the other.

"I'm sorry for attacking you," Galan said to Murin as they walked.

"Huh?"

"I'm sorry for listening to Involore when he told me to attack you guys. I never should've listened to him – ever. In fact, I never should've tried to be a wizard in the first place. I'm obviously terrible at it."

"You're not a terrible wizard, Galan," Murin replied. "You just had a lousy teacher who didn't really care about you. Don't forget: You're the one who finished Involore. Without you, things might have turned out much differently. I think you have the potential to be a great wizard. You just need a new teacher, someone who will encourage you instead of insult you."

"You mean it?"

"Honestly, I do. And if you keep practicing, maybe I'll invite you to go on an adventure with me someday."

"Really?" Galan asked. "So, wait a minute: Does that mean you've decided that you're going to follow your dream and start adventuring?"

"It means I'm going to follow my dream and *continue* adventuring. I'd say that what I just went on was definitely an adventure."

Galan stopped in the middle of the road. They were almost at his parents' house. He turned to face Murin and, looking him in the eyes, put his hand on Murin's shoulder.

"Thank you," Galan said. "Thank you for everything, Murin. For believing in me. For encouraging me. For everything."

"You're more than welcome."

Murin offered Galan his hand, but he didn't take it. Galan wrapped his arms around Murin and squeezed him tightly. Murin hugged him back. They let go, each took a step back, smiled, and nodded. Then, Galan walked to his front door and Murin continued down the road to his family's farm.

"Do you think Murin would ever hang out with me?" Anora asked Luna as they walked.

"I'm sure he would if you asked him," Luna replied. "Do you like him?"

"It doesn't really matter," Anora said.

"Why not?"

"Because I think he likes *you*."

"What?" Luna replied, blushing. "You're crazy! Me and Murin have been friends for like, ever. There's no way he likes me like that."

"I think you *both* like each other like that," Anora replied. "You should've seen your face when I just asked you if you thought Murin would hang out with me."

Luna face was now even redder.

"You two would make a cute couple," Anora continued. "You're perfect for each other."

"Oh quiet," Luna replied, whacking Anora in the arm.

They got to Luna's home and the girls said goodbye. Anora continued down the road and Luna walked to her front door. There was no light coming from the windows so Luna assumed her mother was already asleep. She was right. Luna snuck in, quietly, and found her way to bed. She dropped everything she was carrying, crawled into it, curled up, and started drifting off.

Murin's return home was much different. After briefly checking the stable to make sure the horses made it back safely, he walked to the back door of his family's house. When he saw the patched hole in the door, Murin paused for a moment before going in. He thought about Xavier and wondered how his unicorn friend was doing. Though Murin had no way of knowing it, at that very moment, Xavier was munching on some grass, thinking about Murin and the time they'd spent together.

After thinking about Xavier for a moment, Murin took a deep breath and opened the door. As soon as his family saw him come in, they all jumped up and ran over to him. He gave them a short summary of everything that'd happened and it put a smile on each of their faces, even his father. They surrounded Murin, each taking turns hugging him. First, Murin's siblings hugged him. Then, his mother. Finally, his dad approached him.

"I'm glad you're alright," he said. "I'm proud of you."

"I have something to tell you, father," Murin replied. "But I don't know how proud of me you'll be after you hear what I have to say. Can we talk privately?"

Murin's dad motioned to the rest of the family and they all left the room. Now alone, the two of them sat down, facing each other. Murin's father looked him in the eyes, waiting to hear what his son had to say.

"I've decided that I want to be an adventurer," Murin said, his heart pounding.

"I'm listening," his father replied. "Go on."

"I've always wanted to be an adventurer. And I know you've always wanted me to be a farmer, like you. But as much as I love working with the animals, my heart yearns for something else. And now that I've actually been on a real adventure, I've never been more sure. It's what I want to do. But I feel terrible about disappointing you."

"Disappointing *me*? Son, I couldn't be more proud of you. I'm going to tell you something, but you have to promise not to tell your mother or any of your siblings."

"Of course," Murin replied, leaning forward, eager to hear what his father had to say.

"I've never told your mother this but, when I was your age, I wanted to be an adventurer, too. But unlike you, I was too afraid to confront *my* father. He was a farmer and wanted me to carry on the family business. I didn't want to disappoint him, so I just went along with it. But there's always been a part of me that's wondered what could've been had I mustered up the courage to pursue my dream. By telling me that you want to be an adventurer, you've already displayed a level of courage that I never had. There's no doubt in my mind that you'll make a fine adventurer. You've already saved the world once and you've only just begun!"

"I... I don't know what to say," Murin replied, surprised. "Thank you, father."

"I should be thanking *you*," his dad said with a smile. "If it wasn't for you and your friends, the world would be a very different place right now. When people hear about what you did, you'll be hailed as heroes. But just because you're a famous adventurer doesn't mean you can't still help out around here when you're around."

"Of course," Murin replied. "First thing in the morning, I'll resume my responsibilities."

His dad smiled and Murin smiled back. He really was proud of his son. Mr. Fieldstone didn't really care whether his son was a farmer or not. He just wanted Murin – and all his children, for that matter – to be happy. They exchanged a long hug, then went to go get ready for bed.

The next morning, Murin woke up at sunrise and went outside to take care of the animals. Just as he was finishing up feeding them, his father came outside.

"You almost done?" he asked.

"Just about," Murin replied. "Why?"

"Because you're wanted at the tavern."

Murin finished feeding the animals and walked to the tavern with his father. Along the way, Murin asked his dad what he was wanted for but Mr. Fieldstone refused to answer the question. They got to the front door of the tavern and Murin's dad extended his arm, motioning for his son to go in first.

"There he is!"

"Murin's here!"

"Everyone's here now!"

As soon as Murin walked in, everyone cheered. The tavern was packed with Edgewood residents. Anora, Luna, and Galan were already there. A feast had been prepared and the counter was loaded with meats, breads, ale, wine, and fresh fruit.

"What's all this?" Murin asked.

"This is our way of thanking you," the barmaid answered. "All of you. We heard about everything that happened and wanted to show our gratitude."

"Word travels fast around here, I see," Murin said, joining his friends.

"It sure does," Luna agreed.

Ding, ding, ding! Ding, ding, ding!

The barmaid raised a wine glass and tapped on the side of it with a fork. The roaring crowd calmed down and a moment later the room was silent. All eyes were on Murin, Luna, Galan, and Anora.

"We're gathered here this morning to celebrate the triumphant victory of these four heroes. They uncovered and stopped a conspiracy that would've changed the world forever. It may not be perfect, but there is a lot of good in the world. If it wasn't for these young heroes, there'd be *no* good left in the world – only evil. So here's to Murin, Luna, Anora, and Galan!"

Everyone cheered. The barmaid raised her glass, then took a sip of wine. People around the tavern did the same, raising their wine glasses and mugs full of ale, then drank from them. The barmaid made a plate for each of the heroes first, then started serving everyone else. As the four of them ate, a number of townspeople came up to thank them.

"I can't believe Dessa was behind it all," the village baker said. "Thank you for saving us."

"Yrrr wlmcmmm," Galan replied, his mouth full of mutton.

"Stop by my shop for free baked goods any time," the baker added.

"Sweet," Murin replied. "Thanks!"

"Each one of you is a hero," the village cobbler said, approaching them next. "If you need your shoes repaired, come see me and I'll take care of them for free."

"Thank you," Luna said.

After the cobbler thanked the heroes and offered them his services for free, several other townspeople did the same. The village candlemaker, stonecarver, innkeeper, and glassblower all offered them free good and services.

Everyone had a good time at the celebration, enjoying the food and the drinks. After everyone stuffed their faces, the barmaid tapped her wine glass once again.

Ding, ding, ding!

"For years, Dessa has been Edgewood's leader," she said once everyone quieted down. "She was granted that position because she was the town's elder. But these young heroes uncovered the truth about Dessa and stopped her evil plan before it was too late. As such, it only seems right that they should take her place as the leader – excuse me: leader*s* – of our peaceful village."

"Huh?" Galan said, only catching the tail end of the barmaid's speech, lost in a daydream.

"They're putting the four of us in charge of the town, I think," Murin whispered to him.

"While we've been enjoying all this great food, several of us have talked and come to a decision. From this moment forward, Edgewood will have not one, but *four* leaders: Murin, Luna, Galan, and Anora. If it wasn't for them, life as we know it would no longer exist. It only seems right that they should lead our village. So, again, here's to our new leaders!"

"Here here!" several people cheered.

Everyone raised their mugs and glasses once again. The tavern erupted into applause. The four heroes stood up and took a bow. Murin looked over at Luna and smiled. Their eyes met and she smiled back.

Then, together, they looked over at Galan and Anora. All four of them smiled. None of them could've predicted that things would've turned out the way that they did. They were all excited about their new positions as the village's leaders.

The tavern slowly emptied out. Everyone enjoyed the celebration but had to get back to work. The four heroes stuck around for a while and talked among themselves.

"I can't believe we're the leaders of Edgewood," Luna said to Murin.

"I know," he replied. "It's crazy."

"How'd your dad take the news?"

"Surprisingly well," Murin replied. "He said he's proud of me."

"He should be extremely proud," Luna said. "His son is one of the leaders of his village! I'm glad you decided to tell him you're going to be an adventurer instead of a farmer."

"Actually, I'm going to be both. I promised to still help out around the farm when I can. I love working with the animals, especially."

"Murin Fieldstone: adventurer, village leader, farmer," Luna said. "You're a little bit of everything, just like Thall was. See what happens when you go after what you want? Everything worked out perfectly for you."

"I don't know about everything," Murin said. "That remains to be seen."

"What do you..."

Murin touched a single finger to Luna's lips and she stopped talking. He slowly leaned over to her, closed his eyes, and touched her lips with something else: *his* lips. It completely took Luna by surprise and her mutton-filled stomach instantly turned into a stomach full of butterflies. She closed her eyes and kissed Murin back, the two of them wrapping their arms around each other.

"They're so right for each other," Anora muttered.

Galan watched Murin and Luna kiss for a moment. Then, he looked over at Anora and slowly started leaning in her direction.

"Don't even think about it," she said.

"I wasn't... I was just going to..." he replied.

"Uh huh," Anora said, rolling her eyes.

Murin and Luna eventually stopped kissing and just sat there looking at each other, their faces only inches apart. He took one of her hands into his and smiled.

"You're right," Murin said. "It does feel good to go after what I want. I should've done that a long time ago."

"Better late than never," Luna replied, now smiling, too. "Maybe we can make up for some lost time later tonight."

"I'd like that," Murin said.

"You two are going to be the cutest couple in Edgewood," Anora said.

"And the four of us are going to be the greatest leaders this village has ever seen," Murin replied, raising his mug. "Here's to us. May we lead this town into many years of peace and prosperity."

"Here here!" Luna, Anora, and Galan said.

They all touched glasses and took a sip of their drinks. With big smiles on each of their faces the whole time, the four heroes talked for a while. Even though they'd just found out about their new role as village leaders, they already had a few ideas of how to make their home better. They talked and laughed for much of the morning, reflecting on the wild adventure they'd just returned from and discussing their plans for the future.

38.

"Ow!" Astra yelled.

She was eating some fresh grass when she felt something poke her in the ribs. Before Astra even turned her head, she already knew who it was.

"Xavier!" Astra exclaimed. "You've only been back for a few days and you're already starting to..."

Sure enough, when Astra turned around she saw Xavier standing there. But, much to her surprise, he didn't poke her with his alicorn. In his mouth, Xavier had several long-stem roses he'd picked from a nearby field and that's what he'd used to poke Astra.

"I was going to give these to you," Xavier said. "But, if you don't want them..."

"Xavier," Astra replied with a huge smile, blushing, "of course I want them! They're beautiful. Did you pick them for me?"

"I picked them to give to the first female unicorn I came across. It just happened to be you."

Astra eyed Xavier, suspiciously. He had, in fact, picked them for her. After getting the roses, Xavier passed several other female unicorns on the way to the field where he knew Astra was likely to be. Walking up to her, Xavier dropped the roses on the ground right in front of Astra. She leaned down, inhaled deeply, then picked one of the roses up with her mouth.

"Thank you, Xavier," Astra said, holding the rose with her teeth. "They're absolutely beautiful."

"You know what else would look beautiful in your mouth?" Xavier asked with a smirk.

"You know," Astra replied, shaking her head, "just when I was starting to think that maybe you've changed, maybe you've finally matured a little bit, you go and say something like that."

"What?" Xavier asked, his smirk doubling in size. "I was going to say some fresh grass. It's never looked more delicious. I bet it would look beautiful in your mouth. That's all I was going to say."

"Sure," Astra replied, trying to hold back a smile. She dropped the rose and her tone got a little more serious. "I think you have changed. I *know* you have. You're different, somehow. After everything you went through, how could you not be? You've seen and done more than any of the other unicorns around our age – or any age, for that matter. You *have* matured, Xavier. I can sense it."

"Can you sense this?" he asked, now wearing a supersized smirk.

"What?" Astra replied, taking the bait.

Xavier whacked Astra in the butt with his tail, hard. It was so hard that it startled Astra, causing her to jump. She shook her head and gave Xavier a look. But on the inside, she was smiling. Astra was happy to have Xavier back. In spite of all the mischief that he'd been responsible for over the years, she liked him – a lot. Astra didn't realize just how much she liked Xavier until he was gone. She thought about him every day that he wasn't there.

"I'm glad you're back," Astra said.

"I am, too," Xavier replied.

"What is it like out there in the world, outside of the forest?" she asked.

"Smelly," he replied. "Really, really smelly."

"Ewww."

"Ewww, indeed. But it wasn't all bad. I mean, it was pretty bad. But there are a few things I'm going to miss."

It wasn't *things* that Xavier was going to miss the most. It was the people he'd met that would stay in his thoughts. Xavier was glad to be home but already missed some of the humanoid friends he'd made out in the world. Though he'd grown to like Luna and some of the others, it was Murin that Xavier missed the most. The unicorn thought about his human friend and the time they'd spent together. A smile started to form on Xavier's face, as well as a tear in the corner of his eye. He hoped that he'd see Murin again sometime. Little did he know that the two of them would be reunited before long. But that's another story for another time.

* * *

"Where am I?" Dessa asked.

After chugging the teleport potion, Dessa disappeared from the forest and reappeared on the other side of the continent. She was several-thousand feet above sea level, standing on the side of a massive mountain. Dessa could see far off into the distance and noticed a small town at the base of the mountain. She recognized the town and quickly figured out where she was.

"This isn't good," Dessa mumbled.

She was on Lexander Mountain. It wasn't a place that an elf – or human, for that matter – would want to find themselves alone. Lexander Mountain was known for its massive hobgoblin population. Thousands of them lived on the mountain and in the town below. The town was originally founded by humans, elves, and dwarves, but the hobgoblins took it over during a brutal invasion. Ever since, they've controlled both the town and the mountain.

"This *really* isn't good," Dessa muttered when she heard movement coming toward her.

She turned and started walking fast in the opposite direction. Then, Dessa stopped. Now, she heard movement coming toward her from both sides. With nowhere to go, she stayed put and dug through her bag, looking for something – anything – that might help her escape. Dessa knew that she'd used the only teleport potion she had with her but hoped that there was something else in the bag that could be of use. There wasn't.

Dessa dropped the bag at her feet after pulling out the only weapon she had with her: a small pocket knife that was desperately in need of some sharpening. Looking from side to side, she waited, anxiously.

To Dessa's left, a group of hobgoblins appeared. There were close to a dozen of them and they were all equipped with weapons and armor. She turned to her right and, a second later, more hobgoblins emerged. They, too, were well-equipped and numbered in the double digits.

"Please," Dessa begged. "Don't hurt me. Just let me go. I mean you no harm."

The leader of the hobgoblins on one side of Dessa looked to the leader on the other. They nodded to each other and started walking toward her. She screamed at the top of her lungs and it echoed out over the mountains. With nowhere to go, Dessa dropped to the ground, curled up into a ball, and closed her eyes. Silently, she prayed that whatever was about to happen to her would be over quickly. It wouldn't be.

From The Author

Thank you for reading Bad Unicorn. I hope you enjoyed reading it as much as I enjoyed writing it!

If you liked Bad Unicorn, please take a minute to leave a review on Amazon, Goodreads, or wherever you got it from. Now, I can't say for sure if it's true or not, but I heard that for every person who reads and likes Bad Unicorn but doesn't leave a review, a unicorn is killed by an evil wizard. It's probably not true, but why risk it? Just leave a quick review and you can go to sleep at night knowing there's no unicorn blood on your hands.

Seriously, though: Please leave a review. It doesn't take long and each positive review helps me out a lot. Thank you!

Ellis Michaels Mailing List

Do you want to be the first to know about new releases?

Do you want to have the chance to win free books?

Do you want to know if I decide to give up this whole writing thing to become a Buddhist monk?

If you answered "yes" to any of the above questions, good news! You can by going to my website and clicking "Mailing List" in the top menu.

Ellis Michaels Website

ellismichaels.com

Follow Ellis Michaels On Social Media

Facebook: @ellismichaelsauthor

Twitter: @ellismichaels9

Also By Ellis Michaels

Inside Out (Bloodfeast Book 1)

Back In The Game (Bloodfeast Book 2)

The Final Quest (Bloodfeast Book 3)

Ordinary Hero